# Scandalizing the Duke

**The Wolverton World**

Leslie V. Knowles

Published by Leslie V. Knowles, 2021.

This is a work of fiction. Similarities to real people, places, or events are entirely coincidental.

SCANDALIZING THE DUKE

**First edition. February 23, 2021.**

Copyright © 2021 Leslie V. Knowles.

ISBN: 978-1736493502

Written by Leslie V. Knowles.

# Also by Leslie V. Knowles

**The Wolverton World**
Scandalizing the Duke

Watch for more at https://www.leslievknowles.com/.

For my husband, who is my greatest supporter and the love of my life.

# CHAPTER 1

Charlotte Longborough looked out at the nearly dry Mayfair street below her bedchamber window and grinned. *Finally*. It had been so disappointing to see nothing of London other than the soggy view from the carriage window when she and her sisters arrived in the city. She'd not even ventured to Hyde park, though it lay just two blocks from their aunt and uncle's door. But now, sunlight dawned, a page had turned, and the adventure of her Season beckoned. Flutters filled her stomach and took flight into her throat.

She tugged the window up and took a deep breath. Charlotte loved the freshness of the air after rain. She loved that there were broad green havens like the park in the middle of the city. But most of all, she loved that Aunt Poppy had agreed to sponsor Charlotte's Season and had insisted Elizabeth, enjoy a second one. Aunt Poppy had even allowed Sarah to come, though she was too young to take part in the Season itself.

An unwelcome thought intruded, and she caught her lip between her teeth. Until she arrived in London, it hadn't bothered her to know she was the least interesting of her sisters, but Elizabeth hadn't had a single offer last year. If her beautiful and talented sister hadn't received any offers, how could Charlotte, with her mouse brown hair and ordinary features, hope for one?

Charlotte dearly wanted a family of her own. She wanted a husband who adored her as much as Papa had loved Mama, and babes of her own to hold and care for. Yet, if she did receive an offer, it wouldn't seem right if she married before Elizabeth. Charlotte crossed her fingers, then wondered if it were sacrilegious to do so while she prayed both she and Elizabeth would succeed in making respectable matches by summer.

A soft whuffle, and a tongue that dampened her fingers, made her look away from the view. Amber brown eyes gazed at her with worshipful expression. "What do you say, Harry," she said as she scratched behind the ears of the half-grown beast who leaned against her leg. Even seated, the dog's head reached her waist. "Would you'd like a walk in the park as much as I would?"

She laughed when he barked as though he understood, tail wagging wildly. He'd been a pathetic collection of matted fur and bone when she saved him from an abusive drunkard at an inn along the way to London, and his appearance had been only slightly improved with a bath.

After she rescued Harry, Elizabeth had warned her that such impulsive actions could jeopardize her standing as a well behaved young lady, and that it didn't take much to become the brunt of society gossip. Had that happened to Elizabeth? Surely not. Charlotte was the impulsive member of the family, not Elizabeth.

Charlotte went down to breakfast where she found Elizabeth and Sarah enjoying hot chocolate, eggs and toast with their aunt and uncle. Since they'd come to London, Elizabeth dressed her hair in a softer style than she wore at home, and Charlotte envied her the rich sable color that made Charlotte's own light brown hair look non-descript and boring. Sarah's hair was darker than hers too, and had a glint that was not quite auburn, but made the deep brown glow with life even when confined to her school-room braids. Envy aside, she was glad they were here with her.

She seated herself, accepted a cup of chocolate from the footman, then turned to her Aunt. "Now that the sun is shining at last, may we walk to the park this morning? Poor Harry needs exercise even more than I."

"Oh, yes, please," Elizabeth and Sarah added together.

"Enjoy yourselves," Aunt Poppy agreed with a nod, "But don't linger too long. I, too, look forward to an outing. I thought we might go shopping later."

As soon as they finished breakfast, Charlotte, Elizabeth, and Sarah set out for the park with Harry, their maids, and a trailing footman. The clear sky and light breeze refreshed and lightened their spirits after days of damp gloom.

Once there, Harry made erratic progress as he alternately pulled ahead, then stopped to smell odd places on the park's gravel path. His sudden surges and stops made Charlotte wonder if she should relinquish the lead for the large exuberant creature to the footman until Harry received proper training, At the moment, however, she preferred to keep him on the move. Since it wasn't the fashionable hour to stroll, there were few in the park, though Charlotte saw some nursemaids supervising their charges on the far side.

A gentleman on a distinctive gray gelding trotted by along the row and Charlotte admired the horse's spirited gait. She glanced at the rider when he passed them and her step faltered. Though she couldn't see his face properly, cold dread washed over her, as though the waters of the fast-flowing river back home pulled her under, robbing her of breath. Gooseflesh rose on her arms and she watched his progress with all the horror of her childhood fears until he reached the far end of the park.

Harry jerked against the lead pulling her back to the present. Her sisters had paused for her to catch up and Charlotte took a calming breath before she rejoined them. She struggled to dismiss her reaction to the stranger on the horse. *Surely, she was mistaken*. But the chill of unease remained. *What if she wasn't?*

"There are no people over by the trees, so it might be best if we walked in that direction," Elizabeth said as she scratched behind Harry's ears. He showed his appreciation with a personal sniff in the natural manner of dogs and she gave a startled gasp before carefully shifting his nose to a more genteel location. "Harry is a dear, but he has still to learn his manners."

Sarah giggled and Charlotte gave the lead a sharp tug.

Her disquiet eased when she looked at her younger sister, whose dreams often revealed joys and upsets to come. If actual danger threatened, Sarah would surely be the first to know, and warn her.

Charlotte turned to speak to Elizabeth but Harry suddenly gave a delighted woof and nearly pulled her off her feet when he took off toward the trees. She fought to hang onto the dog's lead and to keep her balance while he hauled her across the grass. She yanked back on the leather lead. "Harry," she cried. "Stay!"

Charlotte tugged to no avail and fought to remain upright while Harry pulled her to where he barked and leapt against a large oak. The abrupt lack of tension in the lead and a protruding rock combined to pitch her forward just before three horsemen thundered out of the trees directly in front of her. She fell to the ground with an unladylike grunt, let go of the lead, and landed in a puddle of mud.

Harry gave another sharp bark.

A man's voice cursed, "Bloody Hell!"

Charlotte ducked her head and the horse's hoof missed her by inches. The damp earth beneath her cheek vibrated when the horse stamped about in a confusion of barking dog, cursing male and the distant cries of her sisters above her head. Instinctively, she froze in place lest she put a limb in the way of anyone or thing that might land on it. The commotion seemed to last forever before a snuffling muzzle at her cheek followed by a tentative wet puppy lick let her know that the danger had passed.

"Oh, Harry," she muttered. "You silly beast. What were you chasing?" Charlotte opened her eyes and focused on a pair of booted feet before a gloved hand reached down to offer her assistance.

"Are you hurt, Miss?"

A man knelt beside her. His baritone voice touched something deep inside, made her nerves spark, and her breath hitch. A peculiar warmth blossomed through her when she looked into vivid blue eyes. Her pulse galloped and her voice trembled when she answered, "I don't believe so."

Charlotte blinked and looked away to the gloved hand he held toward her, and accepted his assistance to stand. She took a deep breath and caught the faint scent of sandalwood and leather mixed with freshly crushed grass and damp mulch. She raised her gaze to observe his squared jaw, clamped mouth and lowered brows before noting that his eyes met hers only briefly before they glanced at her mouth then lowered to her bodice.

A flicker of something—a darkening focus—made Charlotte glance down. The warmth of her awareness turned into the fire of humiliation.

Grass stained her bodice in the most embarrassing locations and mud covered her blue walking dress. Her embarrassment doubled when she saw her rescuer's pantaloons were also splattered with muck.

"I beg your pardon for putting you into more danger than your circumstances had already thrown you." He glanced at Harry, who sat nearby with his tongue lolling.

"It is I who should apologize," Charlotte protested. "Harry is new to the lead, and I should have given him over to a footman to control until he has learned not to give chase without command."

"Dash it all," a new voice made Charlotte look to her right where a sandy-haired man in buckskins and a bottle green riding jacket settled his horse and dismounted. His bronzed skin marked him as a dedicated sportsman. "Tell me you've not maimed the lady."

Elizabeth and Sarah caught up to her, eyes wide and faces pale. "Charlotte, are you hurt?"

"Only my dignity," Charlotte assured them.

Charlotte glanced around to see who else had witnessed her embarrassing downfall and found herself observed by another blond gentleman, the third rider of the group. He also dismounted, doffed his hat and announced, "Any lady who can cause Wolverton to nearly lose his seat must be made known to us. Pray allow us to make acquaintance with these ladies, Your Grace."

Wolverton? *As in the Duke of Wolverton*? Charlotte nearly groaned aloud. She'd made a point of reviewing her aunt's copy of Debrett's Peerage to learn who she might meet during the Season, and the Duke was at the top of the list of unmarried gentlemen she'd assembled.

The duke surveyed her and her sisters, before his lips firmed and his expression shuttered. "I have not had the privilege myself, so you must curb your curiosity, Ravencliffe." He gave Charlotte a stiffly correct bow and told her, "I am sorry to have intruded on your day. As you are unhurt, I shall take my leave. Should we meet again I hope it will be under more favorable conditions." He remounted his horse as did the other two gentlemen. "Lead the way, Norcross," he told the sportsman. All three gentlemen doffed their hats before guiding their horses out of the park at a much more sedate pace.

Charlotte had known it was silly to include gentlemen above her station in her notations, but she had. Along with the duke, Lords Ravencliffe and Norcross would be stricken from her list as soon as she arrived home. First impressions counted, and all three gentlemen would forever associate her with mud and chaos.

THE HUM OF CONVERSATION in the upper room of White's Gentleman's Club should have relaxed Lucien Caldwell, Duke of Wolverton, where he leaned back in his club's leather chair with a frown over his unsettling day. He'd nearly trampled a young woman with his horse this morning. Even if the woman hadn't been pulled into his path by her unruly dog, he'd ignored the ordinance against racing in the park. He never acted impulsively, but he'd challenged his friends and taken off with uncharacteristic disregard for the reason the ordinance existed. He knew better. But for some reason he'd given in to the sudden urge to ignore propriety and ride wild and free.

He studied his half-brother, Tristan, who had just added another conflicting layer of relief and irritation to his disquiet. No longer the skinny gutter-rat of a boy their father scandalized society with by bringing him into their home, Tristan remained lean, but now appeared as respectable as Lucien or any other gentleman in the club. Of course most of the members would never consider a bastard respectable.

He contemplated the single finger of brandy remaining in his glass before telling Tristan, "Anne will be devastated if you miss her come out."

"She will be exposed to ridicule and whispers if I take part in her Season."

Lucien's jaw tightened. The flash of relief he'd experienced when Tristan announced he would be gone during his sister's Season irritated him. It also irritated him that the old scandal still threatened his peace of mind after all this time. The scandalous outrage had never been that the late duke had fathered the boy, but that he'd insisted Tristan be raised along-side his legitimate offspring.

For Lucien, who had been twelve to Tristan's ten years, it had been a blow that left him angry and resentful for longer than he cared to remember, and had resulted in consequences that had impacted them all. Familiar guilt tightened his chest and clogged his throat. At least that aspect of their relationship had been resolved.

Tristan gestured toward the wood-paneled room where a host of gentlemen conversed over wines and spirts. "If anyone here disapproves of my presence and gives me the cut direct, it doesn't hurt

Anne's feelings, or her chances for a good match." He sipped at his own glass and met Lucien's gaze, "But if I take an active part in her come-out, the gossips will have a field day reviving the scandal. Anne will be faced with snide remarks and simpering sympathy." He paused, his eyes reflecting sardonic amusement. "And she won't be able to challenge them to fisticuffs the way we did."

Lucien's knuckles whitened around the glass. He recalled all too well the sudden silences in conversation when he passed his schoolmates, and the embarrassed suspicion that their laughter was aimed at him. He'd learned to disguise his humiliation behind a wall of civil reserve, and when he gained the title, he had vowed he would never allow the family to be gossip fodder again. He defied the gabblemongers by living a pristine life.

Tristan's eyes didn't waver. "If I'm not available, the waters of society will remain smooth and untroubled."

The footman returned and Lucien considered Tristan's argument while the man replaced Lucien's empty glass with a fresh one. The heady scent of aged brandy rose when he swirled the amber liquid.

"You do realize that if you're not at Anne's ball it will draw more attention to the past than if you are. Any lack of family unity after all these years would send a message of discord and create a new scandal at a time when it would affect Anne's future the most." He sipped his brandy and glared at Tristan. "We need no scandals of any kind—real or inferred—to interfere with Anne's Season."

The footman moved on to another patron and Lucien sat forward to argue his point. "The rest of the *ton* might remain calm, but when Anne realizes what you've done and why you've done it, those waters will become very choppy and your boat-full of good intentions will be sunk in a sea of outrage and disappointment. She isn't brainless."

Tristan shifted in his chair. "There is that."

"So you'll at least attend her come-out ball."

Tristan avoided Lucien's gaze when he stood to leave, his expression pensive. "I'll think about it."

Lucien ceased his argument. Tristan would do what he wanted to do—or not—as he always did. Lucien only hoped Anne would accept Tristan's decision as well. As it was, Anne showed a decided disregard for the traditions of rank and the strictures of polite society. She accepted Tristan without question and scorned those who didn't. Though Lucien was proud of her independence, her spirited attitude made him shudder at the social dangers it presented. In her support of their illegitimate brother, he worried she might encourage friends or suitors who were truly unsuitable.

Lucien's thoughts were interrupted when Norcross arrived, took the seat Tristan had vacated, and released a deep sigh. "My mother has decided that she is quite ready for grandchildren and has begun visiting all the families who have marriageable daughters." He shuddered dramatically. "I suspect she is making a list of ladies who strike her as potential daughters-in-law." Tall, athletic, and a viscount since childhood, Norcross had been the target of marriage-minded females long before he reached his majority.

"Fortunately, a list of candidates is not a marriage contract," Lucien assured him. "Nor are you obliged to confine your eventual choice to a list made by your mother. Certainly, my stepmother knows I would never countenance the presumption of anyone else making such a choice for me." The image of a blushing face with large gray eyes suddenly filled his mental vision. He blinked and took a quick sip of his brandy to banish it. His eyes narrowed and he declared, "She also knows I decided long ago that I'll not marry until both Anne and Rowena are launched. I don't need to start a new family until I've seen to the one I already have."

As his youngest sister, Rowena, was only thirteen, he had at least five years grace before he succumbed to the duty of his title and took a wife. His gut clenched when a sudden realization hit him. The crop of ladies he would be considering at that time were currently little girls who still played with dolls.

*Dear God.*

The concept made him slightly nauseous.

*No.*

When the time came, he would find a spinster—or a widow.

# CHAPTER 2

When Charlotte and her sisters arrived home and explained the condition of Charlotte's dress to Aunt Poppy, they learned she was well acquainted with the duchess of Wolverton. In fact, she informed them, they were scheduled to attend her at-home day on Tuesday. Aunt Poppy assured them their visit would remove any ramifications from her disastrous encounter with the duke. It had, after all, been an accident that few had witnessed.

Still, Charlotte's pulse leapt into her throat on Tuesday afternoon when their aunt's carriage rattled to a stop in front of the imposing townhouse that dominated the square. She worried her lower lip and shot a glance at Elizabeth. Her sister had not been introduced to the duchess during her Season since a bout of family illness had prevented the duchess from coming to London the prior spring. Elizabeth adjusted her gloves as she always did when nervous, and Charlotte took heart that she was not the only one with qualms.

"Come along, girls." Aunt Poppy smoothed her auburn hair beneath her hat and rose from the seat opposite Charlotte when the footman opened the carriage door. "Just be yourselves and don't spill your tea." The laugh lines around her hazel eyes deepened when she chuckled. "We shall have a lovely visit. Her Grace is still as charming as she was at our come-out when she was just Miss Holcomb."

Before Elizabeth rose to leave her side, Charlotte whispered, "Do you think we'll meet His Grace, again?"

"I don't think so. At-home days are mostly female venues." Elizabeth murmured, "His Grace will be at his club or remain in his study."

Cold shivers chased across her flesh every time Charlotte's thoughts returned to the moment she'd looked into those brilliant blue eyes, then learned who he was. How should she greet him when they encountered each other? For, as an acquaintance of the duchess, it was simply a matter of time before they crossed paths. Would he acknowledge their chaotic encounter or would he pretend he'd never seen her before? Since they'd not been formally introduced, that was a possibility. She was, after all, not a remarkable person, and he was a gentleman of vaulted rank.

Charlotte straightened her posture when she followed Elizabeth from the carriage. Her eyes widened when she saw pedestals, topped by fierce stone wolves, fortified each side of the broad portico.

Wolves, not lions.

Queasiness gripped her middle and she swallowed hard.

The butler led them up the broad staircase to the drawing room and opened the doors to announce them. The scents of beeswax, fragrant Darjeeling tea, and floral perfumes floated across the threshold and Charlotte relaxed her grip on her reticule when she breathed in the aroma so like Mama's sitting room before she took ill. Mama had always told her not to worry about expectations, just to be the best she could be.

Tall windows provided soft light into a large, elegant room containing pale rose and cream upholstered furniture, and thick patterned rugs of deep rose and sage green. A dozen or so ladies of varying ages occupied the room. Her Grace, a lady of medium height with kind blue eyes and dark blonde hair rose to greet them.

"Lady Elsworth, how good of you to come."

The duchess quickly performed the formalities between her guests, then directed Aunt Poppy to a settee beside her chair. Lady Anne, who resembled Her Grace, guided Elizabeth and Charlotte to join two ladies of their own age.

Elizabeth took a seat beside Lady Millicent Littlemarsh who'd had her come out with Elizabeth the year before. Charlotte sat across from Lady Jane Pomphrey, a young woman with bright red-hair, and who Lady Anne teased for turning down several offers over the past two Seasons. That fact struck Charlotte as a luxury few, herself included, could afford. At least, she amended, so long as she was sure the gentleman was truly kind and honorable. If she waited too long she might become a pitied, fussy spinster like Miss Smythe-Morton back home.

"I believe the offers were made with an eye toward my dowry and with little concern for my company as a wife," Lady Jane explained. "Papa has been most patient with me, but I suspect that will not last if I do not accept someone this year."

Charlotte sympathized with Lady Jane's doubts but knew fortune hunters would not be of concern for her sisters or herself. Though respectable, their dowries were modest.

"I only seem to attract unimaginative gentlemen with no sense of humor" Lady Millicent said with a wry grin. Both ladies were childhood friends whose country homes neighbored the Wolverton's primary estate. Sweet-faced and slightly plump, her brown eyes sparkled with mischief when she lowered her voice and confided, "But this Season I've arranged for Madame Fochet to adjust the necklines of my ball gowns to be a bit more daring than usual in anticipation of catching the eye of a bolder suitor than I have so far." She checked that her mother was still engaged in conversation, then added, "Papa will be fit to be tied of course, but I have noticed that the truly interesting men only dance with those who look a little scandalous."

"That is because they believe those women will not expect a wedding in exchange for a kiss... or more." Lady Jane said bluntly. "Ladies who show more than is proper do not gain husbands, they lose reputations."

"I didn't have her cut it as low as the demi-monde," Lady Millicent protested, "nor shall I lose my reputation by displaying a bit more bosom. Even Papa will only bluster until Mama reminds him this is my second Season. But I hope it will attract the attention of some of the rakes who stand at the periphery of their family's ballrooms." She giggled. "You know they say a reformed rake makes the best husband."

"The problem with that saying is that most rakes never reform," Lady Jane retorted. "Just look around the ballroom next week and you will see a dozen married rakes. Observe their wives. Then decide if you want to flirt with rakes and hope for reform."

Charlotte silently agreed. Though she hadn't observe London society, she'd learned from childhood experience that exterior charm and attractive features could hide inner cruelty, and even dangerous threat. Her thoughts flew to the solitary rider in the park. Her scalp hairs tightened, and goose flesh prickled her skin. She knew better than most how deceiving a handsome face could be.

Mention of ballrooms led them to a discussion of Almack's, their modiste fittings, and the latest styles until Aunt Poppy signaled it was time to go. Before they left it was agreed that Anne and her friends would have luncheon at Aunt Poppy's before going shopping together for dancing slippers the next day.

They had reached the base of the stairs when the door on the ground floor opened. A hint of sandalwood and starch drifted across the entry hall when the duke stepped through from the street. Charlotte's hand clutched the newel post, and she exchanged an alarmed look with Elizabeth.

The duke's expression warmed when he saw Aunt Poppy, and he greeted her with a pleased smile. "Lady Elsworth, it is good to see you. I hope your family is well. What do you hear from Edward? I believe he serves with the $43^{rd}$ on the Peninsula, does he not?"

"He does." Aunt Poppy told him. "We had a letter from him last week, but he doesn't write as often as we'd like."

The duke's eyebrows lifted slightly when he noticed Elizabeth and Charlotte beside her. He handed the butler his hat and walking stick. "My stepmother mentioned that you were sponsoring your nieces this year. Won't you introduce us?"

Aunt Poppy did the honors and Charlotte's cheeks burned when Aunt Poppy commented, "Though I believe you recently encountered one another at the park." Her smile teased even though her words held a light caution.

The duke tipped his head in acknowledgement. His eyes lost some of their warmth and his lips tightened. "An incident that is best forgotten. I should have remained on the horse path, and the dog should have been controlled by a footman until properly trained."

"With luck and a strong footman," Aunt Poppy agreed, "future outings should be uneventful."

They took their leave and Charlotte breathed a sigh of relief. He had asked for formal introduction when he could have ignored her.

She hoped no other catastrophes threatened her Season.

CHARLOTTE MOUNTED THE stairs to the Wolverton ballroom a fortnight later, determined to appear calm and sophisticated, though anticipation made her pulse beat like a hummingbird's wing. She'd been nervous when presented to the queen earlier in the week, but the ritualistic formality of that occasion had tempered her emotions. This, though—this ball—was the real beginning of her Season. She was no longer a child, but a young woman about to take her place in society. London Society. *Breathe.*

Elizabeth had described the splendor and excitement of a London ballroom—the glitter of jewels, the clouds of mixed scents, the beautiful gowns—but she had not prepared Charlotte for the disconcerting sense of unreality that spun round and round in her mind, as though she witnessed the crowd from afar. Hearing people's voices, but unable to distinguish the words. Breathing the scents, but unable to take a deep breath. Climbing the stairs, but unable to step smoothly.

The duke headed the receiving line at the landing, the duchess and his sister at his side. Polite and affable, but slightly distant, his interaction with his guests underscored the aloof superiority of his rank.

Though she'd crossed the titles Wolverton, Ravencliffe, and Norcross from her list, a few peers remained, and she hoped to be introduced to them in the near future. Might it be possible tonight? She took in the grand crowd making their way up the stairs and admitted her list was no more than a fantasy of silliness. Titles had a certain security to them, but she'd do better to encourage a younger son who would be a kind, considerate companion.

It struck her to wonder, as she watched His Grace greet his guests—Did a duke feel as much pressure to choose his future match as did the ladies he met felt to gain one? Foolish thought. *Of course he did*. He was a duke and it was his duty to continue his title and family name. A glimmer of sympathy rose, and she wondered if he found it tedious to be on every lady's list of hopeful matches, for surely, he was. He'd been on hers, sight unseen.

Ahead, Lady Jane Pomphrey reached the landing and he said something to her. Charlotte sighed. It was a pity that His Grace overwhelmed her senses with disquieting flutters. When he smiled widely at something Lady Jane said, the flutters took flight and pushed her heart into her throat. Dear heavens. He had dimples. Not the little poked-in-the-cheek kind, but long melt-your-bones charming ones. Oh dear. *Breathe*.

Uncle Aubrey and Aunt Poppy reached the landing when Lady Jane and her family moved on. Charlotte adjusted her reticule to the crook of her arm and smoothed her white silk gown. "Lord and Lady Elsworth," Wolverton greeted Uncle Aubrey and Aunt Poppy with another of those polite near-smiles. "How good of you and your nieces to come."

He turned to Elizabeth and Charlotte, bowing over their hands. "Miss Longborough and Miss Charlotte Longborough."

He barely made eye contact, but Charlotte swallowed the absurd impulse to giggle. *She never giggled.* But if he had sent her a dimpled smile, she feared she would have lost the battle and given the impression she had more hair than brains.

The duchess greeted her and she curtsied. Lady Anne, dressed in a cream satin and lace gown with yellow trim, also curtsied, and murmured, "We'll talk when I have finished greeting everyone."

Charlotte entered the ballroom proper, and took in the opulent elegance of her surroundings. The room abounded with jonquils, primroses and deep yellow hothouse roses, "Oh, how lovely," she murmured to Elizabeth. "It is as though spring has blossomed indoors."

Cream and yellow brocade curtains framed the tall windows and shimmered in the light cast by several large chandeliers. Wall sconces and mirrors added to the warm glow.

Elizabeth followed their aunt and uncle deeper into the ballroom, then commented, "I'm glad Lady Anne didn't feel the need to dress the footmen to match her color theme." She glanced around as though she checked to see if anyone might hear her, then lowered her voice. "Last year I attended a ball where the hostess dressed the footmen in all pink to match her theme. They blended in with the decorations so completely it was most startling when one appeared at your elbow with a tray." She chuckled when they strolled past a footman in dark blue livery. "You never saw them coming."

When Lady Anne approached them a quarter of an hour later, she was in the company of her brother and Lords Ravencliffe and

Norcross. The duke made formal introductions before the musicians struck up an introductory tune and the guests took their places for the first set. The duke led his sister to the floor as guest of honor. Elizabeth accepted Lord Norcross and Charlotte agreed to partner Lord Ravencliffe.

Charlotte found Lord Ravencliffe's conversation pleasant, and he was kind enough not to refer to the incident at the park, for which she was most grateful.

Her attention often wandered to where His Grace danced with Lady Anne. She hoped no one noticed, and attributed her slight breathlessness to the dance. When the set ended, they returned to where her aunt stood with the duchess. The others joined them, then Lord Norcross claimed Anne's next set and Lord Ravencliffe bowed to Elizabeth before leading her off. Charlotte smoothed her gloves and pretended she didn't know she and the duke were left standing beside each other.

"Will you do me the honor, Miss Longborough?"

"Of course, Your Grace." Charlotte strove to keep her expression composed, but alarm made her scalp prickle and her stomach flipped over. What if she stumbled and made a cake of herself again? She'd completed one set without mishap or clumsiness, but something about the duke made her feel like she'd spun around in circles until she scarcely knew where to put her feet. Her stomach threatened to rebel. She took a fortifying breath and placed her hand on his arm to be led to the floor.

LUCIEN HADN'T INTENDED to dance with anyone other than his sister during the evening, but it would have been awkward had he left Miss Longborough without a partner. Excusing himself would have implied he found her unacceptable, something he was loathed to do without cause. He glanced sideways at her when he led her to the dance floor. Their dance had nothing to do with wide gray eyes or a bosom that needed no grass stains to attract a man's attention. He had acted out of civility and manners, nothing more.

Unfortunately, once the set was over, he would have to dance more sets than he'd planned. She must not be considered to have been singled out, either. The gossips would delight in turning simple courtesy into rumor.

The music began.

For the first few steps they remained silent, then Miss Longborough asked, "Are you acquainted with the Duke of Everham, Your Grace?"

"I am. Why do you ask?"

"I had hoped you might introduce us," she said. "I understand he is fond of dogs."

He didn't miss the hint of humor in her eyes when she answered.

"Oh, that he is," he assured her. "I believe he brings five or six to his town house each Season and keeps an average of twenty-five or thirty at his country establishment at all times."

Her eyes rounded for a moment before she narrowed them. "I believe you are jesting with me."

"I am wounded, Miss Longborough," he said gravely. "I would never deceive a lady. Everham has raised dogs since he himself was a pup." They separated, circled and returned to bow and curtsey before progressing down the line. Her disbelief amused him. At least she was no fool. Everham's obsession with his dogs did skirt the improbable. "He raises bird dogs, though." He informed her while he circled her around to the music. "I doubt he'll take your beast."

"I don't wish him to take my dog," Her eyebrows raised as though surprised at the suggestion. "I wish to see if we would suit."

"You wish to see if—" Humor fled and a shaft of exasperation raised his ire. "I do not play cupid, Miss Longborough." *Impertinent chit*. They reached the end of the row and circled back to the beginning.

"I do not expect you to, Your Grace."

"I should hope not."

He looked down and into the gray eyes that met his with a hint of mirth. Surely, she couldn't mean for him to introduce her to a rival—*Rival*? He frowned. How absurd. He had no interest in Miss Longborough. At least, he acknowledged in light of his physically half-roused state, not beyond the normal reaction of a male to the attractive bosom of a female.

When they met at the top of the line she told him, "Introductions are the only way one can make new acquaintances and form friendships as well as attachments, Your Grace. And you must admit the purpose of the Season is to allow ladies and gentlemen to meet one another."

Lucien recognized her determination and knew, too, that the primary reason Everham was unmarried had everything to do with his utter focus on his dogs and their training. The man smelled of dog at the best of times... and of wet, foul, rolled in something dead, dog at the worst. It would serve her right if he did introduce them.

"Very well, Miss Longborough. Should he attend any of the Seasons' events at which we are all in attendance, I shall make him known to you." Her pink lips drew into a slight pout and Lucien had a sudden urge to taste that lower lip.

"He is not here, tonight?"

"He sent his regrets. His favorite bitch is about to whelp." He experienced a flash of smug satisfaction that Everham attended few social functions when in town, restricting his activities to parliament and the sporting set.

She caught that lower lip between her teeth again and he looked away from the temptation to nibble that lip himself. Unfortunately, his gaze settled on the neckline of her gown and heated his inappropriate thoughts even more. Despite its modest cut, it allowed him an intriguing glimpse at the shadowed depths between her breasts.

"Is the Earl of Grantley here this evening?"

He pulled his gaze from her neckline and realized her eyes had cleared and she'd formed a new plan of action. She didn't give up easily, which only confirmed his suspicion that if one title didn't appear, she'd seek another. He was disappointed to be right. Would it matter to her that Grantley had inherited his title when his elder brother had taken a fall in a drunken horse race and would likely come to a similar end?

"You wish me to introduce you to him as well?"

"If you would be so kind," she said with a smile that set his teeth on edge. "And the Earl of Marley, too, if you would."

*Good Lord, did she have a list?*

# CHAPTER 3

He repressed huff of exasperation.

Obviously, she had searched *Debrett's* in anticipation of the Season. Though the book chronicled title and lineage, it did not reveal finances, temperament or character faults. Marley was a year older than Grantley and had developed a tendency to gambling beyond his means of late.

Despite her branch of the family's lack of distinction, both she and her sister deserved better than the futures those men were likely to provide. He caught his thoughts in surprise. That was her father's responsibility, not his. Lucien had enough on his own plate.

He avoided her gaze and surveyed the crowded ballroom. "May I remind you that I do not play matchmaker for my sister's friends."

She nodded and smiled before saying, "Again, Your Grace, I do not ask you to. An introduction makes no commitment between either party, it only opens the door for exploration and options." She raised her gaze to his and he recognized that she sincerely, if naively, believed what she said when she continued. "You are in no way responsible for the choices either party makes after that."

It was apparent she had no idea how disastrous an inappropriate introduction could be to a lady's reputation, let alone her virtue, in the company of a scoundrel. "I am if I knowingly put an innocent on the road to ruin."

"Are Everham, Grantley and Marley so dangerous to a lady's reputation?" she countered. "From what you have indicated, Everham's greatest deterrent is a love of animals that may border on obsession."

"Not, perhaps, in the literal sense," Wolverton admitted, "but they are unlikely to make stable marriage partners."

"I thought you didn't care for matchmaking."

"I don't."

"But it's as much a form of matchmaking to reject possible suitors as it is to select them." Again, she focused her determined gray gaze on his. "So as such, you should introduce those who request introduction and let the parties involved decide their fate... not you."

*Balderdash.*

"If I make no introductions, I make no such distinctions."

He would not put his sister's friend in the way of any male. Her naive boldness revealed her inexperience, a quality that less honorable men would be quick to exploit. She circled him as the dance steps dictated and he admitted the chit was a delectable innocent who would tempt a cleric into scandal.

He cleared his throat.

"Other than for my sisters, I take no part in the matrimonial games and strategies of the Season. I leave introductions to their mother. I step in only should there be question of propriety or suitability."

They danced in cool silence for some moments after that. Eventually he recovered his manners and sought a new direction of conversation. He nodded to where her sister Elizabeth and Ravencliffe dipped and circled to the music. "I see your sister is dancing. I was led to believe she was not so inclined."

"It's not that she's unwilling," Miss Longborough responded. "It's more that she is seldom asked a second time."

He turned his head to observe that Miss Longborough's sister moved with grace and obvious enjoyment. "She does not appear to be clumsy," he commented, "and she knows the steps."

"Ah, but does her partner appear charmed or disgruntled, Your Grace?" .

Ravencliffe's expression did appear somewhat disconcerted. "I'm not sure." he admitted. "Is it her conversation?"

"It shouldn't be, but I suspect it is. In general discussion, she contains herself to the usual subjects of the weather and upcoming social events. But she's told me that when dancing, many gentlemen make the mistake of asking about her interests... and she tells them." Her eyes gleamed when she told him, "Elizabeth has unusual interests."

The dance separated them, and Lucien absorbed his partner's explanation. When the dance brought them back together, he asked, "How unusual? What are they?"

"She likes tools." She grinned at his involuntary start of surprise. "Her embroidery is appalling, but her wood carving is exquisite."

Lucien wondered now who was being less than truthful. He shot a glance over to the petite woman who circled her partner and found he could not picture her—or any other woman of his acquaintance for that matter—wielding saws, chisels, or whatever other tools were involved in woodworking. "She...*er*...makes wooden objects?" Perhaps he had misunderstood.

"Wood is as much a passion for her as," her face lit with mischief, "raising dogs is for the Duke of Everham."

Lucien gazed into the slate gray eyes that should have reflected the coolness of stone but that sparkled with amusement and life. Without thought, he asked, "And what is your passion, Miss Longborough?"

Her eyes blinked and a dusky rose tinted her cheeks before washing her neck and shoulders. He knew that faint flush traveled well beyond those soft shoulders, and he had to check his sudden urge to haul her off the dance floor to find a secluded area in which to discover her rosy warmth. *Dear, God*. He certainly had more control than that. What was it about this young woman that raised his lust at the same time as she trampled on his dignity?

Her gaze met his, first with question, then it sharpened. "I enjoy gardening." Her voice held a note of restrained civility that revealed her irritation. The warmth of her expression had chilled to the stone cold of slate after all, and Lucien discovered that his sister's friend was not quite so frivolous as he'd believed. The chit might be naïve, but she was no fool, and his response to her far too inappropriate for a respectable miss.

Silence hung between them while he searched for an innocuous response. In the end he could only say, "Then you do not share your sister's unusual interests?"

"I may not share them," she murmured quietly, "but I enjoy the fruits of her labor."

Thankfully, the music finally ended, and he was able to escort her back to her aunt. He bowed to them, took his leave, then scanned the ballroom for his missing half-brother. His irritation at his wayward thoughts refocused onto Tristan. He had eventually sent Lucien word he would attend their sister's ball, so where the devil was he?

THANKFULLY, AUNT POPPY was in conversation with Lady Littlemarsh and paid Charlotte no attention once the duke was gone. Charlotte watched the duke with a mixture of irritation and confusion while he crossed the room, and decided the man was as annoyingly pompous as they came. Except for that startling question about her passions, he had held himself in aloof disapproval simply because she had asked him to introduce her to a few eligible gentlemen.

She bit her lip and admitted that perhaps she'd overstepped propriety there. If she couldn't introduce herself to a gentleman, though, why couldn't she ask someone to do it for her? Was that why he'd asked about her passions? Did he think her common?

At first, she'd believed his question flirtatious and a little scandalous. But then she'd realized he expected her confess something vulgar—like performing acrobatics upon the stage. Her ignominious catastrophe in the park made him think she was some hoyden with no sense of propriety or dignity. Dignity, *humph*. The man had enough dignity for everyone in this overcrowded ballroom. And what's more—

"Charlotte?" Elizabeth's voice interrupted her indignant thoughts. "Charlotte, why are you scowling like that?"

Charlotte suddenly remembered exactly where she was. "I wasn't scowling." She smiled to give credence to her claim, and asked, "So how did you enjoy your dance with Lord Ravencliffe?"

Elizabeth laughed before she took Charlotte's arm and led her to some chairs along the wall, "Far more than he did, I'm afraid. He asked the usual things about how I liked town, and did I enjoy the lovely spring weather, but he eventually asked how I spend my free time." She gave a rueful little shake of her head. "I truly tried to keep our conversation on acceptable topics. But when he asked me about embroidery and painting, I had to confess how wretched I was at such activities... and he kept asking." She hesitated, then her expression turned sheepish and she blurted. "So, I told him."

She chuckled. "He was more polite about it than some of the gentlemen who've asked. He merely made a slight misstep and paled before recovering himself. He even rather kindly asked about my current project."

At that moment, Ravencliffe came into view. He neared the card-room, followed by a rather boisterous younger man chortling over something that had been said before they came within hearing distance.

"When I saw you stand up with the Longborough Amazon I knew you would be unable to suppress your shock when she spoke of oak woods versus walnuts or—" He gave a choked laugh. "Whatever else she took it in her head was fit conversation for a ballroom. Last year Lord Alton quit the floor in the middle of the set, he was so appalled."

Elizabeth gasped and turned pale. It was all Charlotte could do to remain seated, but she didn't want to draw attention to themselves.

The earl responded with apparent bored disinterest. "I agree the talk of carving and polishing various woods was most unusual. However, the lady is hardly an Amazon. If anything, she is quite petite and dances most gracefully."

His mild disclaimer didn't slow the man's commentary. "She is a freak of nature," he assured the earl. "I hear her sister's making her come-out this year. I wonder if she's as strange." He shook his head. "I doubt it, though. There couldn't be two freaks in one family." He hesitated a moment before adding, "Though there *is* word of taint in the line so perhaps they are all freaks."

The two men reached the card room and their voices faded from hearing. Charlotte turned to her sister with dismay. Elizabeth stood stiffly, her face ashen. "Oh Elizabeth, pay no attention to that oaf. He is obviously no gentleman."

"Oh, but he is." She gazed at Charlotte, her eyes suspiciously moist. She firmed her lips. "That was Lord Marshburn, the Earl of Dovehurst's heir. He is not the only gentleman to have expressed similar sentiments, nor, as you heard, is he the first to react quite so publicly."

Lords Alton and Marshburn were two more names to cross off her list, Charlotte decided without regret.

In all Elizabeth's stories about the glories of a London Season, her sister had never once mentioned the Lord who had left her standing abandoned on the dance floor. *How humiliating*. Charlotte's heart ached now that she understood the pain Elizabeth had hidden beneath rueful humor whenever she'd regaled her sisters with stories about her failed Season.

Elizabeth straightened her spine and adjusted her gloves. "I wish I could pretend to be a proper miss long enough to capture someone's interest, but neither do I wish to pretend to be someone I am not."

Charlotte linked her arm with her sister's and drew her from the room. "Mama taught us to worry less about what people expect and more about being ourselves," she reminded her. "You are perfect exactly the way you are. You have a unique gift, and any man who does not see that is not worthy of you. That oaf is not worthy of anyone, let alone a woman of unique quality."

She steered Elizabeth down the wide hall. "Let's pay a visit to the ladies retiring room to wash our hands before joining the others in the ballroom. I believe Mr. Hook asked for the next set, did he not?"

Charlotte was grateful to find the retiring room empty. Both she and Elizabeth needed time to calm themselves before returning to the ballroom. Charlotte hated that people considered Elizabeth odd simply because she preferred woods to embroidery threads.

Elizabeth took advantage of the basin to cool her flushed face then turned to Charlotte with what Charlotte recognized as a determined smile. "Don't worry about me," she said. "I refuse to let the small minds of pompous men ruin my enjoyment of the Season's entertainments. If that means that I sit with Aunt Poppy as an observer when we attend balls, then so be it."

Charlotte gave her sister a hug. "There has to be someone special for you. It may be that such a man will not be found in the fashionable ballrooms, but in some of the other places of intellect and variety London provides. Perhaps Uncle Aubrey could escort us to a scientific lecture or demonstration one day."

At that moment, a reed-thin woman in her late twenties entered the room and crossed to another of the basins. Her bright rose gown was dirt smudged and she held her right wrist tightly to her middle. She kept her face averted from them while she poured fresh water into the bowl with her other hand. The pitcher slipped and she automatically tried to catch it before it fell. When she did, she gave an involuntary exclamation of pain at the movement and water sloshed from the pitcher, splashing her gown before she was able to return it to the table.

Charlotte and Elizabeth hurried to her side. "Are you alright?"

The woman shook her head in denial. "It is nothing." She once again cradled her wrist against her body. "I—I merely—" She stopped. She closed her eyes briefly, then spoke in a calm, low and firm manner. "I injured my wrist in a fall in the garden when I went out for a respite from the heat. It is not serious, but I wanted to soak it in some cool water for a few moments." She gave them a tentative smile. "I did not realize how heavy the pitcher was."

"Are you sure that's all?" Elizabeth asked. "Perhaps we should have Her Grace summon a physician to be sure it isn't broken."

At this, the lady's face blanched and her voice took on a note of panic. "No, please do not disturb our hostess. Truly, it is but a minor hurt of the moment and will be fine. I beg you return to the dancing without further concern."

The woman's agitation made Charlotte believe there was more to her story than she'd told them. She said she had been in the garden, and Aunt Poppy had been quite clear from the moment they'd arrived that they were not to go beyond the terrace of this or any ballroom for any reason. Had someone assaulted the woman in some way? The panic in her voice seemed more than concern about making a scene in a public place.

"My husband was with me when I fell, and he encouraged me to soak my wrist while he called for our carriage. He will be waiting for me in the hall as soon as he has made the arrangements." The woman shot a nervous glance at the doorway. "Please. I thank you for your concern, but I shall soon be home."

It was clear that their continued presence made her more uncomfortable than the pain from her wrist.

"If you insist," Elizabeth acquiesced, "we'll go."

As they quit the room Charlotte surveyed the hallway and did, indeed, spy a gentleman speaking to one of the footmen. Charlotte caught her breath and cold shock froze her lungs. He wore his light brown hair in the latest style and dressed in the black and white of fashionable peer instead of the ordinary clothes of a land steward, but nothing else about him had changed.

She'd not been mistaken that day in the park.

The man in the hallway was Albert Franklin as surely as her name was Charlotte Longborough.

She hadn't seen him since she was eight years old, but she recognized the man who'd locked her in a tool shed and threatened her life before letting her out hours later. The injured woman they'd left said he was her husband—so he had married again. And the woman's injured wrist told Charlotte he had not changed in any other way.

Charlotte had, though, and when they passed him in the hall, she averted her face to avoid giving herself away.

He was a guest of the Wolvertons. Would she be able to avoid being introduced to him? What would he do when he realized who she was? She was no longer a child.

Would anyone believe her now?

# CHAPTER 4

Lucien moved through the crowd away from the Longborough chit, his progress slowed by various guests who approached him. His sister's ball was the lauded crush that hostesses craved, and he had learned to hate. Too many people, too many gossips, too many expectations. Most of the guests had a daughter, sister, or cousin of marriageable age.

By the time he reached the other side of the room, he'd decided that this year's crop of hopeful young ladies must be the largest on record. Tall, short, plump or lean as greyhounds, each of them had a female relative with determination, and the erroneous belief that he needed a wife and full nursery.

He had enough obligations. In addition to his sisters and stepmother, there were the numerous estates to run and his responsibilities to the House of Lords. He didn't resent his duties but chose not to add to them. He maintained a polite facade when faced with hopeful mamas and their giggling, simpering charges, of course, but kept the contacts as brief and distant as possible. He prayed his sister did not simper when out of his sight. He glanced away from Lady Ormsby's giggling daughter to where Anne smiled serenely at the gentlemen vying for her attention. She wouldn't dare do so in his company.

*Charlotte Longborough does not simper.*

The thought renewed his irritation. Neither did she show proper awareness of demure behavior. She must have a list. And surely no proper lady prepared a list of marital prospects. He looked around the ballroom at all the hopeful faces, then admitted the truth. *They all did*. Or at least their mothers did.

Nevertheless, proper young ladies did not brazenly request introductions to one man while dancing with another. Everham, Grantley and Marley of all people. Not, he assured himself, that he was offended that she clearly did not include him on the list. That assurance brought him up short. Why would he care if he were on her list? Too many ladies already made it clear his name was on theirs. He selected a glass of champagne from a passing footman and took a thoughtful sip. Even so, he was surprised to note the idea stung. Why wasn't he on her list?

He excused himself from the giggling brunette and her mother when he saw his great-aunt approach.

"A most excellent crush, Wolverton," Lady Althea Ridley announced. It always impressed him that she still had the carriage and complexion of a woman far younger than her seventy-six years.

"I'm glad you approve, Aunt." He took her hand and bowed over it, then straightened and acknowledged her silver-haired escort. "Wentworth." He turned back to his aunt and gave her a knowing smile. "Anne will be pleased you are here."

"Pish-Tosh," she answered with a dismissing wave of her hand. "She knows I would be the last to miss her come-out. What will please her is a full dance card and a drawing room full of flowers come morning." She turned and placed her hand on her escort's arm. "Once we have our dance, Wentworth, you will lead me to my grandniece before you go to the card room."

As they swept away to take their place for the next set Lucien saw that Tristan had finally arrived and was conducting Anne onto the dance floor.

He did not see either of the Longborough sisters.

THE FRAGRANT SCENT of roses greeted Charlotte when she followed Elizabeth down the stairs the morning after the ball. A collection of flower vases filled several tables about the drawing room. A few contained lilies and one held cheerful yellow jonquils. She took another appreciative breath and counted nearly a dozen bouquets. *Oh My.*

Lady Anne had told her they would be the measure of her success with the gentlemen to whom she had been introduced. Though she had enjoyed the ball and had never lacked for a partner, Charlotte had wondered if she would receive any flowers. Did this mean she and Elizabeth were properly launched into the Season?

Elizabeth selected a card from the nearest bouquet, pink and white roses interspersed with lacy green ferns, glanced at it and passed it to Charlotte. "These are for you."

Charlotte smiled in delight as she sniffed the fetching arrangement. Their peppery floral aroma captured the promise of summer to come. She read the message on the card, then chuckled as she read aloud.

"*So lovely a dancer,*
*so lovely a smile,*
*so lovely your laughter,*
*and gaze for a while.*"

She grinned as she tucked the card back into the bouquet. "I do hope Mr. Seldon does not aspire to making his fame with poetry." He'd been the earnest young man who'd been her partner for the supper dance.

Elizabeth laughed as she handed Charlotte three more cards, "The white, yellow, and dark pink roses are also for you. At least these don't include poetry." She gestured to the six additional vases that filled the room. "You most certainly charmed everyone last night."

"Surely they aren't all for me." Charlotte protested. How terrible if Elizabeth was ignored. She quickly checked the other cards, dismay gathering when the next four were also for her. Finally, she saw her sister's name on the arrangement of jonquils and daisies. "Here," she said as she passed the card to Elizabeth, "These are for you."

Pleased surprise warmed Elizabeth's expression as she took the card. "They are from Lord Ravencliffe. "*Flowers that bloom naturally in the wood are as sweet as those cultivated in the garden.*" She studied the flowers, and then smiled. "Jonquils are not the usual choice for floral acknowledgements, but neither are they odd." She smiled at Charlotte. "He knew we overheard Lord Marshburn last night. How kind of him to find a way to assure me I am not beyond courtesy."

"Kindness had little to do with it, I'll wager." Charlotte declared. "I suspect he found your conversation a refreshing change from bland observations on the weather and gossip." Certainly, Charlotte appreciated the way he had defended her sister to Lord Marshburn. He was handsome, too. And titled. And intelligent. *And perfect for her sister*.

She selected the card from the last bouquet. "Oh, here. Lord Ravencliffe is not your only admirer." She reached into a bouquet of white roses and handed a second card to her sister. "Mr. Sheffield also sends his regards."

Mr. Sheffield had been the only other gentleman to ask Elizabeth to dance once the rude Viscount had made the rounds of the card room. "Neither gentlemen are actual admirers." Elizabeth said as she fingered the petals of one of the roses. "Lord Ravencliffe wanted to offset the unkindness of Lord Marshburn's comments, and Mr. Sheffield, as his friend, is following suit. I doubt either of them would have done so had not Lord Marshburn spoken so dismissively."

"I say they're both more interested than you give them credit for."

"And I disagree," Elizabeth said as she leaned down to bury her nose in the floral perfume. "But I don't intend to let that interfere with enjoying the first bouquets I've ever received." She stood and surveyed the overflowing room. "In fact, as there is ample proof of our social success when we receive callers this afternoon, I shall remove mine to my room so I may enjoy them all the more."

Once Elizabeth and her bouquets were gone, Charlotte returned each of the cards to their respective bouquets. Most were from gentlemen who had been pleasant but made no lasting impression. Though several of the titled gentlemen from her list had attended that evening, they had found other partners, and she still had no idea if they would impress. There were no flowers from the one who most invaded her thoughts. The same one who refused to introduce her to possible matches.

Since His Grace had been almost surly in that regard, she asked her aunt about her list of gentlemen over breakfast. "Aunt Poppy, is it true that the Duke of Everham keeps a host of dogs with him when he comes to London? His Grace said he has at least twenty-five or thirty more at his country estate."

"Everyone knows the Duke of Everham is obsessed with his dogs," Aunt Poppy agreed. "Other than in Parliament, one never sees him in public without several on lead."

So, the duke had not deceived her, though Aunt Poppy did not sound as derisive as His Grace had. "He would not comment about Lords Marley or Grantley, though I got the impression he did not approve of their behavior."

Aunt Poppy's eyes widened. "Tell me you did not ask him about them." Her horrified expression told Charlotte more than her admonition. "Beyond the indelicate nature of such a question, Wolverton is especially disapproving of gossip. Promise me you will come to me or your uncle if you wish to know more about a gentleman."

Aunt Poppy spread a dab of marmalade on her toast and confessed, "As to the gentlemen in question, I'll grant you that both the late Lords Marley and Grantley had scandalous reputations. But that does not mean the sons are unworthy," she assured Charlotte. "Take Wolverton himself, for example. He is the pattern of propriety. In fact, some speculate his father's actions are responsible for his own pristine reputation."

Charlotte set down her fork. "What did his father do?"

"Oh," her aunt flushed. "It was long ago and really isn't something one should dwell on. As it is, Mr. Sheffield has become a respectable gentleman despite his unfortunate position."

"What does Mr. Sheffield have to do with the actions of Wolverton's father?"

Aunt Poppy gave her a startled glance. "Mr. Sheffield *is* the scandal," her aunt clarified. She wiped her fingers on her napkin and straightened her cutlery as though organizing her thoughts at the same time. "As you have been introduced, I suppose you should know of the situation, but," her eyes shifted to where Sarah sipped her chocolate and nibbled on toast. "Perhaps now is not the time."

Sarah drained her cup and set down the narrow crust remaining of her toast. "It is alright, Aunt Poppy." She pushed her chair back and placed her napkin beside her plate. "I've finished. I'm going upstairs to write a letter to Papa, so you can tell them all about the scandal without worrying about me." She gave them all a saucy grin. "Though I already know. His sister, Rowena, told me all about her family while you and the duchess selected fabrics at the modiste's shop."

Aunt Poppy gasped but waited until Sarah was out of the room before she explained, "Mr. Sheffield is the former duke's natural son by the current duke's first nurse. If that were not enough, when the child's mother died several years later, Wolverton's father brought the boy into his own home and expected Her Grace to raise him along with the legitimate children. It caused quite a stir for several years." Aunt Poppy flushed again before adding, "But, as I said, Mr.

Sheffield has turned out well and is generally accepted by most families."

Elizabeth, who had returned from her room in time to hear the story, spoke up. "When Anne introduced him as her half-brother and his name differed from hers, I assumed he was Her Grace's son by an earlier marriage." She put a piece of toast on her plate.

Aunt Poppy took a sip of tea before responding. "As I said, it serves no purpose to dwell on an embarrassing family situation. Both the former duke and the woman in question are no longer alive and that which is in the past should remain there. It is known, but not discussed." She rose from the table in a manner that indicated she had said all she intended. "Don't forget we have fittings at Madame Fochet's this afternoon, and we are to attend the opera this evening."

Charlotte absorbed this information and realized how vague her introduction to the duke's younger brother had been. She remembered that he had arrived late, so had not been announced at the door. Not only that, now that she considered her aunt's revelations, he and His Grace had remarkably similar coloring and features. Indeed, with her focus on her list of prospects, she had made the same assumption as Elizabeth without questioning the resemblance of the two men.

"Who would imagine Mr. Sheffield to have such a background?" Charlotte mused. "I wonder how many other scandals we are unaware of."

Elizabeth set down her cup. "I'm beginning to think quite a few."

Two hours later Charlotte knew that assumption was correct as she caught fragments of gossip flowing through the rooms at Madame Fochet's modiste shop. A repurposed townhouse, the ground floor provided a parlor for those waiting for fittings or private consultations. The upper floors contained bolts of fabric, and workrooms where seamstresses filled orders and made alterations.

Several ladies in the parlor chatted over books of patterns and samples of cloth.

Most on-dits were nothing more than revelations of who escorted whom and what they wore, but occasionally the scandalized voices took a sudden dip in volume before the huddled participants gave collective gasps, then censorious declarations or titillating giggles gave away the manner of the transgression.

Curiosity—alright—*nosiness,* had Charlotte straining to hear the whispers around the room. By the time the hems on her new dresses had been marked, she overheard that Lord Hobart had a new mistress, Lady Jordan was enceinte with a child believed to be fathered by someone other than Lord Jordan, though no one knew who, and Miss Rosemary Somms had been discovered in an attempt to elope with a gentleman whose name she refused to divulge and had been sent into the country in disgrace. Charlotte also learned that Lord Bascomb had crashed his phaeton after taking a dangerous turn at high speed at yesterday's races in Middleton and that Mr. Percy Philmont had taken a tumble into the Serpentine after a particularly long night of carousing.

She knew that the Duke of Everham's dog had, indeed, whelped a litter of eight puppies, and at least three ladies feared their husbands would pick one to bring home to their children.

Soon after she'd seated herself in the main salon to wait for Elizabeth to be finished with her fittings, an irritated male voice, from the private viewing room nearby, caught her attention.

"You will wear what I tell you to wear, Sophronia. You know you have no taste and that you invariably combine the wrong colors with ridiculously modest designs. You are neither an innocent nor a crone and you will display what charms you have in any manner I decide fit my requirements. We have been invited to dine with the Earl of Dovehurst before the opera and I will not have him or his son think I am shackled to an insipid female."

Charlotte stiffened. *Albert Franklin*. Her stomach clenched and her hands chilled. His irate tone resurrected her childhood terror and the threats he'd made when he'd found her spying on him near the riverbank that ran between the property he managed and Papa's.

"Now go back into the fitting room and tell Madame Fochet to lower the neckline another full inch and it is to be done within the hour so you can wear it tonight."

Unable to help herself, Charlotte rose and drifted toward a table of design books provided for the patrons. The table's location next to the private consultation room allowed her to verify that the voice did, indeed, belong to Albert Franklin. She fingered the pages before peering around the wall. Madame Fochet stood beside the thin woman Charlotte recognized from Anne's ball. Vivid red silk clung to the woman's narrow form and the wide cut neckline already dipped lower than Charlotte's. *Oh my*. Another inch would bring the fabric perilously close to exposing the woman's bosom entirely.

The low cut on Charlotte's own gown for the evening had made her blush though she'd been assured that the neckline was the latest in fashion. The neckline on the red dress, however, exceeded those she had observed so far. A glimpse of the woman's downcast expression as she turned to enter the dressing room convinced Charlotte the woman dared not object. Charlotte had seen that same expression on his first wife's face many times in the months she had spied on her neighbors. Charlotte's eyes stung and she blinked away tears. *Poor woman*.

Albert Franklin moved into sight and stood with his back to the doorway. She ducked away before he caught sight of her.

A few moments later Madame Fochet emerged with the red gown and summoned a helper to whom she gave swift, quiet instructions before returning to the private viewing room to assure him that the seamstress would complete the required alterations immediately.

"Matilda will bring you and Lady Dalton tea while we make the adjustments, M'lord."

*M'Lord? Lady Dalton?* Charlotte moved to a corner seat out of sight of the private consultation room. He must have inherited a distant title since his first wife's death.

# CHAPTER 5

When they took their seats in Uncle Aubrey's theater box that night, Charlotte surveyed the vibrant colors and brilliant jewels on display as the audience filled the opera house. Her pulse thrummed and her breath quickened with excitement. She'd dreamed of seeing a stage performance from the first moment she'd read one of Shakespeare's plays. Her sisters had often acted out plays for their own entertainment at home, but to be in a real theater, with real actors, made her positively giddy.

Conversations and laughter filled the great hall and musicians at the foot of the stage tuned their instruments, filling the hall with sound and her spirits with celebration. Perfumes of every description mingled with the more subtle scents of talcum, wax and spirits. Even the occasional whiff of over-heated and under-washed personages failed to override her delight in the evening's promise.

"Oh, how splendid," she breathed. Leaning forward, Charlotte gazed out over the railing to the pit area where several young men congregated as they greeted one another and ogled the young ladies sitting with their families and escorts. She ogled them back until one of them caught her eye and winked at her, which made her gasp in surprise and then chuckle at his audacity.

She quickly shifted her gaze to the boxes on the opposite side of the theater where she saw the Earl of Ravencliffe enter a box followed by Lord Norcross and an unknown, rather dashing, gentleman with light brown hair. Each of them escorted ladies whom Charlotte had not yet met. When she asked who they were, her aunt eyed them with careful attention before stating, "I am not acquainted with them... and am unlikely to be."

"Why not...?" Charlotte's eyes widened and heat burned her cheeks when she realized the implication of her aunt's assessment. "Oh."

She returned her gaze to the box and the questionable ladies who were now seated and laughing at something the gentleman with the brown hair said. They did not appear particularly different to her. True, the necklines of their gowns were quite low, but so were several of the gowns she saw on many of the ladies to whom she had already been introduced.

She turned to Elizabeth and whispered. "Do you think Aunt Poppy is right?"

"I'm afraid so." Elizabeth answered. "I have seen them before at various public entertainments, but they have never been included on the guest lists of any private balls that I've attended."

Charlotte stared, fascinated by the women. Though she was not supposed to, she knew that some women sold their favors and that many gentlemen engaged mistresses for their pleasure—which she had reasoned out had to do with mating. Of course, no one had ever explained the terms, but she had overheard enough to know that much. She also knew that mating was how babies were made, which was why true ladies did not allow gentlemen to kiss them before their betrothal, and that they most certainly did not allow any other favors or familiarities to their person until actually married.

She had always assumed that women who were free with their favors would look different from ladies of genteel upbringing. To be sure, she had seen some women on the streets in the lesser areas of town who did have the hard, course features of a woman who would lower herself for coin. But the women in Ravencliffe's party were well dressed, with tasteful jewelry and the finest of silks. How could anyone believe them less than respectable? What made them different from ladies like her aunt or the women in the streets?

While she watched, though, she realized that there was a subtle forwardness in the way the couples interacted. The ladies didn't object to the familiar way the unknown gentleman touched their arms or waists or backs—which he did frequently. In fact, they appeared to encourage it.

If the ladies were not true ladies, then that meant that their escorts might well enjoy their company for more than supper when they left the theater. The thought made her glance at Elizabeth. Charlotte had considered Ravencliffe as a possible match for her, but if he publicly consorted with women of ill repute perhaps, she needed to reconsider.

She knew from her visit to Madame Fochet's that many of the ladies there had whispered about whose husbands kept mistresses while they pretended they didn't know if their own male relatives consorted with such women. How could they pretend not to know, if the men attended public venues in their company and where the respectable world could see them together? The idea of an unfaithful husband made her shudder with disgust. But did a wife have any say in the matter? Annoying as it was, men were excused all manner of bad behaviors.

Charlotte studied Ravencliffe and his guests. Neither he nor Lord Norcross were as obvious as the third man's familiarity toward the women, but there was still something about their behavior that was less formal or—*proper?*—than they had displayed at Lady Anne's ball. Charlotte frowned. She'd overheard women speak of men's needs when they'd whispered about mistresses. Did that mean all gentlemen engaged such women? She glanced at her Uncle Aubrey. Surely not all of them. Then, again, her aunt and uncle did disappear with a frequency that put her to the blush. She was quite sure Uncle did not keep a mistress. But had he before he married Aunt Poppy?

Her troubled thoughts were interrupted when the duke and Lady Anne entered the box with her mother. The duchess invited them to attend their box for refreshments during the intermission and Aunt Poppy and Uncle Aubrey accepted with delight.

His Grace, Charlotte noted, gave a slight start when he glanced across the theater to where Ravencliffe and his party filled the earl's box. She might have missed the fleeting tightness of his lips, before they relaxed into what she recognized as resigned amusement, had she not been so aware of his presence.

That slight twitch of his lips when he spied the Ravencliffe party made her pulse leap in the hope that those elusive dimples would bracket his smile once again. Unfortunately, his expression settled into the polite public persona that kept all but his family at a distance. He radiated dignity mixed with a masculine air that made her breath quicken, though she didn't like the fact that she was drawn to a man who acknowledged her only because he was too polite to ignore a friend of his sister's.

When his gaze turned to Charlotte, her breath hitched. For a mere instant something lit his eyes before the flame vanished, replaced with the cool assessment she had come to recognize as his usual demeanor. He wouldn't have asked her to dance last night had he not been caught at her side when the set began. Still, though he'd frustrated her with his attitude about introducing her to other gentlemen before he'd returned her to her aunt's side, she'd been aware of his whereabouts every moment.

"Be careful not to lean too far over the railing," he warned with what stuck her as mocking amusement at her fascination with the crowd, "Lest you fall into the pit." He stepped closer to observe the group of young men below.

"I assure Your Grace I am not so foolish as to make such a spectacle of myself."

He gave a slight bow of acknowledgement. "I stand corrected."

He greeted Elizabeth before turning back and adding, "I recommend you observe the gentleman in the bilious green waistcoat and mustard colored cravat in the fifth row. That is the Earl of Grantley behaving in his usual form." When she looked, the gentleman in question was engaged in a friendly tussle over the possession of a flask. "Should you still wish to make his acquaintance after the evening is finished, he will be at my aunt's garden party on Friday a fortnight from tonight and you may ask her to do the honors."

The sardonic twist to his lips made it clear he doubted that after the performances, both onstage and off, she would not choose to ask.

She smiled brilliantly. "I am sure she will. She struck me as a most gracious lady when we were introduced last night."

"More likely, she will graciously decline," he informed her. "She doesn't approve of his current behavior." His eyes met hers with cool assessment before Uncle Aubrey asked him a question and he turned his attention to the conversations between his stepmother and her aunt and uncle.

When Anne took a seat beside Elizabeth and Charlotte, Charlotte debated whether she should mention her aunt's assessment of the ladies in Ravencliffe's box. Before she could decide, Anne gave a sharp little gasp, then turned to her friends with laughter lighting her eyes.

"I wonder how Lord Ravencliffe will manage to pay his respects during the intermission without offending Mama and your aunt," she said with a giggle. "My brother warned me that Lord Ravencliffe is to host the Marquess of Clarehaven this Season. He is held to have a most scandalous reputation, and Lucien decided it best to warn me to avoid his company as much as possible."

She turned her attention to the Earl's box and grinned. "It is obvious the ladies in their company are not ladies, and they dare not bring them to our attention, nor would it be good form for the gentlemen to abandon them while they come alone. Yet, they cannot pretend they have not seen that we occupy our box this evening." Chuckling in delight she added, "This should be most interesting."

After the Wolvertons returned to their box Charlotte tried to become engrossed in the performance taking place on the stage. Unfortunately, she couldn't keep her attention from drifting to the questions that now plagued her about men. Before coming to London, she had never contemplated the difference between men and women other than their accepted duties and roles in life. Did men really have different needs as well as duties? If so, what exactly were they? And how were they different than for women?

The curtain came down for the intermission and she realized with a start that she had lost the thread of the comedy being portrayed on stage. When Elizabeth commented that the soprano had less range than one would expect from a leading performer, Charlotte blindly agreed with her assessment. She parroted the same observation to Her Grace when they visited the Wolverton box moments later.

"If you will excuse me," His Grace said shortly after they entered the box, "I must pay my respects to others before the performance continues." That said, he gave a quick bow to them all, and left. Soon after, Lords Ravencliffe, Norcross, and the earl's guest entered the box without their escorts.

When the gentlemen made their bows to the duchess and Aunt Poppy, Anne nudged Charlotte and tipped her head in the direction of Ravencliffe's box with a grin before whispering, "I vow I should have known they would find a way." Charlotte looked across the theater to see the duke at Lord Ravencliffe's box. "The women are not deserted, the men can pay their respects, and Mother and your aunt can pretend they don't know where Lucien is while they do."

The women in the opposite box apparently knew the duke though Charlotte had not seen the earl introduce them. Did His Grace consort with such women? If all men had needs, and there was no denying that the Duke of Wolverton was a man, then it made sense he did. As she watched, one of the women placed her hand upon his arm as she made a comment. He grinned, and those devastating dimples could be seen all the way across the theater. Charlotte bristled when he leaned low over the woman's shoulder and said something in her ear that made her laugh and tap his arm with her fan. Charlotte decided his behavior was proof that he had never belonged on her list.

It struck Charlotte that Anne knew a great deal more about men and their needs because she had brothers to observe. Anne had immediately understood the situation and found it funny rather than shocking. With no brothers of her own, Charlotte had no practical understanding of males or their interactions with females, whether respectable or not. Clearly, she needed to explore this question. It was one thing to know men and women were different and quite another to understand exactly how and why.

She was pulled from her musings when Lord Ravencliffe presented the brown-haired gentleman she'd observed earlier. "May I introduce Lord Clarehaven?

Charlotte rose and curtsied along with her sister and Lady Anne. Lord Ravencliffe introduced each of them in turn and she extended her hand.

"I am pleased to make your acquaintance," he said as he bowed to her. He straightened, his eyes fixed on Charlotte's bosom and he murmured, "Very pleased."

Charlotte's eyes widened at his blatant flirting. She might not know a great deal about the private aspects of male and female relationships, but she recognized a man who believed every female found him irresistible. He clearly supposed his heated gaze would make her swoon with romantic bliss. But handsome as he was, he did not send shivers of awareness down her spine. Amused instead, she bit the inside of her cheek and smiled demurely as he released her hand.

Lord Ravencliffe cleared his throat, and she saw the Marquess's lips quirk before humor lit his expression and he turned to Uncle Aubrey, who was now the only male in their party. "You are most fortunate to be surrounded by such lovely ladies." He smiled ruefully, bowed to each of them, then made his excuses. "It has been an honor, ladies. However, I have seen a gentleman with whom I have been corresponding for some months and will need to speak with him before the intermission ends."

Once he and the others had gone, her family took their leave of the duchess and Lady Anne. Charlotte found her attention returning to Wolverton and the women of dubious virtue. Though Lord Ravencliffe and his guests returned to the women moments later, it was not until the warning gong sounded for the second act that the duke quit their box. That fact caused her to lose a bit of her enjoyment of the evening. The curtain rose and Charlotte forced her attention away from the questionable women and focused on the performance.

The soprano's range was, indeed, a bit narrow, even for a comedic role.

After the performance ended and they waited outside the theater for Uncle Aubrey's coach, Charlotte noticed Lord and Lady Dalton a short way from where she stood. The vivid red dress had indeed had its neckline lowered and Charlotte gasped to realize Lady Dalton wore the scandalous French stays brought to England by escaping immigrants. The stays did little more than support underside of the woman's bosom, and the dress revealed as much of her as possible without quite exposing all. She stood with distant dignity, while a middle-aged gentleman ogled her as he chatted with her husband.

How distasteful it must be for her to be subject to such rude attention. Lord Dalton's demands did not surprise her. Charlotte suspected the lady's cool demeanor was her armor against the scandalous gown her husband had forced her to wear. He had treated his first wife as nothing more than chattel over whom he held complete control. His attitude had not changed with his second, as demonstrated by his demands in the fitting of her dress. She did not doubt that if Lady Dalton's wrist injury had truly been the result of a fall, Lord Dalton had been the cause. Changing one's name and location did not change the man.

LUCIEN NOTICED THAT Charlotte Longborough had drifted slightly away from her family's party, her attention on Lord and Lady Dalton and the Duke of Dovehurst. Her earlier liveliness had turned troubled. What had upset her? He noted the deep décolleté of Lady Daltons gown and wondered if she was shocked by the generous display. Modest country life didn't embrace the more extremes of evening fashion, but a low-cut gown shouldn't cause such a disturbed alteration in her demeanor.

He stepped to her side.

"For someone who has recently left a comic opera, your expression is far too serious. Is there something amiss?"

"Not at all, Your Grace," she said as she turned her attention to him.

He studied her face for a moment before accepting her denial. Whatever had disturbed her thoughts lingered only a moment in her eyes and posture before she regained her usual humor. For that brief moment, though, her demeanor spoke of more maturity than he'd believed her to possess.

"I thought the entertainment to be quite diverting, do you not agree?" she asked.

Her comment, however, revealed the naïveté he expected from someone in her first Season. "As comedies go, I agree. Though the farces often become more silly than entertaining."

"Do you prefer drama, then, Your Grace?" Her eyes glinted with renewed humor that dispelled whatever had deceived him into thinking her more mature than she was.

"Drama offers more in the way of depth and reflective thinking," he assured her. She would do well to expand her tastes to weightier matters than frivolities of lovers hiding in closets while servants aped their employers behind their backs. "It raises questions about one's role in history and one's obligations to others."

"But don't comedies, especially farces, do the same thing?" she asked. Her tone was not one of question but of challenge.

He clarified, "Comedies may entertain, but they do not enlighten or improve their audience."

"I beg your pardon for disagreeing, Your Grace." She did not give the impression she wished his pardon. Her eyes sparkled and her eyebrow lifted. "They point out the absurdities and hypocrisies of social situations and historical events and make us laugh while acknowledging our own foibles."

How could she attempt to dignify the ridiculous contrivances he'd witnessed tonight as worthy of discussion? Histories and tragic dramas had meaning. They reminded people that the mistakes of the past had consequences. People who didn't learn those lessons paid the price of those consequences. He'd learned that lesson the hard way.

"Making light of serious issues allows the public to treat those subjects as though they hold no importance."

Her posture stiffened, revealing her irritation. "Making light of the issues they address makes it possible to bring such things to light in a less disturbing manner, and in so doing, they at least bring them into the light." A gentle breeze fluttered the ruffle on her dress, and she seemed to realize the challenge in her stance and relaxed her posture. Her voice modulated into a reasoning tone. "Histories and dramas scold, condemn and moralize." she said with a smile. "Comedies acknowledge that we are human." Her eyes, nearly black in the semi-darkness of the street, glinted with a flash of sudden amusement. "I would wager that theaters have far greater attendance when they present a comedy than when they present a drama or history."

*Audacious chit*. What made her so confident in her assessment? "And you, fresh from the country schoolroom, are an authority of the role of theater in human commentary?"

His words made her flush, though whether from anger or embarrassment, he wasn't sure. Perhaps he'd reacted too strongly. It was her first Season, after all. She still had a lot to learn about life.

"I have read a great many plays though I have not had the privilege, until now, to see one performed on a real stage," she admitted. "But I believe Mister Shakespeare had it right. The world is a stage and the people in it play their parts as written by Providence. The theater, whether imitating life in the country or town, merely condenses those human stories into a three-hour performance."

He recognized a certain truth in her statement, and she'd voiced them with a dignity he had to admire. There was a brain beneath that lovely caramel brown hair.

A new carriage pulled up and several brash young men moved to claim it. They rushed forward to race each other for the forward-facing seats, laughing and wagering as they jostled for position. In the melee, one young man crashed into Charlotte's back who, with a cry of alarm, fell forward. Lucien quickly caught her in his arms and hauled her up against his chest before she hit the pavement.

"Watch what you are about, sir!" He ordered sharply. At the same time, he registered the pleasure of holding a well-endowed female in his arms. "You and your unruly friends nearly knocked this young lady to the ground."

The young lady in question currently had her face buried against his chest and he was acutely aware of the full feminine curves pressed against the rest of him. He closed his eyes for a moment and breathed in the scent of wildflowers. He made himself release his hold to set her upright lest she realize how much she affected him. Holding her upper arms gently he leaned down to look into her eyes and asked, "Are you alright?" He realized his mistake when his gaze shifted and fastened onto tempting plump lips that made him want to scoop her back up and kiss her senseless.

"Yes. Yes, of course," she murmured. Her face flamed in obvious embarrassment.

The young man's voice intruded. "I am sorry." His boisterous demeanor had altered to apologetic as he bowed toward Charlotte. "I do beg your pardon. I am glad you are unharmed, Miss." He shot a glance at Lucien and correctly interpreted his expression. "I shall remove myself immediately." With a quick final bow, he took his place in the carriage and they drove off.

"You appear to spend much of your time in the path of disaster, Miss Longborough," Lucien teased as he placed her hand on his arm to guide her back to where her family's carriage had finally arrived. Thankfully, the dim light of the street concealed his discomfort of body. Too bad it did nothing to relieve the disturbance to his peace of mind.

*Bloody hell, he'd nearly forgotten himself and created a scandal in front of a public theater house.* With careful civility, he assisted her and her sister into the carriage where her aunt was already seated.

# CHAPTER 6

"I had an odd dream last night," Sarah murmured at breakfast the next morning. She looked sideways at their aunt and uncle to see if they'd heard her before making eye contact with Elizabeth and Charlotte. "I'm not sure what it meant, but..." She pleated her napkin with precise folds, undid the folds, and repeated her actions as she said, "I was at a strange outdoor menagerie during a wild thunderstorm with frogs croaking and snakes slithering through the mud."

"A rat chased a hedgehog in circles while a hawk swooped down and carried off a mouse. Then Harry chased a weasel over the barriers and up a tree. Everything was so strange and at the same time it all made perfect sense."

She surveyed her sisters with solemn concern. "What woke me up," she whispered as she sent another worried glance to where Uncle Aubrey sat reading the Times and Aunt Poppy reviewed her appointment calendar. "Was a red fox caught in a poacher's trap." She took a short tight breath. "It had Cousin Edward's eyes."

Charlotte's heart lurched and her lungs constricted. Cousin Edward had russet-red hair the exact shade of the foxes that inhabited the wild areas near Uncle Aubrey's estate and that, along with his clever mind and quick reflexes, had made him known by most of the family as their resident fox.

"Are you sure?" Elizabeth asked as she, too, checked to see that their aunt and uncle had not picked up on the sudden tension Sarah's revelation sparked. "He was *trapped*– not...?"

"His hind leg was caught, and he was bleeding and in pain." Sarah clarified. Her voice held a wobble of distress. "Should I tell Aunt Poppy? Would she understand?"

"Grandmamma was her mother, of course she would understand," Elizabeth assured her. It was no secret that Grandmamma had dreams, but few knew of Sarah's. "But we don't want to alarm her until we hear something official. There is nothing she could do at this time and it will only make her worry more."

Charlotte nodded her head in agreement. *The fox was hurt but not dead.* "If Edward has been injured, he may well recover before we receive word from him. There is nothing to be done but wait and see." She reached out to comfort her little sister who, Charlotte knew, wished her dream had been clearer– or that she'd not had it at all. "Don't trouble yourself, Sarah. If Edward were in mortal danger you would have seen that... and all injuries are painful. I'm sure all will be well."

Sarah's expression eased, though she still glanced at Aunt Poppy before taking a piece of toast and nibbling on it. Charlotte poured herself a fresh cup of chocolate and hoped she was right.

Determined to follow her own advice, Charlotte finished her breakfast, then asked her sisters if they'd like to take Harry for a walk in the park. Elizabeth chose to remain home to work on a project, and Sarah reminded her that she'd already been invited to join Rowena Caldwell and her governess for an outing.

When she crossed through the park entrance a little while later, she couldn't help but remember her first disastrous venture with Harry. Though His Grace had been at several of the same entertainments she'd attended since the opera, she didn't think he'd changed his opinion that she courted disaster. If anything, it was as though he avoided her as much as possible without quite appearing to be uncivil. His sisters and stepmother, at least, welcomed her company and blamed the park incident on the duke for racing in the park.

Today was warmer, the sky entirely free of clouds, and the grounds equally free of mud. Harry trotted smoothly along beside her on his lead. This outing was as much a test to see if Charlotte could now handle him safely as it was an opportunity to enjoy the clear spring day. She was pleased that John, the footman assigned to his training, had made great strides with Harry after a few weeks of work. He accompanied her and her maid, ready to step in if Harry misbehaved.

Before starting out, the footman had warned her to let go of the lead instantly if Harry forgot his lessons and attempted to chase the park's wildlife. After her earlier experience, she didn't need to be told the folly of trying to hold back a dog that, though not fully grown, already nearly outweighed her. True, the young wolfhound still occasionally found it impossible to resist investigating fascinating scents, but he no longer wove back and forth tripping her with his lead, nor did he tug her forward when he saw squirrels in the distance.

Sarah had grinned and warned Charlotte not to ruin her new green frock if Harry forgot his lessons. The Wolverton carriage had arrived at that moment, and Lady Rowena had informed her that Lady Anne would be enjoying a morning ride in the park with Lord Merton. Charlotte made a mental note to congratulate her friend on her popularity. A wide circle of beaux already surrounded Lady Anne, and she'd ridden out with Lord Swathmore only the day before.

Though Charlotte had also been invited on a few carriage rides and had danced every dance at the balls she attended, she and Elizabeth weren't nearly so popular. Lord Seldon, who'd included a poem with his flowers, had been one of those who taken her on promenade, but he had done so with two other ladies since then and that was fine with Charlotte. He had been fun, but not sparked her interest. So far, no one had. Well, no one whose attention was sparked in return, she amended.

As though that thought had conjured him up, she saw the duke with Lords Ravencliffe and Clarehaven walking their horses along Rotten Row, stopping occasionally to exchange greetings with their acquaintances.

Among those acquaintances, she noted, was a somewhat carelessly dressed gentleman who held multiple leads as he maneuvered four spaniels across the grounds. A veritable giant of a man, he controlled the dogs with casual ease.

Charlotte had taken a path away from the carriage traffic but still avoided the trees that had been her downfall so recently. She quickly realized that the gentleman's path might intersect with her own and turned the lead over to the footman. John took firm control of the leather and gave a command to Harry when he spotted the dogs ahead. Harry's ears perked and his body quivered with anticipation, but he sat beside the footman and Charlotte breathed a sigh of relief that she'd avoided catastrophe.

The spaniels spotted Harry and set up welcoming yelps that Harry answered with delighted woofs as he leapt forward and dragged the dismayed footman over to meet them. The racket attracted the attention of everyone in the vicinity and Charlotte realized she had once again become the center of a public scene despite her best efforts.

*Blast and botheration*!

Surprisingly, the owner of the spaniels had managed to keep hold of his dogs though their leads hopelessly tangled. They all leapt and jostled to check out the lumbering beast that delightedly danced around them, lowering his forepaws in an attempt to get them to play. John Footman managed to haul Harry away from his would-be doggy friends and the other man did the same, scolding the dogs by name.

"Archie! Hunter! Sit!" He tugged the other set of leads and commanded, "Toby! Rufus! Down!"

To Charlotte's amazement, the dogs obeyed his commands with little more than whines of disappointment, but they settled, and he was able to straighten out their leads.

"Once again, Miss Longborough, you are at the center of disaster," Wolverton drawled after he dismounted. Charlotte cringed to realize he'd come to her footman's assistance with Harry. On the evening of the opera his comment had reflected amusement, but this morning his voice held a note of disapproval. "As large as your beast is, four dogs working as a pack could inflict a great deal of damage."

"Oh, no, Wolverton", the dog owner protested. "I confess it was Toby who issued the first challenge to the lady's pet, but my dogs know better than to attack another canine."

"Nonetheless," the duke countered, "of the four times I have been in her proximity, Miss Longborough has come to grief in all but one." He studied Charlotte from his superior height making her feel like a scolded child having to look up in order to observe elders. "Fortunately, she managed to attend my sister's come-out without causing chaos."

"That is most unfair, Your Grace," Charlotte protested. "I could not avoid the accident the other evening, and today I turned my dog over to the footman as soon as I realized that Harry might take exception to other dogs in the vicinity." How dare he reprimand her like an unruly ward– and he most certainly was *not* her guardian. She turned her attention to where Harry now sat between John and Wolverton, his avid attention still on the spaniels though he remained still. "And what is more," she stated, "they did no actual harm."

"She's right, Lucien" Lady Anne's voice joined the conversation and Charlotte turned to see that Lord Merton had guided his carriage to where they all stood. "All is well." She gave Charlotte a cheeky grin. "Did he introduce you to His Grace?" When Charlotte looked at her blankly, Anne laughed aloud. "Lucien do your duty."

The duke scowled at his sister, but a hint of a devilish light replaced his disapproval when he formally introduced her to the Duke of Everham. Square faced with a strong, Norman nose and gentle brown eyes, the duke gave the appearance of a large country gamekeeper in fawn skin pantaloons and brown wool jacket. He ordered his dogs to stay as he took the few steps nearer to bow over her hand. "I am most honored, Miss Longborough."

Charlotte caught her breath when the overpowering odor of dog inundated her. "As am I," she murmured. The duke's person and clothing gave every appearance of being clean if somewhat rumpled, but the odor was unmistakable. Involuntarily, she glanced to the duke whose expression of *I-told-you-so* had her fighting to keep her own expression neutral.

Everham straightened and beamed at her. "Always glad to meet a fellow dog lover though, as you can see, I favor spaniels." He studied Harry where he now lolled against Wolverton's boots. "Large as he is, he looks to be a bit young– perhaps eight or nine months. Am I right?"

Charlotte took a discreet step back when he released her hand. She tried to breathe through her mouth as she admitted she didn't know precisely how old Harry was and told him the story of the dog's rescue. During her recitation most of their observers, including Lord Merton and Lady Anne, returned to the promenade but Lords Clarehaven, Ravencliffe, and the duke remained.

When Charlotte finished her story, Lord Clarehaven commented, "Irish hounds can be fierce hunters and are most protective of their owners."

"Harry is embarrassingly friendly with everyone." Charlotte chuckled as she noted that Wolverton stood scratching Harry's ear as though entirely unaware of his actions. "So far he has no awareness of either his reputation or his size."

"He may well discover both should you ever be in distress," Everham assured her with a gallant bow. "Though I hope you are never put in the position to find out."

Charlotte was grateful for the slight breeze that helped to freshen the air. She tried to put a little more distance from the pungent duke without being rude. Standing to his right, and therefore slightly upwind from Everham as he did, the duke made no attempt to hide his smug amusement at her discomfort.

"I say," Everham suddenly said. "My bitch, Roxy, just whelped. Would you like to visit her pups? They are all spoken for, of course, but they are an excellent litter." He took them all in with a proud glance. "Not a runt in the bunch."

"If I remember correctly," Wolverton said, "The pups haven't yet opened their eyes. Might it not be better to wait until they are a little more independent and, therefore, more entertaining?"

Everham's expression dimmed for a moment. "To be sure, you are correct. Most ladies–" He bowed slightly in Charlotte's direction, "prefer to watch them scamper and tumble. Perhaps I shall arrange a viewing day once they are more of an age."

"An excellent idea," Wolverton stated briskly. "In the meantime, we have kept Miss Longborough standing far too long for true propriety." He turned to her. "I believe your footman might do well to handle your beast as you return home."

"It was my intention, Your Grace." Charlotte hated that he supposed her incapable of coming to that conclusion on her own. "If you will excuse me."

The duke had certainly made it clear he saw her as little more than a lodestone for disaster and embarrassment. What was more, she was beginning to believe he might be right.

AFTER MISS LONGBOROUGH and her beast crossed the park, Lucien remounted his horse, bid Everham a good day, and rejoined his companions to finish their ride. To his annoyance, Clarehaven watched her until she was out of hearing distance, and then said with a chuckle, "What a delightful Season this promises to be. You said she is a Longborough?"

"Despite her family's reputation, she is an innocent and a friend of my sister's." Lucien warned him with a tight smile. "So, unless your intentions are honorable, I suggest you find another lady with whom to comport yourself this Season."

Clarehaven looked back to where Miss Longborough had reached the end of the park. He gave Lucien a sardonic smile before he asked, "Are you sure that delicious morsel is off limits, Wolverton? As I understand it, she isn't a relative and you aren't courting or bedding her, so why do you care if I enjoy a bit of flirting... or perhaps a bit more than flirting?"

Cold fury engulfed Lucien at the idea of Clarehaven attempting to seduce Charlotte Longborough—or *any* unmarried miss—he amended. Only the knowledge that it would create a scene kept him from knocking the insufferable rake from his horse. "The Longborough sisters are ladies and close friends to my sister," he warned the Marquess coldly, "As such, I consider them to be equally under my protection."

The Marquess gave him a knowing grin and said, "I think you want to bed her yourself."

"You are mistaken." Lucien denied the Marquess's accusation. Then he realized that on the most basic level it was true. It wasn't only his temper Charlotte Longborough raised when she challenged him. His body came to attention and ignored his intellect whenever she was near. He was still half-aroused from their unexpected encounter.

*Damn Clarehaven for his sly innuendo.*

Lucien's humor was not improved when he arrived home an hour later and discovered Lord Jeremy Bascomb in his drawing room with Anne, drinking tea and munching sweet biscuits along with Merton and Swathmore. When had Bascomb been introduced to his sister, and why had his stepmother allowed it? Bascomb was a scrapegrace who attracted scandal with all the reckless determination of a rebellious son.

As soon as the men left, he told his stepmother, "I hope you will not encourage Bascomb, Mama. He is too wild and undisciplined to play court to Anne. For that is all he would do—play."

"I am aware that he has yet to mature, Lucien," his stepmother informed him. "But since you have declined to attend the Winterstone's musical evening and Anne is not comfortable singing solo, I thought to ask Lord Bascomb to join her in a duet. He has an excellent voice."

Lucien shuddered with distaste. Such evenings, where the guests attempted to entertain each other, inevitably made one aware of precisely how few people actually had the talent they believed they had. Young ladies with thin slightly off-key voices warbled, while their sisters, cousins, or friends plunked determinedly on the pianoforte or scraped the protesting strings of their violins. A musical evening was always an excellent reason for spending time at one's club.

He wasn't fooled by his stepmother's reasoning. She'd orchestrated matters with all the cunning of a general and knew exactly what would make him agree to escort them to the musical.

If Jeremy Bascomb were to perform a duet with Anne, they would have to rehearse together—something Lucien had no intention of allowing. Of course, that meant that, in addition to providing escort, Lucien would be obliged to add his own baritone to his sister's soprano in an odious duet of sentimentality.

Annoyed and disgruntled, he gave a resigned sigh, and bowed to duty.

The next week, soon after they arrived at the Winterstone's residence, he watched his sister hold court with half a dozen other young bucks who stood not a chance in hell of gaining his approval, but who would fill Anne's Season with laughter and excitement until the right prospect came along. Bascomb was among them, but she grinned at Lucien over their heads and he relaxed. That cheeky grin told him her heart was not in danger from any of her currently fawning beaux.

He also saw that his stepmother had commandeered seats in the second row of the chairs arranged down the center of the grand salon. At the end of the long room, a pianoforte dominated the musicians' dais. A refreshment table had been placed against the side window wall, with plates of sweet biscuits, tarts, and cream cakes to be enjoyed during the intermission. The usual scents of perfumes, starch, and hopeful females floated on the air.

Ravencliffe, Norcross, and Clarehaven joined him a few minutes later. He wouldn't have expected the Marquess to attend so mundane an entertainment had he not greeted Lucien with a sly grin and commented, "There is nothing like a musical evening to whet a man's appetite to hear a woman sing a more erotic song." He checked the room with an amused and calculating eye. "Lady Middlesham looks to be in fine form tonight, do you not agree?"

His companions glanced toward the lady in question, a tall lushly endowed brunette who'd recently come out of mourning. At least, Lucien thought, Clarehaven's current quarry was a widow and, from the way she returned Clarehaven's gaze, a willing one.

Lucien shifted his attention from Lady Middlesham to a trio of ladies dressed in matching dresses and made a slight groan of disappointment. "Lady Montfort is here with her daughters in tow. They will undoubtedly subject us to one of her original compositions."

When Clarehaven raised a questioning brow, Ravencliffe explained, "She imagines herself to have great talent as a composer of string music and her daughters as virtuosos of the violin." He grimaced. "One cannot tell, however, if it is the composition or the performance that makes listening the greater trial."

Lucien agreed. Lady Montfort's regular contributions to the various entertainments provided during the Season were an excellent example of why he'd avoided such evenings in the past. Who else would he have to endure this evening before adding his own idiocy to the mix? Anne still held court and he noted that she'd now been joined by Ladies Pomphrey, Littlemarsh, and the Longborough sisters.

Miss Charlotte Longborough was another reason he'd not planned to attend. He'd known she and her sister would be there, and she disturbed his peace of mind more than he cared to admit. As Clarehaven had so annoyingly pointed out, his natural instincts went on alert whenever she was near. And, as he'd told Clarehaven, she was off limits to any but a prospective bridegroom. A role he most definitely had no intention of taking on himself.

His gaze focused on Charlotte Longborough, whose expression revealed a hint of nervous vulnerability that must mean she had little confidence in the quality of her voice. At least the low pitch of her speaking voice meant she wasn't going to be a screeching soprano. She laughed at something Lady Littlemarsh said, and his pulse jerked in response.

Over the past weeks she had become a regular member of his sister's circle of friends and it disturbed him that he often found himself listening for her voice among the feminine chatter in the drawing room. He looked away and saw her elder sister held a musical score but no portable instrument, which must mean she would pound upon the pianoforte.

He took a fortifying breath before taking his seat beside his stepmother. Only for family would he suffer the exhibitions of non-talent and occasional, but rare, competence he would endure tonight.

# CHAPTER 7

When Charlotte and her family entered Lady Winterstone's drawing room, Charlotte's trepidation mounted at the number of guests who stood in clusters and had already seated themselves for the coming entertainments. Though not so crowded as a ballroom, there were far more people than she was used to, and singing beloved songs at home with her sisters was a far cry from performing for people used to the stages of London.

Of course, she reminded herself, this gathering was meant to display the accomplishments of the newest members of society as much as to provide an evening's entertainment. The native talents of the performers would vary greatly, for everyone was expected to contribute. Elizabeth had practiced her piano selection with diligence all week, and Charlotte had chosen a song that complemented both her taste and contralto limits. Still, she found her nerves had left her mouth parched and she hoped Lady Winterstone had included a pitcher of plain water along with the lemonade and wine punch.

Charlotte spied Lady Anne surrounded by several gentlemen who vied for her attention. Excusing themselves from Aunt Poppy and Uncle Avery, Charlotte and Elizabeth crossed the room to join their friends.

"I do hope you don't prove to be spectacularly talented," Lady Anne greeted them with a broad smile. "For I'm not, and it's difficult not to be jealous of those with superior skills."

Lady Millicent agreed, and added, "A little talent is fine, so long as you don't make us feel inferior. I'm scarcely able to carry a tune, though I haven't yet set the dogs to howling."

Charlotte laughed. "You have greatly eased my mind."

Charlotte turned her attention from her companions when she heard their hostess greet the Daltons. Lady Dalton leaned carefully on her husband's arm and walked with a slight limp.

"Lady Dalton," Lady Winterstone said, her voice reflecting her concern, "How have you hurt yourself? Are you in need of medical assistance?"

"My wife tripped over her own feet this morning and twisted her ankle." Lord Dalton told her with a rueful chuckle. "But we could not miss your gathering."

"I'd most certainly have understood had you sent your regrets," Lady Winterstone assured them. "I wouldn't want you to injure yourself more, simply to attend a musical evening."

"If we sent our regrets every time my wife had an accident," Lord Dalton spoke before Lady Dalton could answer, "We'd miss half the Season's entertainments. Why she's hurt herself twice this past week alone." He patted his wife's forearm and gave her an indulgent smile. "I love my wife, but she's a bit clumsy."

"He has the right of it," Lady Dalton flushed and said quietly, "I have long gone through life somewhat out of balance. Please don't concern yourself over a silly fall."

"Then I hope you enjoy yourself." Lady Winterstone said as she led them to a pair of vacant chairs. She excused herself and Lady Dalton took a seat when her husband told her he wished to speak to some gentlemen at the far side of the room before the performances began.

Charlotte realized Lord Dalton hadn't recognized her at Anne's ball, but feared he would remember the Longborough name when she and Elizabeth performed. He'd undoubtedly recall the child who'd made a pest of herself before he locked her into that shed. Yet, if she were ever to appease her conscience, it must be now.

She slipped into the seat beside Lady Dalton and took a quick breath before saying in a low voice, "I beg you will pardon me for saying this, but I'm unconvinced that you're accident prone."

Lady Dalton's startled gaze met her earnest one. "I beg your pardon?"

Charlotte reached out, placing her hand on the woman's arm in reassurance. "I mean..." She hesitated, knowing that she could be wrong, but unable to ignore her instincts. "I don't think your *silly fall* was an accident, nor do I believe you fell in the garden when I first saw you at the Wolverton ball."

The woman's eyes widened, and Charlotte saw she remembered the incident. "Of course, I fell." She glanced across the room to where Lord Dalton stood. When she answered, her voice shook. "I have... dizzy spells."

"Your husband indicated you were simply clumsy." Charlotte reminded her.

"The spells make me clumsy."

"I think your husband makes you clumsy."

Lady Dalton's eyes rounded in alarm and she made to pull away from Charlotte's grasp. "Whatever could you mean by that?"

"I mean I believe he mistreats you and that you're in danger."

"You must not say such things about my husband," she whispered. "He'd never purposely hurt me. Both my wrist and ankle were my own fault. No one is more devastated when I am hurt than he."

Charlotte saw the defensive light in Lady Dalton's eyes and knew saying more would be pointless. "Very well," she said as she stood. "But if you ever need assistance, you have only to ask and I'll do what I can to help. You see, I knew your husband when I was a child and know his true character."

Charlotte was grateful Anne and Elizabeth were engaged in conversation with Lady Winterstone about the order of their performances when she rejoined them and didn't notice her unease. She had tried. She had offered to help. Though she didn't know what she could do. But if ever Lady Dalton called on her, she'd find a way. She would not fail her.

She swallowed several times, fighting the memories, but they were as vivid as the morning she'd inadvertently witnessed the outgoing and handsome Albert Franklin backhand his wife for over-sweetening his tea. The force of his blow had sent Mrs. Franklin to the ground. She struggled up, her lip bleeding, and apologized before quickly pouring him a fresh cup. Charlotte's throat had locked, and she'd frozen in place lest he see her in the shadow of the large oak bordering the back of their garden.

Such violence had been far beyond Charlotte's experience, and she'd been fascinated despite her fear. She'd begun to watch them as often as she dared. It wasn't the last time he hit his wife over the next year.

The one time he'd caught Charlotte spying, he'd locked her in the tool shed with the threat of drowning her in the river if she did it again. Terrified, she'd stayed away, never telling anyone what she'd seen for fear he would hear of it and follow through on his threat. She had never forgotten, however, that a handsome face could hide an ugly character.

Charlotte glanced over to where Lord Dalton was talking with Lord Winterstone and fought the urge to hide before Lord Dalton realized who she was. She was no longer a child. She was no longer in danger of being locked into a garden shed. She was no longer afraid—

Her throat locked, her breath caught as it had long ago, and her stomach flipped. She closed her eyes and admitted the truth. *I'm still afraid.*

She opened her eyes, clasped her hands together, and vowed she would not let fear keep her from helping Lady Dalton if she ever called on her for help.

Lady Winterstone stepped in front of the chairs and asked that everyone take their seats so the performances could begin. Charlotte sank onto a chair between Elizabeth and Lady Anne, grateful that no one had noticed her distress. She folded her hands in her lap and made herself breathe slowly until the trembling ceased and her pulse slowed to a steady pace once more.

When she calmed, Charlotte checked the program the footman had given her when they arrived. Hers would be the last performance before the intermission. First, however were the three ladies currently stepping up to the dais. Glancing at the program again, she read:

*Spring's Sweet Promise—an Original Composition by Lady Montfort Performed by Lady Montfort, Misses Francis and Daphne Montfort*

The matron and her two daughters took their places, violins in hand and she heard a faint groan from one of the gentlemen behind her. The ladies began to play, and Charlotte quickly understood why.

By the time she took her turn, Charlotte was no longer nervous about the quality of her voice. Certainly, she couldn't be any worse than any who had sung thus far. She, at least, could carry her tune accurately and, she believed, with clarity of tone.

Her awareness of Lord Dalton near the back of the room gave her more concern.

When Lady Winterstone introduced her, Charlotte steeled herself, and took note of his reaction. First puzzled, then assessing, she knew the moment he made the connection. His gaze hardened with clear intent when he saw she remembered his threats. She looked away first.

# CHAPTER 8

The refreshment intermission was announced when she finished her song, and she quickly moved to join Elizabeth and Anne lest Lord Dalton approach her. Several gentlemen offered to supply them with lemonade or punch, but their offers were rendered unnecessary when the duke, Lord Ravencliffe and Lord Norcross approached carrying glasses of lemonade.

"You have a pleasing voice, Miss Charlotte," The duke commented as he handed glasses to her and Lady Anne.

"You are being kind," She took a grateful sip of lemonade. "I dared not attempt anything more taxing than a ballad."

"If only more ladies knew their limitations and confined their efforts to their range." He glanced across the room at a young lady who had attempted an aria earlier. "You did well."

Lord Norcross chuckled as he agreed. "The old ballads soothe the soul while operatic arias generally dramatize chaos of feeling."

The duke muttered something about feelings of homicide or suicide and Charlotte had to swallow quickly to quell a sudden chuckle. His Grace's comment came as a bit of a surprise. She had not guessed that beneath his sober exterior lurked a dry sense of humor.

In the short time she'd known him she'd seen he didn't compete for attention, but when he entered a room people noticed. She also acknowledged that it was more than his title that made people pay attention. When he spoke, people listened and when he showed displeasure, people moved out of his way. But, having met his family, she knew without a doubt that he would not raise a hand against a woman.

Lord Ravencliffe offered the glass he carried to Elizabeth. "I see you are to begin the second half of the evening with one of Herr Beethoven's sonatas. Some feel his music is rather controversial, though I must say I appreciate his ability to stir the soul. Do you enjoy music as well as woodworking?"

Charlotte noted that Elizabeth flushed at his directness, before she told him, "I find playing the pianoforte to be more interesting than plying a needle in the evenings." With a smile she confessed, "I become a bit restless away from my tools, and the dexterity required for the pianoforte fills the need to do something with my hands. Herr Beethoven's pieces challenge me."

"That is to be expected," he replied. "The creative mind is always at work even when the body is at rest."

Charlotte eyed the man, looking for an undercurrent of derision or mockery, but he appeared genuinely curious. Perhaps he might do for Elizabeth after all. Perhaps the women who'd occupied his box at the opera were the guests of Lord Clarehaven and not of his choosing.

When Lady Winterstone called for her guests' attention a few minutes later, Elizabeth took her place at the pianoforte while the rest of the guests took their seats. Charlotte saw that the audience had diminished slightly in the interim, but whether from other obligations or consideration of their musical sensibilities was anyone's guess.

Thankfully, the Daltons were among those who'd left.

DAYS LATER WHEN THE duchess and Lady Anne called on Aunt Poppy and the Longboroughs, Anne fairly danced through the door with unsuppressed excitement. As soon as the three younger women excused themselves to walk in the park, Anne announced, "I have had my first offer and the Season is not yet half over."

"Who?" Both sisters spoke at once.

"The Marquess of Ailsbury. Can you imagine?" She chortled. "He told Lucien that I was a fine filly of a female who was sure to produce a sturdy heir and spare."

"Ailsbury?" Charlotte gasped, "But he is older than Uncle Aubrey. Surely Wolverton did not allow him to pay his addresses to you."

"Of course he didn't," Anne laughed again.

Not only was Lord Ailsbury close to sixty years old, but he was a thickset, loud, horse-mad widower whose wife had died giving birth to his eighth daughter. His only heir had been stillborn years earlier. Charlotte knew this because Aunt Poppy had told her he was just out of mourning when he arrived at the ball.

"How could he think your brother would approve such a match?" Elizabeth asked.

"I don't know either," Anne said, "But the point is, I have received my first offer of the Season." She giggled, obviously enjoying the situation. "An absurd one, to be sure, but an offer none the less." She raised her hand to her forehead in a parody of drama. "The greatest pressure is removed. No matter if I remain a spinster, no one can claim I never had an offer."

Charlotte burst into laughter. "You will never be a spinster."

"I know I won't," Anne assured them gleefully. "I just said that to make the point... and to make you laugh. Even Lucien laughed when he told me about Ailsbury's assessment of my *finer* qualities—apparently I show promise of being an excellent breeder—and my brother is always grim when he talks about whom I should and should not encourage."

"Who does he warn you to avoid?"

"Let me see if I can remember them all." She gave an exasperated sigh. "He adds to the list daily." She checked around the park and nodded her head in the direction of each as she named them, "Mr. Theodore Hook because he is a nodcock who plays practical jokes and leads all his friends into trouble. Lord Jeremy Bascomb because he is a rake and a friend of Mr. Hook and is just as much trouble. She took an exaggerated breath. The Earl of Marley because he is following in his father's footsteps at the game tables...and with equally bad luck. The Earl of Grantley because he is likely to break his neck on some fool wager– Lucien's description, not mine. Lord Everham," She glanced at Charlotte with a quick grin, "For odiferous reasons over and above his inability to give attention to anyone or anything that does not have four legs or fur... and, of course, the Marquess of Clarehaven."

The Marquess currently cantered along Rotten Row, nodding to various gentlemen and stopping at the carriages of chaperoned young ladies along the way. Clarehaven saw them, tipped his hat, and directed his horse in their direction.

"According to Lucien he is a remorseless rake who will ruin me then quit the country leaving the family in scandal and me in disgrace, as he is reported to have done to an unnamed lady some years ago." She ceased ticking off names and huffed in frustration. "I vow it is a wonder Lucien has allowed me to ride out with anyone, for he gives every gentleman who calls a threatening stare before granting permission for the outing."

"He allowed you to ride with Lord Merton and Lord Swathmore." Charlotte reminded her.

"Only because Lord Merton is a pleasant, but most unimaginative, somewhat boring gentleman, and Lord Swathmore is a distant cousin who is hoping to convince my brother to buy him a commission in the horse guards. He wouldn't dare do anything to upset Lucien, so therefore I am safe with him." She sighed. "Lord help me, but if Lucien keeps vetting my beaux, Lord Ailsbury might well be the only offer I receive."

Lord Clarehaven reached the pedestrian path and dismounted with a flourished bow. "Good morning, ladies. How is it you are in the park alone together?" He gave them a knowing grin. "Are you planning scandalous adventures?"

"One does not court scandal, my Lord." Elizabeth told him. "It tends to find its victims without encouragement."

"Nor are we alone, sir. We are properly escorted by both a footman and maid." Lady Anne declared as she directed his attention to the servants who followed before adding, "I do confess I hope for an innocent adventure or two," She laughed. "Though poor Charlotte has already dealt with more than she expected."

He studied Charlotte a moment then smiled with devilish charm. "Perhaps I can offer you my assistance in adding to your tally. Planned adventures have the added appeal of anticipation." He lifted one eyebrow in an exaggerated leer that made them all laugh.

"I shall keep that in mind should the Season threaten to disappoint." Charlotte retorted. "Though the type of adventures that create anticipation may court the very scandal we wish to avoid."

That made him chuckle before he countered, "Scandals are only scandals if they become public."

Clarehaven's attention shifted behind them as another of Uncle Aubrey's footmen caught up with them. "Your uncle sent me for you," he panted. Clearly, he had rushed to find them, "You must return at once."

Icy fingers chilled Charlotte's heart and dread settled like a stone in her belly. Only bad news would cause her uncle to send for them in such a manner. Their cousin Edward was fighting the French on the Peninsula. Had something happened to him? *Please God, not Edward.*

They hastily excused themselves and hurried back to the house and into the drawing room where the duchess sat beside Aunt Poppy on the settee. Sarah sat white faced in an armchair while Uncle Aubrey stood holding a letter as he paced the room in deep thought. All their expressions reflected distress and worry, but poor Sarah sat frozen in misery, her eyes red rimmed and heavy with unshed tears.

Uncle Aubrey stopped his pacing at their entrance and lifted the letter in his hand, "Edward has been injured." He announced without preliminary. "He is being sent to Portsmouth from Lisbon."

"How bad is he hurt? Do you know?"

Though the eldest of the Elsworth sons, Edward had begged Uncle Avery to buy him a commission and allow him to defend England against Napoleon. It had taken months of arguing and cajoling, but Edward had finally convinced his parents that since his younger brother Charles, who was still at school, was too young, it was his duty, and they had finally let him go.

Uncle Aubrey let his arm drop to his side and his normally cheery expression saddened. "His leg was broken. He writes that he is being sent home as a cautionary measure, but I doubt he would be sent home if all that were needed was time for him to heal. From what I have heard at my club, the leg could fester from the conditions in the field, to say nothing of the dangers of the voyage to England."

He began pacing again. "I'm sorry to cut your Season short, but we must leave for Portsmouth immediately in order to prepare for his arrival. Once he is in Portsmouth, we'll travel on to Alderstone so he can recuperate at home. Your things are being packed as we speak."

"May I offer a suggestion?" The duchess took Aunt Poppy's hand in hers but directed her words to Uncle Aubrey. "Rather than move your entire household to Portsmouth and then again to your estate, why not leave your nieces with me? You will travel faster, and arranging care and lodging for your son will be simpler." She turned her attention back to Aunt Poppy. "Rowena would certainly love Sarah's company and I'm more than willing to sponsor your nieces for the rest of the Season."

"I'm not sure–" Aunt Poppy began.

"A capital idea." Uncle Aubrey gave a sigh of relief before asking, "Wolverton won't mind?"

"Of course not," The duchess said with conviction. "We've plenty of room and he will be escorting Anne already. Why would he mind?"

# CHAPTER 9

It was late afternoon when Lucien signed the last of his correspondence and reached for the dark blue sealing wax on his desk. His morning had been interrupted by that fool Ailsbury with his outlandish offer, and then he'd needed to send detailed instructions for the transfer of funds to his steward for estate repairs. He sealed his reply to his man of business, and had rung for a footman to deliver it when a commotion outside his door caught his attention.

An all too familiar low-pitched voice filtered through the study door from the entry hall. His stepmother and sister had not returned alone. Then a dog's bark startled him, and he strode across the room and flung open the door.

Charlotte Longborough's shaggy gray beast gave a delighted woof and sent Lucien staggering back into the room when he leapt up and licked Lucien's face in greeting. Dog breath filled his nostrils before he could regain his footing and push the beast down.

"Harry, down." Dismay, concern, and amusement succeeded one another on Charlotte Longborough's expressive face as she tugged her dog away from his person. "I am so sorry, Your Grace. I promise he will stay in the garden and not bother you again."

The dog settled to the floor but his whipping tail and quivering nose told another story.

"Oh, Lucien, I'm so glad you are home." His stepmother's calm voice announced as she came to stand beside Charlotte and her mongrel. "Lord and Lady Elsworth have been called to Portsmouth. Their son was wounded and is returning to England to recover."

Lucien eyed the various trunks and valises in his entry hall and completed the obvious statement. "So you invited the Longboroughs to stay with us until they returned."

"I knew you would understand," his stepmother declared. "Now why don't you join us in the drawing room for tea while Timmons and Mrs. Abbot sort out the luggage and find appropriate shelter for Harry?" She assessed his rigid posture and removed a long grey strand of dog hair from his lapel with a wry smile. "I suspect we've interrupted your concentration for the moment, so you might as well come hear what we know about Lieutenant Elsworth."

Lucien eyed the great gray beast. Was it possible he had grown even more since their encounter with Everham and his dogs? He turned his attention to the silent cluster of ladies who formed a frozen tableau in the hall and his gaze noted the combination of laughter and uncertainty in Charlotte Longborough's expression. Catastrophe on two legs had just walked into his home, and he could not in all conscience send it away.

Feeling a bit of a martyr, he simply inclined his head and gestured for them to precede him up the stairs. "After you, ladies."

THE BENEFIT OF ADDED sponsorship by the Duchess of Wolverton became quite clear when Charlotte entered Lady Isley's ballroom a few nights later. As beloved as her aunt and uncle were, they had not the prestige of the Caldwell name or the Wolverton title. Once word circulated that Her Grace had taken them into her home, she was called upon to introduce both Charlotte and Elizabeth to half a dozen gentlemen who had politely ignored their presence until then. Elizabeth, she was gratified to see, was no longer disregarded. Charlotte danced with each of the gentlemen, but accepted their sudden attention with ironic good humor. Many of them were on her list. Few would remain there, however. Their attentions were clearly meant to garner favor with the duke and not two young women of little importance of their own.

Their earlier acquaintances remained, though they offered no more likelihood as matches. Mr. Hook, and his friends in particular, made them laugh with droll stories of their less scandalous practical jokes and adventures. Charlotte knew Mr. Hook and his friends still pursued adventure with too much enthusiasm to take on the responsibilities of family obligations. They were, however, quite entertaining.

When the irrepressible Mr. Hook led Charlotte to the dance floor for the second time, she laughed delightedly as he regaled her with yet another of his silly escapades. Though he had once indicated his family intended him to stand for office, he clearly intended to enjoy high spirits until such time as his obligations required he rein back his behavior. He returned her to the duchess' side when the set ended, and Wolverton claimed the next with a solemn determination that took her by surprise.

"I hope you do not take Hook's attentions seriously," he stated as they took their places. "While there is not real harm in him, he is still far too–"

"Enamored of adventure to settle into respectable propriety," Charlotte interrupted with a laugh. "Just as I am too sensible to take him seriously." Perhaps she could yet convince the duke she was not a flighty hair-for-brains female. In the few days since they had taken up residence at Wolverton House, she had noted that the duke was far less aloof with his family. His sisters adored him, Harry fawned over him and his staff thought he could do no wrong.

"I realize your impressions of me have been skewed by unfortunate events, but I truly am not a widgeon-head." She raised her eyes again and smiled lest he think her insulted. "But I thank you for your attempt to warn me against inappropriate attachments." Her smile broadened into a teasing grin, "Though, of course, I know you do not act as matchmaker for your sister's friends."

He rewarded her impertinent reminder of their dance at Anne's ball with a choked laugh and a brief glimpse of those elusive dimples.

"*Touché*, Miss Longborough. I shall mind my own business."

THE FOLLOWING WEEK, Lucien entered his study and shut the door closing off voices of the women as they chatted about the evening, then said their goodnights and made their way to bed. He poured himself a generous portion of brandy and settled heavily into the chair beside the fireplace. What terrible sin had he committed that caused the Almighty and his stepmother to settle three more females in his home? And not just any females– Charlotte Longborough and her sisters.

His entire life had been disrupted beyond recognition in less than a week. The frequency and intensity of feminine social imperatives had escalated beyond tolerance. As had his obligations as escort. Prior to the inclusion of the Longboroughs, escorting his sister to private balls and Almack's had only required he arrive with her and take her home from each occasion.

With two unrelated ladies in tow, however, he was expected to dance. With *them*. Tuesday it had been Lady Isley's ball, tonight it had been Almack's. *Almack's*. Where a single invitation to dance could be taken as a half step to courting and a second dance during the same evening gave expectations of public declaration.

Elizabeth Longborough posed no problem. During their single set she merely chatted about the weather and the exhibit she'd viewed that morning. Miss Charlotte, on the other hand tantalized his senses all the while she had once again apologized for their presence and assured him he would not even know they had joined his household. *He did know*. Every moment he spent in proximity to her, he was aware of her wildflower scent, the perfection of her skin and the lively sparkle of her eyes. He shifted in his chair, but it didn't ease the aching result of her presence in his home.

A soft, regular cadence caught his attention and he turned with resignation toward the sound. *And then there was the dog.* The beast slept with canine abandon on the rug in front of the fireplace. Harry was supposed to reside in the garden at the back of the house, yet it seemed the dog could pass through walls to appear in his study with regularity. How a beast the size of a small horse could slip by his butler and footmen with such ease and frequency defied logic. Yet there he was. Again.

He muttered a curse and took a deep swallow of his drink.

When Tristan had taken his own rooms in St. James Street two years earlier, Lucien hadn't realized how much he'd miss male company in a house that now overflowed with discourse on fashions, embroidery, and social engagements. How ironic that the one family member he'd least wanted in his life when he was twelve was the one he most preferred to talk to now.

He didn't desire Tristan's company at the moment, even if his brother had been in town. Which he was not. Lucien only wanted a bit of balance to all things female. *And one female in particular.* He could go to the club and most likely run into Norcross or Ravencliffe where they would agree that Almack's was the bane of mankind and a detriment to one's familial loyalty. They could discuss the tensions mounting with the Americans or the war on the Peninsula, but he doubted that anything would take his mind from of eyes the color of smoke and a contralto voice to match.

Leaning back, he took another sip, savoring the rich aroma and slight burn as the warmth flowed across his tongue and down his throat. He closed his eyes, then quickly opened them when the image of those smoky eyes filled his mind.

Quiet routine and peace of mind had departed the day his mother installed the Longborough sisters in Wolverton House. He couldn't step out of his study without bumping into some swain come to take Anne or one of the sisters on carriage rides in the park or excursions to an art exhibit or concert. He'd noted Elizabeth received fewer callers than Anne or Charlotte but, nonetheless, his public rooms were crowded. More annoying, his awareness of exactly where Charlotte Longborough was at any moment left him irritated and... aroused. *Damnation!*

At Lucien's feet, Harry's eyes suddenly opened, and he lifted his head as though testing the air for whatever had penetrated his consciousness. He rose and padded over to the closed door, whining at Lucien to release him. Lucien's frustrated contemplation evaporated. *Intruders?* The hairs on his arms rose and he strained to listen for whatever had disturbed the dog. The silence beyond the door told him nothing.

He carefully removed the firearm he kept in a locked drawer in his desk. He rose and crossed the room to ease open the door. The dog instantly slipped through the opening and trotted silently up the stairs. Lucien followed swiftly, keeping close to the wall to avoid creaking stairs while remaining less visible to anyone who might realize he had not yet gone to bed. Once at the landing he saw the dog's tail disappear through the library door and waited to see what kind of commotion, if any, the dog's entrance would spark. When no sound emerged, Lucien worked his way to the library door easing it open further so he could slip into the room, then froze in surprise.

Charlotte Longborough paced beside the window at the far end of the room clad only in her nightgown, her slender feet bare. Harry sat nearby, his head following her movements as she made her way back and forth as though searching for something.

Moonlight filtered through the window casting pale silver into the room and revealing her shape through the soft cotton that floated around her like a cloud. *Holy mother, Joseph and Gabriel.* Lucien swallowed hard and fought the sudden hot, tight swelling in his groin. Miss Charlotte Longborough had a figure to make a man forget his honor for the driving need to touch, taste, and claim her.

"Miss Longborough?" Lucien put his firearm on a table and crossed the room as he spoke. "Miss Longborough," he repeated, then—"Charlotte, what is wrong?" He reached her side and settled a hand on her arm. "Charlotte, why–?" Her gray eyes turned in his direction, but she stared blankly with no conscious recognition, and he realized that she walked in her sleep.

What did he do now? Somewhere he had heard that one should not wake a person in this condition, but what *did* one do? When he'd touched her arm, she'd stopped her pacing, but now she turned and began again, this time she muttered something indistinct, but of concern. She repeated herself as she continued her restless pattern.

Her path brought her near him again and he gently caught her shoulders, stopping her by the simple act of enfolding her in his arms. *Now what?* Her eyes, when he took her shoulders, remained focused on something she saw only in the dream that had sent her roaming the main floor. Once his arms encircled her though, her eyes closed, and her frantic muttering stilled. She settled against him, her own arms coming around him as she lay her head against his chest with a sigh. Lucien registered the soft pressure of her breasts against his chest and the narrow taper of her waist as she relaxed against him... and fought to keep his hands neutrally around her shoulders.

He needed to return her to her room.

That warning thought surfaced in complete opposition to his body's desire to take her to his bed and explore the feminine curves pressed against him. Her wildflower scent teased his senses, and her pliant form filled his imagination with ideas he'd tried to suppress from the first moment he'd seen her grey eyes, pink lips and grass-stained bosom.

He loosened his hold with the intent of guiding her to the hall, but she resisted and burrowed closer. Her hands now moved in slow exploration of his back and his body tensed in full alert. He stifled a groan and slid one hand up to stroke her cheek with the back of his fingers. She turned her head to follow them with a murmured sigh of pleasure. Her breath warmed his knuckles. Good intentions turned to smoke. He opened his hand to cup her cheek, tilting her face up to meet his before brushing her soft lips in a tantalizing, testing kiss.

In that moment of exploratory contact Lucien knew she'd never been kissed before, but in the next, her mouth adjusted to his and she pressed closer, instinctively responding to the call of male to female. Despite his conscience, he gently deepened the kiss, coaxing her mouth open before tasting the warm sweet flavor that was Charlotte Longborough.

He knew the instant she came awake. Her soft lips stiffened, and her roving hands froze stiffly against his back. Reluctantly he raised his head and looked into eyes that now held a mixture of shock, outrage... and interest.

Damnation. *He knew better*. Scrambling to pull himself together, he searched for words to explain his behavior and their embrace. "Sleeping Beauty awakes."

"I– I beg your pardon?" She dropped her arms from around him and a deep pink flush flooded her features as she stepped away, her confusion clear in the quaver in her voice.

"You were sleepwalking," he told her. "I followed the only course I knew of to wake you without harm." He dared not look away or she would recognize his guilt. He'd kissed her for no other reason than he could not resist the temptation. Her fingers went to her mouth as though to verify she'd been kissed, and it was all he could do not *to gather her into his arms and kiss her again.*

He cleared his throat. "Do you often sleepwalk?" *Heaven help him if he knew she roamed his halls at night.* "You were talking in your sleep, though I could not make out what you said."

He soldiered on in an attempt to behave calmly, as though there were nothing unusual or scandalous in kissing a sleepwalking woman awake.

He gestured to Harry, who still sat alertly watching his mistress as though keeping guard. "Harry must have heard you leave your room. He led me in here. You were pacing... and, er... muttering." He found himself floundering in a way he had not done since his childhood when facing his father's discipline. He looked down into those puzzled gray eyes and blurted, "I didn't know what else to do. I beg you forgive me if I have offended."

Charlotte had not moved during his disjointed explanation, but she watched him with an intensity that disturbed him more than if she had raged at him for compromising her virtue– *Lord help him, he'd compromised her.* In his own house. Which he shared with his stepmother and sisters. If anyone woke and found them in the library together– and her in nothing but her night clothes– he would be leg shackled by the end of the month.

"You must return to your room," he said abruptly. "Take Harry with you."

He turned and strode to his own room where he spent the hours until dawn chastising himself for giving in to the temptation to kiss her.

Kicking off his quilts, he told himself Charlotte Longborough was a determined, marriage-minded catastrophe who, he would swear, fate had literally thrown into his path. The genuine shock and embarrassment in her eyes each time they clashed made it clear she'd not engineered any of their encounters. Yet there was something in her expression when caught unaware that invited him to take her in his arms and... *nonsense*. It was his own desire that saw sensual invitation where there was nothing but innocent curiosity.

*Of course, she was curious*...after all, she'd made a list of eligible mates and had come to the marriage mart to find a husband. Husbands meant kisses and all the mysteries of the marriage bed about which she had probably overheard just enough to wonder. Devil take it, curiosity was not an invitation.

# CHAPTER 10

Back in her room, Charlotte climbed into the bed and pulled the thick quilts up high enough to all but bury herself, then lay in wonder and confusion. *He kissed me.* Her lips still tingled from the hot pressure, the shocking intrigue of his tongue against her own. *The Duke of Wolverton kissed me.*

In her dream she'd been hurrying, watching for Edward's ship along the Portsmouth docks. She searched without success until she'd become aware of a sense of warmth and security, the likes of which she'd never experienced before. She'd clung to that security, that feeling of being sheltered, protected... *cherished*. Then she'd responded to the seductive invitation of moist heat against her lips. She'd needed to accept the enticing demand until she realized she was not dreaming and the arms holding her close were real.

*He kissed me.*

Her body still quivered with the heat that warmed her blood... and the absolute certainty that she hadn't wanted him to stop.

She knew she sometimes walked in her sleep, and she knew why she had tonight. Though she and her sisters hadn't made any particular fuss about being left behind when Aunt Poppy and Uncle Aubrey hurried off to meet Edward's ship, they all worried about his injuries. Staying behind had been the most practical solution. But they would all worry until they received further word from Uncle Aubrey... And when she was worried, Charlotte walked the floors in her sleep.

She stifled a groan of mortification. It had been years since she'd last experienced a sleep walking incident. Why did that particular quirk in her nature have to reassert itself in front of the one man who already considered her lacking in admirable traits?

But, he'd kissed her– and *she'd kissed him back.*

How would she face him in the morning?

LUCIEN ENTERED HIS breakfast room the next morning and nearly backed out of the room at the sight of six bright-eyed females waiting expectantly for him to take his place. His glance went to Charlotte whose cheeks flushed and she quickly looked down at her plate. *Good, God. Surely she hadn't told...* He cleared his throat. "Good morning, ladies," he said as he went to the sideboard to make his selection.

Their chorused response raised the hairs on the back of his neck. He knew better than to think it a coincidence that they had all decided to have breakfast downstairs. Sitting at the head of the table, he surveyed their cheerful faces while the footman filled his cup with the strong coffee he preferred with breakfast. He took a fortifying sip and resigned himself to the inevitable before asking his stepmother, "To what do I owe the pleasure of your company this morning?"

"You promised Rowena you would take her to the Exeter Exchange Menagerie this morning and we," she gestured to everyone at the table, "are joining you."

He had made the offer when they'd arrived in town to keep Rowena from feeling left out of the festivities of the Season. He didn't remember specifying a day. "I thought today was Great Aunt Ridley's garden party." he commented as he sliced a chunk of ham. "Which does not begin until three." He put the bite of ham into his mouth and chewed with deliberation as he awaited her response.

"That is tomorrow." she replied.

He glanced out the window to realize heavy clouds darkened the morning sky. "If it does not rain."

"Oh, it won't rain," Sarah assured him, then her eyes widened, and she glanced to her sisters in dismay.

Did the child think he would take offence at her speaking at the breakfast table? He knew many of his fellow members of parliament believed firmly that children should be seen but not heard and banished them to the nursery for their meals until they left the schoolroom.

"As the Menagerie is on the upper floor of the exchange, the weather need not be a concern." He smiled at her so she would know he took no offence. "I was referring to Aunt Ridley's garden party."

"So was I," Sarah murmured. "I..." She flushed, then looked toward her sisters, took a quick breath and said, "If it rains today, it will be clear by tomorrow."

Two hours later they climbed the stairs toward a hallway from which the pungent odor of the captive animals filled the air. Once on the first floor they discovered barred rooms containing a wide spectrum of exotic animals including a lion, a tiger and, to Lucien's amazement, two elephants. *How in the name of all things holy did they get not just one, but two of them up the staircase to the main floor?*

Rowena and Sarah stood before each room in fascination sharing their book lessons and impressions with each other. His stepmother, Anne, and the Longborough sisters did much the same, though with less giddy animation.

"I had no concept of how large elephants were in actuality," Elizabeth commented. "I believed the illustrations in books exaggerated."

Charlotte wrinkled her nose before removing a scented handkerchief from her reticule. "Nor did I realize how unique their aroma would be."

Lucien shared her sentiments, though he refrained from resorting to burying his nose behind a square of cloth to mask the strong odors trapped within the building. Fortunately, the younger girls satisfied their curiosity about the exotics before he gave in to the temptation.

"It is a bit chilly and damp to visit Gunther's for ices," Lucien announced as they entered the carriage once they had made their way downstairs. "Perhaps a visit to a confectioner's for cream cakes before returning home would make a pleasing finish to our outing."

"To say nothing of how pleasant the scent of freshly baked goods would be in contrast to the menagerie," Anne said with a chuckle. "I believe I shall be content to learn about the unique animals of the earth from books in future."

They all laughed at that and Charlotte discovered the duke's genuine laughter revealed a side she'd not seen until now. More than the reappearance of those elusive dimples, it altered her perception and her heartbeat. It softened his usually taciturn expression. His genuine amusement unsettled her almost as much as the fierce desire she'd glimpsed the night before when he'd claimed his kiss to be nothing more than an attempt to wake her safely.

How could she wake safely with Wolverton's lips on hers and his arms pressing her to his body? Her mouth dried and her pulse quickened. Not Wolverton's lips, but *Lucien's.* How could she think of him by his title after the intimacy of their shared kiss?

Charlotte was the last to alight the carriage and, as he assisted her down, Lucien's firm grasp on her hand sent a warm tremor through her. They had not had occasion to speak privately to one another since the night before, and though his action was properly impersonal, she could not help remembering the intriguing comfort of his embrace. When he shot her a narrow look of assessment, she felt that heat rise to make her cheeks burn.

"Again, my apologies if I upset you last night," he murmured. "You need not worry it will be repeated."

"And I shall place a chair at the doorknob to ascertain that I remain in my room." She met his eyes briefly, then dropped her gaze before hurrying to catch up to the rest of their party at the confectioners.

Lucien ordered a selection of cream cakes, tarts and sweet biscuits. There were few customers in the shop, which did indeed, smell far sweeter than the menagerie. They chatted about their plans, including Aunt Ridley's garden party. Lucien remained with them and Charlotte noted that he consumed two cream cakes, a strawberry tart and four sugared biscuits. Who would think a man of such sober habits would have a sweet tooth?

When he told them he intended to meet Ravencliffe and the Marquess at Tattersall's the next morning, Sarah asked, "Are you planning to buy a horse?"

"I may," he answered. "I have considered purchasing a new mare for my stables."

"Is it true some less scrupulous traders sometimes use paints or dyes to give the appearance that a pair are matched when they are not?" she asked. She took a sip of her chocolate and glanced over at her sisters before turning her guileless eyes back to his. "I've heard they use shoe blacking to cover white stockings and blazes."

"That's true," Lucien agreed. "Though I'm not looking for a pair."

"That's good," Sarah announced with satisfaction. "Because I wouldn't like anyone to be cheated."

Lucien chuckled. "Nor would I. Though such tricks are far more common at country markets." He reached for another cream cake. "Tattersall's has a reputation to maintain, so such instances are rare."

THE MORNING OF LADY Althea Ridley's garden party dawned as clear and sunny as Sarah had promised, so the hour-long carriage ride to the estate near Richmond was as pleasant as Charlotte could have wished. The duchess, Anne, Elizabeth and Charlotte chatted pleasantly while the duke cantered beside the carriage on his horse.

When they arrived, they were directed through the entry hall and morning room to the terrace overlooking the gardens at the back of the house.

Lady Ridley's garden was a riot of late spring blooms that had been laid out to give the impression of comfortable space. Charlotte surveyed the carefully tended flowers and realized how much she missed her own gardens at home. Tending young plants always calmed her.

They descended the stairs to the ground level where Lady Ridley welcomed them.

"How fortunate the weather has cooperated for your garden party," the duke said to Lady Ridley after Elizabeth had greeted their hostess. "After yesterday's dark clouds I feared you might be forced to cancel."

"You know Aunt Ridley would never allow the weather to interfere with her plans, Lucien." Lady Anne teased as she greeted her aunt. "When she selects a date for an outdoor event, she sends an invitation to the Almighty Himself to guarantee good weather."

Lady Ridley laughed. "I'll admit that my entertainments have been blessedly free of inclement weather over the years, but one mustn't tempt fate by trying to order it to one's liking, especially in spring." She gestured to the terrace where French doors led into the house. "I always make a contingent plan in case the good Lord decides to deny my requests. Had the weather remained uninviting we'd have gathered in the music room and entertained each other for the afternoon." She gave an amused smile. "I firmly believe that if you have an alternate plan you won't need it, but if you don't, you will." A footman approached and spoke quietly, and she excused herself to speak to another of her guests.

Charlotte didn't know quite what to do now that they had greeted their hostess.

Anne solved that problem when she linked arms with her and Elizabeth and said, "Come, we must circulate."

They strolled across the gravel path that wound around the formal garden. Near a fountain they saw Ladies Jane Pomphrey and Millicent Littlemarsh chatting with Mr. Hook and Lord Bascomb. Millicent's cheeks glowed pink and Jane appeared to be trying to hold back laughter. Lord Bascomb must be in rare form to make Jane relax her usual disapproval of rakes.

When they joined them, Lord Bascomb bowed over their hands then turned to Elizabeth and declared, "I have recently been told the drollest rumor and you must answer me truly. Did your grandmother, or did she not, use a potion or cast magic spell upon your uncle to make him fall in love with your aunt?"

Charlotte gasped and realized that was what had so amused Jane. Where had he heard that piece of gossip? She'd thought it confined to the boundaries of their village.

"I cannot imagine who would believe such nonsense, can you?" Lady Millicent said. Her expression was one of uncertainty, and Charlotte guessed she was half-embarrassed that Bascomb had raised the subject and half hopeful it was true.

"It is an old tale told by the ladies who envied his devotion to our aunt. No potions or spells were involved, I assure you," Elizabeth told him with a smile. "Even if such magic were possible, Grandmama would not condone such means to procure a mate for anyone. Whether by contract or love, marriage weaves its own spell to establish its success. It is called cooperation."

Lord Bascomb nodded his head and grinned before he added. "And where there is no cooperation, it casts its own curse."

Before the conversation could tread into more family matters, Charlotte scanned the garden for a way to change the subject. She saw the duchess at the far side of the garden. "I beg you will excuse us," she said. "I believe Her Grace is signaling us to join her." With that, she curtsied and turned it that direction. Elizabeth followed suit, and a clearly amused Anne did as well, before they slipped around the group and escaped to the collection of tables and chairs where the duchess sat visiting with friends.

As they made their way to the table Anne assured them, "I know what people say about the Longborough family, so you needn't have worried about any revelations Lord Bascomb might have brought up." She chuckled at their wary response.

"When Lucien first learned of our acquaintance, he questioned my furthering it on the grounds of rumor regarding some of your relatives, but Mother told him she'd met you and that he needn't worry. I taxed mother about it after Lucien left for his club and she told me some of the more fantastic rumors that passed about the ballrooms when your uncle offered for your aunt. Imagine anyone believing in witches, or of accusing someone of casting some magical love spell in order to marry a titled gentleman." She laughed merrily. "I don't know how people can still believe such silliness."

The sisters exchanged surprised glances before Elizabeth queried, "You knew our grandmother was accused of witchcraft?"

"Oh yes," Anne said. "According to Mama, the gossip was most diverting. Some said your grandfather rescued your grandmother from being burned at the stake, others claim she cast a spell on Lord Elsworth to propose to your aunt, and still others—" She lowered her voice as they passed a cluster of young ladies and gentlemen, "Said your aunt was already married to a gypsy." She laughed outright as she added, "How could she be married, if she married Lord Elsworth?"

"Don't worry that I'll hold such stories against you." Anne assured them, "Scandalous as many might find such suppositions, I find them wonderfully droll. I agree with Mama that most rumors emerge from a tiny grain of truth, and the final product is generally a mountain of imagined and incorrect detail. Perhaps one day you will share those grains of truth with me, but for now I shall simply enjoy your company and tease Lucien with the absurd stories I've heard."

Charlotte's pulse jumped in alarm. "I pray you'll not disclose any more stories than he already might have heard," she protested. "He's been gracious about our staying in your home, but I wouldn't like to cause him to question his generosity."

"Don't worry," Anne said before they reached her mother. "Lucien has more sense than to act upon silly rumor. He may be strait-laced and eminently proper, but he's fair minded and is entirely familiar with the salacious inaccuracy of the scandal-mill."

# CHAPTER 11

The duchess looked in their direction as they approached. She gestured to the empty bench near her chair, then introduced Elizabeth and Charlotte to the ladies with whom she sat. They exchanged pleasantries for several minutes before Lady Templeton, a lady of impressive girth and strong opinions, returned to the subject of their prior conversation.

"I tell you," Lady Templeton stated as she accepted a fresh cup of tea, "I do not approve of the styles that we are seeing of late. Did you see Lady Dalton's gown at the opera? Utterly shocking."

She gave a theatric shudder and shook her head before continuing with a sniff of disdain. "Jezebel red with an indecently low neckline. And those shocking French stays that do nothing to conceal the bosom. Even if the garment were not indecent, it is a fashion followed by our enemy. I cannot imagine what she was thinking with such a vulgar display. Why, her appearance was more scandalous than any of the courtesans who attended." She stopped abruptly and glanced over at the unmarried ladies who sat nearby.

Charlotte, Elizabeth and Lady Anne lowered their eyes at Lady Templeton's slip, and Charlotte worked to keep her expression innocently neutral lest the woman curb her comments. Lady Templeton cleared her throat and adjusted her seat before continuing. "I do not understand why Dalton allows her to go about like that. He has ambitions in the diplomatic core, you know. Yet if a wife shows no awareness of proper dress and decorum, how is she to further her husband's interests?"

Charlotte was tempted to tell them that it was Lord Dalton and not his wife who had chosen that shocking gown. Before she could decide if she should admit to eavesdropping, Lady Templeton added, "To say nothing of how her poor health becomes an impediment to hosting diplomatic events. As it is, I understand that she took another severe chill and did not join Dalton at the Harris rout. If you will recall, she missed several events last Season for similar reasons as well. Such skimpy clothing leaves one most susceptible to exposure related illnesses."

She looked up to where Lady Ridley had just greeted the newly arrived Daltons and lowered her voice. "At least she is well covered today. Perhaps Lord Dalton has finally put his foot down."

Charlotte turned to see Lady Dalton dressed in an afternoon gown of salmon pink with ruffles that rose high on her neck and sleeves that disappeared beneath the edge of her short gloves. Her pale complexion had a pallor that underscored Lady Templeton's assessment that illness had prevented her attending the recent ball but raised Charlotte's suspicions.

Such modesty of dress on a warm day struck her as unusual and she wondered if it served to hide bruises. Mrs. Franklin had been in the habit of resorting to high necklines and long sleeves in the days following the frequent abuses Charlotte had witnessed. Ten years might have passed, and Albert Franklin might have come into a title since he had left their village, but he had not changed—and Lady Dalton was in danger of suffering the same fate as Martha Franklin.

When the Daltons exited the terrace away from where Lady Ridley had greeted them, she breathed a sigh of relief that he had not seen her. After the evening at Lady Winterstone's, he knew she was in the city. She hoped he would assume her childish spying had ended when he locked her in the shed. She wished it had.

A question from one of the matrons lead Charlotte to agreeing that she enjoyed gardening, and Her Grace asked if she'd yet visited

Lady Ridley's orangery. Charlotte's negative and request for directions allowed her and Elizabeth to escape before the Daltons paid their respects to the duchess. Crossing the lawn, Elizabeth saw Lady Jane and excused herself to join her while Charlotte continued to the orangery. She was relieved to go alone so she could calm her thoughts.

A glassed ceiling allowed the light and warmth to provide the climate needed for the exotic fruit to grow so far from its native Mediterranean homeland. Charlotte breathed in the sweet fragrance of oranges that permeated the air as did the rich earthy scents of mulch and loam. The trees had been arranged around the room in great wooden planters and a combination of wicker chairs and wooden benches provided resting places for guests to enjoy the room in comfort. A potting table stood near the end of the room and Charlotte moved toward it, needing to be as far from the inquisitive garden party guests as possible.

Ironically, though it disturbed her that stories of her family's less than conventional past were bandied about as entertaining party conversation, she resented the assumption that they were too absurd to be believed. Of the three examples Anne had cited, two were true.

Their grandmother had, indeed, been declared a witch, but she had most certainly not cast a spell on Uncle Aubrey. The accusations had been the result of their grandmother's dreams, for Sarah was not the first of the family to receive the cursed gift of dreams and intuitions. But Charlotte's other aunt had, in fact, married a traveler. Since her Aunt Lily had not taken part in a Season, few people beyond their home village knew or cared that the Longborough sisters had a second aunt.

Yet Anne's comments on the more salacious rumors about her family paled beside the horrible certainty that Lady Dalton had suffered a severe beating. Charlotte's stomach churned and clenched. She wondered what excuse Lord Dalton had used to justify his most recent mistreatment. Lady Dalton might deny it, and society might not believe it, but Charlotte had no doubts that the lady suffered regular abuse.

A faint sound brought her out of her reverie, and she turned to see Lord Dalton enter the orangery. "Miss Charlotte Longborough, I believe?" he said as he strolled toward her. "I would never have recognized the wild child of Stedbury had you not performed the other evening."

Time had not lessened his good looks in the ten years since she'd last seen him, but she knew his handsome face hid sadistic anger and no remorse. He stared at her with a blend of derision and male interest. "You are most definitely no longer a child—I wonder—are you are still a bit wild?"

Blood drained from her face before it returned to fire her skin with anger. She raised her chin and stood stiffly. "I am a lady, though you should not need to ask."

She prayed he did not see the tremors that chilled her hands and weakened her knees as she faced the man who had beaten his first wife so unmercifully. He didn't know she'd seen what he did in the end, only that he had once caught her spying, and assumed his threats had ended it.

"Does that mean I succeeded in teaching you not to spy on your neighbors?" he asked. His face darkened and his voice lost the pleasant, cultured refinement he'd used as greeting. "I had hoped I taught you to mind your own business." He took a step closer and his eyes narrowed. "But you felt the need to question my wife some days ago."

Charlotte's breath hitched, ice invaded her veins, and she swallowed hard.

"I saw you sitting with her at the Winterstone's," he fairly growled. "Though she swears you did no more than discuss the evening's program, I know better. Musical selections do not leave one's wife agitated and wary." He took another step, and his aggressive stance made the hairs on Charlotte's arms rise. "Do not approach her again, Miss Longborough. I should dislike seeing you peering over garden hedges at me or my wife while we are in town."

His expression chilled. "I understand you have been the center of more than one fiasco in the park already. Put your nose where it ought not to be and you may discover that you are far more accident prone than you have proven thus far."

"On the subject of your behavior," he said as he closed the space between them, "a *lady* knows it is not wise to go off by herself—even at a respectable garden party. Nor does she slip away for a *tryst* in the middle of the day." He cocked his head and an unpleasant smile formed on his lips, but not in his eyes. Her skin crawled as she realized he looked at her with lust as well as fury. *If only she had not come into the orangery alone.*

"Ahhh. I know... You liked to watch your neighbors as a child... did you come hoping to *observe* a tryst?"

"You are impertinent, sir." Her alarm rose, chilling the heat of anger but she strove for calm. "I came only to see the orangery. I enjoy gardening and wished to see one firsthand." She disliked the expression in his eyes and the way he crowded her. "I expected to be alone." Charlotte quickly assessed possible escape routes from the situation.

"I would not expect the wild child from your adventurous family to engage in so solitary a hobby–" He lowered a brow. "Though I suspect you still spy."

Alarm sent another shiver of chills along her spine at his menacing words. He was not the first to believe her to be of wanton character because of her family's history. She took a step around him toward the entrance, but he stopped in front of her, blocking her path.

She took another step away, wanting to push past him and escape, but sensed that he would react as any predator and chase her down. She forced herself to behave as though his words didn't fright-en her and reached to touch a still green fruit that hung nearby. "I prefer gardening because it soothes. One prepares and seeds the soil so that blooms may grow." She eased one more step away as though to inspect another fruit which had begun to take on the color for which it was named.

He blocked her movement by reaching out to catch her arm and turning her back to face him. He leered and his voice roughened. "I prefer the expediency of plowing a woman's body to grubbing in the dirt."

Charlotte gasped at his effrontery and tried to break away from his hold on her arm. "How dare you speak so to me?" She struggled, shock and panic escalating. "I am a virtuous lady. Let go of my arm and do not accost me in future."

"I think not, m'dear," He caught her other arm and pulled her against him. "You pretend innocence with gasps of outrage yet invite me to play with double entant phrases about how you like preparing the garden for planting seeds."

His eyes gleamed and Charlotte struggled to break away when he pulled her closer and whispered against her ear. "I know all of your family history, Miss Longborough. My father regaled me often with tales of his youth and the infamous ladies of his day. The Longborough name played prominently among them. Did you know he nearly offered for your mother's youngest sister despite of your grandmother's infamy?"

He leaned back and watched her face when he told her, "Of course that was before the little fool eloped to marry a gypsy." Disgust and derision filled his expression, and he gave Charlotte a sharp shake. "A *gypsy*, for God's sake– and you think yourself a lady and put on airs when you are no more than a commoner's child yourself. Your grandfather may have been a baron, but I am a viscount. My word against yours will still hold."

Then his hand wrenched her face toward his and his mouth came down hard on hers. His assault forced her lips apart shocking her with the deep thrust of his tongue. At the same time, he pushed his leg between her knees and pressed her hard against the potting table behind her. Shock and revulsion made her gag at his invasion, then fury made her react. She bit hard and kicked him in the shin at the same moment. He jerked back, a speck of blood glistening against his lip.

"So, you did like what you saw, did you? Rough it will be, then." he snarled and released her arm to swing his own back in preparation for a blow that never came. In a flurry of movement, she was suddenly freed from his hold and stumbled before catching her balance.

Lord Dalton's face turned white and his eyes widened in shock as he was forced face down onto the floor, his arm twisted behind him.

"Did he hurt you, Miss Longborough?"

Charlotte caught her breath at the sight of Wolverton, eyes feral with fury, standing over Lord Dalton, his hold on the man's arm threatening to dislocate the socket.

"Nothing that washing my mouth will not cure."

Despite her attempt to appear in calm, her voice trembled. Now that nothing restrained her, her knees nearly buckled and bright spots danced in her vision. Blinking hard, she fought to gain control of her body's reaction to her tumbling emotions. Her hands sought the support of the bench behind her and she tried to take slow deep breaths to no avail. *She would not faint in front of him.* She would not. *Then the bright spots grew and turned black.*

# CHAPTER 12

The scents of starch, wool, sandalwood, and oranges teased at the edge of Charlotte's consciousness before she became aware of the solid wall of muscle that supported her. Gentle fingers brushed her cheek, and she opened her eyes to see Wolverton peering at her in concern.

"Miss Longborough—Charlotte—are you all right now? Do you need your sister or my mother to attend you?"

Memory rushed to the forefront. She tensed, then sat up and looked around for Lord Dalton.

"He's gone." Lucien assured her. "I would have challenged him for behaving in such a manner, but to do so would have created a greater scandal and ruined your reputation. I warned him off. He won't bother you again." His eyes glinted and narrowed. "Nor will he spread slanderous tales about you or your family."

"How did you know—? When did you—? Charlotte didn't know how to ask if he'd heard the terrible things Lord Dalton had said before he tried to force himself on her.

"I didn't know you were here." He scowled and Charlotte realized that he would have blamed himself had he not arrived in time to prevent Lord Dalton from harming her. "This morning, before I left for Tattersall's, your sister Sarah asked me about orangery's, and I promised I would bring her some fruit from my aunt's. That I arrived before he could do you ruinous injury was a most fortunate coincidence."

Those piercing blue eyes studied her and Charlotte tried to think of a response that would disguise the new flutter of entirely different emotions that filled her senses as he held her. Her voice trembled. "A most fortunate coincidence, indeed."

The note of irony that laced her agreement made his gaze sharpen and his features reflected a grim approval that she had recovered from her faint. "Speaking of coincidence," he tapped the tip of her nose with his forefinger and smiled as though to lighten the mood. "Clarehaven nearly fell prey to the same trick your sister asked about yesterday. A new breeder had a pair of matched blacks that caught the Marquess's eye and I believe he might have purchased them had not a young stable lad tripped and spilt water onto one of the horse's forelegs. Shoe blacking melted away and revealed both a white sock and an inflamed fetlock. The breeder has been banned from future sales." He chuckled. "One would almost think Sarah's reading matter is controlled by the fates."

Far from reassuring her, his words gave her a moment of disquiet. For Sarah to have approached Wolverton with so timely a question could only mean she'd had one of her intuitions after Charlotte and the rest of the women in the household had departed. Bless Sarah and her intuitions. Bless the duke and his kindness to her sister. *Bless the fates that he assumed both incidents mere coincidence.*

"Do you feel able to stand?"

Charlotte blushed. As wonderful as it felt to lean against his broad shoulders, it would not do for anyone to enter the orangery and see them. "You must think me the most missish of ladies," she declared as she stood and smoothed her skirts. "I have never fainted before and do not understand why I did now—" she faltered, then spoke with determined calm. "I have never done so before."

"You received a shock. Dalton's behavior was crude. And unforgivable of an honorable man."

"Did you know Lady Dalton is not his first wife...?" Charlotte had known nothing of Lord Dalton's rise in rank and wondered how much society knew of his past.

"I did not." Lucien peered at her in surprise. "How would you know such a thing?" He stopped abruptly. "How long have you known him?"

"He was the estate manager for our neighbor when I was a child," she said. "I have not seen him since I was eight."

"Then it was no accident that he spoke to you?"

"I did not invite him, if that is what you mean," Charlotte protested. "I had hoped to avoid him. He held no title when I knew him, and I was surprised to hear him named Dalton."

"But you recognized him at some function?"

"I saw him first at Lady Anne's ball, but he didn't recognize me until the Winterstone musical."

"I find it difficult to believe he would accost you in such a fashion, and particularly if he had not seen you since you were a child." Lucien gazed at her, his eyes reflecting an unspoken question.

Charlotte stiffened away from his support. "He did not like me as a child," she informed him. "He merely found a new way to show his disregard for me as an adult."

She stood abruptly and found the need to blink away the brightly colored dots that threatened to overwhelm her again. This time she succeeded in keeping the darkness at bay and she stepped away.

*He didn't believe her claim that she hadn't invited Dalton into the orangery*– she could see his doubts clearly in those piercing eyes. It would do no good to tell him what she'd witnessed all those years ago. If he doubted her word as an adult, he would give even less credit to her childhood memory.

"Thank you for coming to my rescue, Your Grace," Charlotte said with cool dignity. She turned away from the temptation to seek the security of his embrace again. "I must join my sister lest my absence be commented on."

LUCIEN WATCHED THROUGH the window as Charlotte crossed the garden and accepted a glass of lemonade from one of the circulating footmen. Her face still had a slight pallor– and she had been truly struggling to get away before Lucien intervened. Every instinct in him wanted to give Charlotte support rather than let her return to the garden alone, but to do so would only spur gossip as damaging as the circumstances he'd interrupted.

Certainly, he could not be seen leaving the orangery with her. He had to wait until her presence was noted in the normal course of events before he could join the rest of the party. He would have to make a public show, later, of coming back to the orangery to gather oranges for Sarah and Rowena lest his attention to the orangery be linked with Charlotte's.

What did he know of Dalton other than what he had just witnessed? He vaguely remembered some story that Dalton's title had come to him via a most convoluted and exhaustive search for heirs some six or seven years ago. Equally vague was his recollection of Dalton marrying his current wife, an orphaned heiress, a year or so later. He remembered nothing about a first wife.

Why would a grown man dislike a child? Why would he attempt to assault her after... ten years? It made no sense. Yet he didn't believe she lied. She approached life with a directness that he found disconcerting at times, but he knew did not include deception. He didn't think she'd told him everything, though.

When she crumpled to the floor after being manhandled by that despicable—vile enough words failed him in his fury—he'd been ready to kill the swine. Instead, he'd hauled the man up by his twisted arm and taken great satisfaction in the cry of pain Dalton made when the shoulder slipped from the socket.

He had ordered Dalton off his aunt's property, warning him to stay clear of Charlotte in the future, and that no malicious rumors be bandied about or Lucien would personally see to his ruin... at dawn. For if Dalton spread scandalous falsehoods about her family, a challenge would be the only way to end it. Then there would be another taint of scandal attached to the Longborough name—and his own. As it was, he wouldn't be able to give the man the cut direct when next they attended the same event.

Thank God Charlotte's sister Sarah had taken to reading about greenhouses and orangeries recently or Charlotte might have come to greater grief than fainting from shock.

CHARLOTTE SIPPED HER lemonade in a vain attempt to settle her nerves. She checked the various groups of guests to be sure the Daltons had left, and her pulse finally slowed when she overheard someone say Lady Dalton had become ill again and Lord Dalton had hurried her home. She looked around for Elizabeth and saw her sitting with the duchess and the ladies she'd been introduced to earlier.

She wasn't ready for light conversation, so she wandered toward a narrow bench tucked in a visible but less crowded corner of the garden. Fissures of heat and cold still alternated along her spine and her hands shook. She didn't feel she could ask to leave early without raising speculation, but after being trapped in the orangery, she needed the comfort of knowing people were nearby until she could seek the sanctuary of her room.

She sat on the secluded bench and set her lemonade beside her, then folded her hands tightly in her lap. She was used to the fact that people talked about her family and that the highest sticklers of society considered associating with them to be a bit suspect. She didn't like it, but she was used to it. But for someone as despicable as Lord Dalton to sneer, fury rose, and she wanted to howl her frustration to the world. How could a man of his ilk feel he was somehow superior to Aunt Lily's husband whose only supposed sin was to have been born a gypsy?

Did an unconventional background make her or her sisters any less ladies worthy of respect? *It most certainly did not.* Nor did the fact that Elizabeth liked working with wood or that Sarah had stronger intuition than most. Charlotte vowed she would prove to all those doubters that lack of convention didn't mean lack of character.

To do that, though, she must continue to pretend she didn't notice the subtle probing that sometimes entered conversations with new acquaintances. Questions with innuendo and promiscuous hints she now realized they tested. Was that why Dalton's renewed threats had taken a lecherous form?

She breathed in and savored the scent of fuchsias, iris, hyacinth and, was that cardamom? Charlotte heard a soft giggle followed by a sigh and a man's low whisper followed by another muffled giggle. *Who?* The giggles assured Charlotte that their private time was mutually desired in contrast to her own upsetting encounter. In the past, curiosity would have tempted her to peer through the hedge to see who indulged in a bit of flirtation. But heat and chills still skittered along her spine and she took another calming breath. She was finished with spying forever.

She finished her lemonade and returned to the center of the garden party. Lady Jane and Elizabeth now sat a bit apart from the ladies, and Charlotte smiled brightly as she joined them. Lady Jane shifted on the bench to make room for her, then continued her description of the gown she'd ordered the day before.

"Madame Fochet suggested a most unusual coral silk that nearly duplicates the color of my hair," she told them. "I had serious doubts but allowed her to make it up into a new design. I am going to wear it to the Swathmore ball. Wait until you see it," she clapped her hands together as though she could contain her excitement if she held them together tight enough. "Wait until *Lord Chalmers* sees it." She blushed as her words revealed her interest in the tall fair-haired peer who had asked her to dance at Almack's the previous Wednesday.

It wasn't until Charlotte saw Lady Millicent strolling with Lord Bascomb that she noticed Lady Anne walking with Lord Clarehaven. Knowing that the duke disliked both men's rakish ways, Charlotte suspected Anne flirted with the appearance of danger because she considered her brother overly protective. Anne was far too sensible to encourage the attentions of a libertine but, considering her own experience earlier, Charlotte wondered if she should warn Anne how vulnerable a woman was to a man's strength if he refused to behave as a gentleman should.

LATE AS IT WAS WHEN they returned from the Westbrook ball the next night, Charlotte found she couldn't sleep. Lady Westbrook had engaged a quartet to play the occasional country dance and all the guests mingled with good cheer, but Charlotte had noticed small details to the conversations that she'd failed to pay attention to before.

Prior to the incident at Lady Ridley's, she'd been flattered with the interest she'd seen in her dance partners' eyes. Now that same interest made her uncomfortable. Quickly stifled laughter and hushed whispers made her wonder if they discussed her or her family. Did she read too personal a stake in the unending shuffle of petty gossip that was the underlying purpose of routs, card parties and balls? She felt exposed and vulnerable and she didn't like the feeling one bit.

The downstairs clock struck three and she cast aside her coverlet in disgust. If her mind wouldn't shut down without help, she would help it. The library downstairs had a full shelf of bound sermons. Perhaps reading some would soothe her peace of mind. Or at least, put her to sleep. After donning slippers and her flannelette wrapper, she lit a candle and crept downstairs.

The library fire had been banked for the night, but the room still held a bit of warmth along with the comforting smell of paper and parchment. Unlike many libraries, this one had not been filled to impress the eye with matched leather sets of imposing sounding tomes. Not that there were not impressive titles to choose from, but it was obvious that they had been acquired for the knowledge contained rather than for impressing guests. Fine leather, course leather, and pamphlets of heavy paper all combined to provide a topic of interest for anyone and everyone. Anne, when she'd taken them on tour of the house upon their arrival had whispered, "The naughty books are on the top shelf behind the books on agricultural science."

Raising her candle, Charlotte stepped to the bookcase flanking the fireplace where she remembered seeing the sermons. She started to pull one from the shelf, but the memory of Anne's whispered words made her stop. *Naughty books?* What made them naughty?

She glanced up at the far wall. The shelves reached to the ceiling, far above her, but a library ladder rested along its track on the right side of the far wall. Charlotte tried to control her curiosity, but the spark had been lit. *How* naughty? Did they detail scandalous behavior? Did they reveal what happened beyond kissing?

Her mind flashed back on Lord Dalton's brutal kiss and how he had shoved his tongue into her mouth making her gag both literally and figuratively. At the same time, she remembered the sensations she'd experienced when Wolverton had kissed her awake. He, too, had opened his mouth to hers, his tongue inviting hers to tangle with his in a dance of sensation and pleasure. How different those kisses had been from one another. She looked up at the top shelf again. Had reading naughty books taught the duke how to make her feel pleasure instead of revulsion? What could they teach *her*? Before she could change her mind, she shelved the sermon then moved the ladder to the left and climbed until she could reach the top shelf.

# CHAPTER 13

Back in her room, Charlotte's eyes rounded as she translated the French text that explained the meaning of terms she had never heard before. Wavering candlelight lit illustrative drawings beside the descriptions that made her blush even as they made her feel oddly unsettled.

She turned the page and dropped the book in shock. *Surely not.* She picked up the book again and carefully studied the illustration. The artist must have exaggerated the dimensions of the man's organ in order to draw it clearly. She had once inadvertently seen a man rising nude from the river near her home and he had most certainly not been of the same proportions shown in the book... nor had it appeared rampant.

She turned another page and gasped to see a new drawing, this time illustrating a man lying atop a woman whose bare limbs wrapped around his back and his man part pressed into her most private place. Well, that answered *that question.*

A soft footfall in the hall made her aware that the staff were stirring. Dear heavens, was it that late? She closed the book and tucked it under the covers with a flush of guilt. What if the maid discovered her reading such a book? What if *anyone* caught her reading the book? She couldn't return it to the library in the light of day, nor, if she were honest, did she want to return it until she had read further. It embarrassed her at the same time as it fascinated her. Where could she hide it until then? She dared not get up to find a place lest the maid enter to light the fire, so she slid it between the bottom of the pillow and its embroidered slipcover, then lay back down to feign sleep.

A knock on the door, then Elizabeth's voice woke her. "Charlotte? Are you ill? You never sleep this late."

With a start, Charlotte saw that the shadows from the window light were short and the light as bright as noon. A check of the mantle clock confirmed it was half past noon and she sat up as disoriented and groggy as if she not slept– which she hadn't. Not until the early break of day.

"I am fine," she assured her sister when she opened the door and peeked in. "I did not fall asleep until late."

"Is something bothering you?" Elizabeth crossed the room and sat on the edge of the bed. "I thought you rather quiet last night as though your mind was distracted."

Charlotte had not had an opportunity to be alone with Elizabeth since the incident with Lord Dalton and she suddenly needed to warn Elizabeth about him and the chance that their current access to the upper reaches of society might be brief. Much as she hated to admit that she feared the censure that would rise in the opinion of most of the families with whom they had been introduced, Charlotte knew she dreaded that moment.

"I was," she admitted. "A most distressing incident occurred yesterday at Lady Ridley's party. Fortunately, nothing came of it and I believe the problem is controlled for now, but you need to know what happened."

Elizabeth's eyes widened and she reached out to take Charlotte's hand. "Tell me."

So she did, leaving out her childhood secret. She didn't know if she could ever admit to anyone how she'd spied on their neighbors, then not revealed the truth of what she witnessed... and Dalton would certainly not make that public.

When she got to the part where Lord Dalton had attacked her claiming their relationship to gypsies made her unworthy of respect, Elizabeth's face paled. Charlotte quickly made it clear that he'd managed no more than a brutal kiss before the duke had pulled him away and she'd fainted. Relating the story aloud, her anger grew again.

"It isn't right." she finished. "Uncle Rafe is an honest man. He doesn't deserve to be seen as a thief or swindler simply because he and Aunt Lily travel the country and own no land. I know it is shocking that she ran off to marry someone so much lower in status, but they love each other, and they *did* marry. And we don't deserve to be deemed wantons because Aunt Lily married him."

She turned to Elizabeth, her voice tight with frustration. "Anne thinks she knows our background, but she laughed at the idea that we could be related to gypsies. Perhaps we should arrange to go home. Papa will understand."

"He might understand," Elizabeth agreed with a sigh, "But he would be disappointed that we didn't stand up for the family. We knew when Aunt Poppy offered to sponsor our Season that we were unlikely to be invited into the highest levels of society, but it didn't stop us from coming." She chuckled, then continued. "Yet here we are, guests of the ever proper and upstanding Duke of Wolverton." Her smile stretched into a grin. "And Sarah assured us the wolves in her dreams were friendly."

The last bit surprised a laugh from Charlotte, and she hugged Elizabeth before climbing out of bed. "I am glad we are family," she said with conviction. "And we know family is more important than anything... especially misguided rules and spiteful gossip."

As soon as Elizabeth left her to dress, Charlotte wrapped the book in a shawl and tucked it into the traveling bag at the back of the clothes closet. Further edification would have to wait until late afternoon since they were to view an exhibition of art at the museum with a small party of Anne's friends in little more than an hour. Mindful of the time, she rang for the maid.

When they returned, she retired to her room on the pretext of a nap and locked her door before retrieving the scandalous book to further explore the mysteries it solved. Some images made a certain sense, but others made her suspect the author's understanding of human dexterity was greatly flawed and to wonder at the brazenness of his imagination. Whether probable or not, whether *possible* or not, Charlotte appreciated the thoroughness of the book to her education regarding men and women. It made noticeably clear exactly what would have happened if Lucien had not arrived when he did, and exactly why society insisted men and women not be allowed time alone together before marriage.

She'd also appreciated the fact that she needed to return the book to the library as soon as possible. She'd waited until everyone was abed after they returned from the Pomphrey rout. Once the house had quieted for the night, she slipped down the stairs and into the library, book still wrapped in her shawl.

Charlotte slipped the naughty book behind the thick tome on modern methods in cattle breeding and stifled a giggle. She understood a great deal more about *human* breeding than she had before climbing this ladder the night before.

She hid the evidence of her education behind the cattle book where she'd found it the night before, then descended and shifted the ladder back to the right side of the wall. She let out a breath, relieved to have completed her task without anyone the wiser. She turned to leave as the door opened and Wolverton stopped in obvious surprise.

*Blast.*

"I THOUGHT YOU'D RETIRED." Lucien took in the sight of Charlotte, again in night rail, though this time with a pale pink quilted wrapper adding a moderate layer of propriety to her dishabille. It didn't matter. Her backlit form had been burned into his memory and no salute to propriety was likely to erase the image any time soon... if ever.

"I had," Charlotte admitted, "But– I couldn't sleep. I remembered seeing some books of sermons..."

"If anything will put a person to sleep," he acknowledged with a slight smile, "it is a book of sermons." He stepped over the threshold and placed his lamp on the reading table in the center of the room before studying her face. "I hope your difficulty in sleeping isn't because of Lord Dalton's crude behavior yesterday. I noticed earlier that you looked a bit heavy eyed. Were you unable to sleep last night as well?"

"I confess I did not sleep until nearly dawn," Charlotte said as a pink flush rose from the neck of her night clothes and she looked away. "Perhaps I should have tried sermons last night."

He crossed to where she stood and took her hands in an attempt to soothe her. He could see she'd been far more frightened than she admitted. Dalton's *so you like it rough* flashed in his memory. Fury rose to realize what those words might mean. "Charlotte?" he probed carefully, "Did anything...*more*...happen before I intervened?

Now her face blossomed deep rose and her eyes closed. "No. He kissed me. That is all."

"I hope he didn't make you afraid of kisses." He stroked the back of her hands with his thumbs. "While a lady is not encouraged to kiss anyone but her fiancé, I wouldn't like to think you'd be afraid of such intimacies once you have accepted an offer. Not all kisses are brutal."

The pink became scarlet and he felt the sudden jump of her nerves. "I know," she whispered. "Yours were not."

*Dear God save me from virgin confessions.*

His voice tangled in his throat before he managed to choke out, "I'd hoped you wouldn't remember that. I assure you I meant only to wake you–"

She reached up and touched a restraining finger to his lips. "I know," she whispered again. She lifted her face until the lamplight revealed her clear gray eyes and added, "It made a difference, you know."

"A difference–?"

"You and he are different men. He is repulsive and his kiss repulsed. You are not and your kiss made me want more."

Lucien froze, stunned by temptation.

*I pray to God and the devil answers.*

"That is a dangerous thing to say to a man." His voice barely made it past the constriction of his throat. "It tempts him to give you more."

She said nothing, but her eyes shimmered with the curiosity that plagued his dreams and kept him half aroused just to know she might be in any room he entered.

She swallowed and he watched her throat work. He wanted to taste the fine skin, to stroke his tongue along the tender spot at the base of her ear, the edge of her jaw, the corner of her lips—plump, luscious lips. He closed his eyes to shut out the temptation and tamp down the flaring heat that melted his conscience and tempted him to teach her all that could happen beyond kisses.

He opened his eyes again when she released a broken sigh. She licked her lips.

"Would you kiss me again?"

He lost the battle with his conscience, lowered his mouth to hers and feasted on the glory of her mouth. Soft and pliant, the warmth of her body melted the rest of his resolve. He cupped her bottom to pull her higher and tighter against him until he pressed, hip to hip, the intimate dip at the top of her thighs. *Heaven*.

She made a pleased sound and wrapped her arms around his neck.

"Relax your mouth," he coaxed, "Let me taste you."

She opened her lips, then met his tongue with a tentative exploration of her own that made him groan with the pleasure of it and press her hips tighter to his.

That elusive scent of wildflowers floated up from her skin and he broke the kiss to run his tongue along her jaw to that tempting spot where the skin was most sensitive. Her breath hitched and her fingers curled into his hair pulling him closer. She touched her lips against his neck, then stroked her tongue along his skin in imitation of his caress. He took her mouth again in a deeply searching kiss that made his heart pound, his lungs seize, and his body throb. Her mouth was magnificent. *Delicious.*

The clock struck the hour and his conscience struggled against the pleasure of the moment. He wanted to resist mindful intrusion, but the spell cracked, and he eased his embrace. When Lucien finally raised his head, he recognized the alteration in those beautiful gray eyes. Innocent curiosity had been replaced with a new awareness that made her interest all the more tempting. Her pulse matched the frantic beat of his heart, her panting breath was as shallow and agitated, her skin as flushed. Her nipples pebbled the soft cloth of her night clothes.

She was glorious.

And no longer as innocent as she should be.

Cold sanity washed down his spine. Dalton had shown her the brutal side of lust, but he, Lucien, had introduced her to the hunger of passion. If he didn't stop now, he would ruin her as surely as his father had ruined Tristan's mother.

He settled her back on her feet and stepped back. "We must cease this. I should not have taken your words as invitation. I beg your pardon."

LUCIEN'S SUDDEN RETREAT left Charlotte bereft and slightly disoriented. His hands had held her so tenderly while he'd inundated her senses with his kiss, but now supported her forearms while she worked to breathe normally. His words penetrated her understanding, and she raised her eyes to his. "*Invitation?*"

She took a step back and folded her arms across her waist. "I did not– I didn't mean for you to..." Her hands clenched and she took a bracing breath. "It wasn't an invitation."

His features tightened, his expression more severe than she'd ever seen it. Moments before his gaze had burned with heat, now it chilled the fiery emotions he'd kindled. She refused to pretend she didn't see the implication.

"Anne said you objected to us when we were introduced because people questioned our family's past. Those were the same reasons Lord Dalton cited before he tried to take advantage of me. But that doesn't make me a wanton."

"That was never my impression." Lucien moved to the fireplace where he leaned against the mantle. "My objections at the time were based on concern for Anne's reputation through association with someone whose name I knew only through vague rumor." His hand lifted in a dismissing gesture. "Once I had the particulars of your history, I knew the rumors were nothing more than village gossip and ignorant superstition. As for your gypsy uncle, my man of business verified that he is both skilled with horses and scrupulous in his dealings."

"What do you mean, once you had the particulars– You had us *investigated?*"

"Of course." He appeared surprised she might object. "I couldn't allow Anne's Season to be tainted with scandal."

Charlotte took a step back, her spine stiffened, and her chin rose. "How dare you pry into our lives? Did you think we would sully your family by being the same room with you?" Realization stuck. Her voice dropped to a horrified whisper. "The same *house* with you."

Her eyes burned with furious tears that threatened to overflow and she blinked hard. She would not give him the satisfaction of seeing how much it hurt to know he'd had them spied upon like common criminals. She raised an eyebrow and stared him in the face before declaring, "No family is without some past scandal." She looked meaningfully at the miniature of his brother on the mantle. "I believe this is an occasion where it is the pot calling the kettle black."

She turned on her heel and swept out of the library and up the stairs before he could respond.

# CHAPTER 14

Lucien left the house and headed for his club where he knew he would find refuge from the aching residue of his unrelieved lust. Guilt knotted his belly. He abhorred violence against women for any reason, but other than that, he'd behaved no better than Dalton. He'd not forced her kisses, but he'd given in to his desires for a woman whose words had revealed how little she understood about passion and a man's reaction to it.

Once at White's, he made a point of strolling through every public room before settling down with a brandy while he watched for Ravencliffe. Dalton was not in evidence, nor did Lucien believe he would attend any future social event to which his own family had accepted invitations. He would alert his friends to watch for Dalton at any other venues his family might attend without him.

Dalton had been about to strike Charlotte for resisting his aggressive embrace, but was Lucien much better because his kiss had been more seductive? That question made him stifle a curse and grip his glass until his knuckles whitened. He should have come here directly after seeing his family and the Longboroughs home instead of disappearing into his study until time to meet Ravencliffe as they had agreed that morning.

If he'd come to the club, he would not have noticed the faint light under the door to the library. He would not have found Charlotte. He would not have kissed her. He would not have discovered that he was as weak as his father and as despicable as Dalton. The chit was under his protection and he'd ignored honor by giving into the driving need to taste her mouth– her skin– *Damnation!* He took swallow of his drink and worked to ease the fire that still licked his blood with the heat of his own personal hell.

Her parting accusation had been like an echo of his own past. He had shouted much the same to his father when he was sixteen and embarrassed at being caught with a willing maid in his room. That confrontation had led to retaliation that haunted him with guilt, and to his determination to redeem his honor through absolutely blameless behavior.

He closed his eyes and sighed. He'd failed that pledge tonight.

Had Tristan's mother held the same fascination for his father as Charlotte held on him? Never had he regretted his youthful spite more than he did tonight.

UNABLE TO FACE LUCIEN at breakfast the next morning, Charlotte requested hot chocolate and fingers of toast in her room. Her abandoned response to his kiss mortified her, as did her defensive attempt to embarrass him with her childish exit. She'd been as small minded and petty as the same people whose gossip fueled everything. She had no business bringing up the scandal she'd learned about from Aunt Poppy. The only time she had met Mr. Sheffield he'd been all that was kind and proper in his behavior. Neither he nor the duke deserved scorn for their father's actions any more than she and Elizabeth deserved derision because of her aunt's elopement.

Charlotte took a final sip of her chocolate and frowned as she admitted she owed him an apology though she wasn't quite ready to do so. She set the cup down, rose, and rang for the maid to remove the tray. Crossing to the vanity, she poured warm water into the bowl and dipped a face cloth into the tepid water. Stroking the cloth along her neck, she shivered with the memory of Lucien's lips and tongue following the same path. Kisses he'd admitted he should never have given her. She rinsed the cloth and scrubbed her face vigorously, the abrasive action offsetting the compulsion to relive the seductive temptation of his touch.

He owed an apology to her as well.

An inquiry to the maid assured her that Wolverton attended parliament that morning. Cowardly as she knew it to be, she breathed a sigh of relief that she would not encounter him before she knew how she could apologize without letting him think she forgave his investigation. When she finished dressing, she made her way to the family sitting room in search of Elizabeth or Anne.

She found them both laughing at the mess Elizabeth had made of her latest attempt at embroidery. It amazed Charlotte that Elizabeth had such a difficult time with a needle and thread when she could carve the most delicate of flowers in wood. Of course, Elizabeth freely confessed that she gave less than half her attention to the needlework and the rest focused on mentally solving her latest wood project. She sat next to Elizabeth on the settee, held out her hand for Elizabeth's embroidery hoop, and began to pick out the tangled stitches.

LUCIEN WAS IN HIS STUDY when the clock in the hall chimed the hour and he realized it was time to dress for dinner. He'd avoided Charlotte by attending parliament that morning, but he might as well as stayed home for all the attention he'd been able to focus on the matters under discussion. Guilt had made him retreat to the study when he returned, where he'd pondered the situation created by his lack of control.

How could he have been so weak... so lacking in honor and control as to take advantage of an inexperienced guest in his home? Charlotte had suffered a shocking attack and he'd given in to his own desires under the guise of ... What? That his inappropriate behavior was justified to show her pleasure instead of threat? What had he been thinking?

He hadn't been thinking. He'd been feeling. *And she'd felt perfect in his arms.* The memory sent heat to his lower regions and he gave a huff of disgust. He'd kissed her for no other reason than he wanted to. He'd allowed himself to ignore his own code of honor as well as that of a gentleman.

He rose from his chair and strode up the stairs to his room. The family dined at home this evening before attending yet another ball where he would fulfill his role as protector for his sister and her guests. His conscience did not miss the irony of his role considering his behavior to one of those guests. If he suspected any of Anne's admirers of behaving in a like manner, he would thrash the man within an inch of his life.

A swarm of suitors filled the drawing room twice a week and Anne's dance card quickly filled at every ball, but so far none stood out as a serious candidate for her hand. His thoughts shied away from who might claim Charlotte Longborough. She, too, seldom sat out a set.

Once Anne's choice was secured, he would not have to cross the threshold of the Almack's marriage mart to drink another glass of tepid lemonade for at least five more years.

*This Season can't end soon enough.*

Then Charlotte Longborough would no longer be in residence.

A small hitch interrupted his breathing, and he wondered why that thought didn't relieve his frustration.

His stepmother, Anne, and both Longborough sisters were already in the drawing room when he entered it an hour later. Fashion demanded that unmarried misses wear white, which often made them blend into one another on the dance floor. Variations in the color and style of the trims seemed to be the primary distinction and only the female portion of the attendees paid any attention to those. He never had. But tonight, Charlotte's gown, though the proscribed white, shimmered with silver when caught by the light. If the gown shimmered, Charlotte glowed.

*Damned if he didn't want to kiss her again.*

Rowena and Sarah entered the room a few moments later, chatting happily. Grateful for their interruption to his wayward thoughts, he asked the younger girls about their day. Then, when Timmons announced dinner to be ready, led them all into the dining room.

Soon after they'd seated themselves for dinner, Sarah asked, "Does your brother have a fondness for rats as pets?" Startled, Lucien peered at the youngest Longborough. "I beg your pardon?" Her sisters' appalled expressions reassured him that his hearing had not been faulty. Since taking up residence, Sarah had made occasional odd comments that caused her sisters to exchange glances before filling in the blanks of the child's conversational path. It was a trait he feared would hinder her matrimonial prospects despite the fact that she would be a beauty when she came of age. As often happened after making such a comment, Sarah blanched, and her gaze skittered between her sisters.

"A pet rat, Sarah?" Elizabeth asked. "What have you been reading now? No one would choose to have a rat living in the house. They are vermin of the worst kind."

"I think bed-bugs would be worse," Rowena spoke up.

"What do you know of bed-bugs?" The duchess demanded. "We have never had a bed-bug in this house...and never shall so long as I breathe."

"I heard one of the maids telling the cook that—"

"I believe Sarah asked a question," Lucien put in before the conversation could go any further afield. "Tristan is quite firm in his dislike of rats," he said. "Why would you think he might make one a pet?"

"I... I just had an odd dream about a rat and... *in my dream... for some reason*..." Sarah's face had paled to parchment white and Lucien feared the girl would faint before finishing her sentence. "It seemed connected to him–somehow?"

Charlotte's face had also paled. "Was that a good thing or a bad thing?" she asked.

"I don't know." Sarah told her. "I never actually met Mr. Sheffield so... It made me wonder if the rat was a pet of some sort. It was a confusing dream similar to one I had recently where a rat chased a hedgehog, though this time there was a weasel and..." She stopped and her large blue eyes turned to Lucien. "I just wondered."

Lucien smiled to ease the child's disquiet. "Dreams are often disjointed as I am sure you know." He picked up his utensils and cut a bite of roasted pork. "I don't know why the absurd seems perfectly normal in dreams, but it does. Don't worry, there are no rats either at Wolverton House or Tristan's apartments."

# CHAPTER 15

"I wonder what people would do if we danced a waltz?" Anne quietly mused as they climbed the stairs for the Swathmore ball a few hours later.

"Whatever are you talking about?" Charlotte asked. "We have often walltzed."

"I don't mean the country waltz," Anne clarified. She slowed her steps and whispered, "I meant the continental waltz. You know, the one they say allows a man face his partner and hold her in his arms while they move to the music."

"That cannot be right." Elizabeth said. "Such behavior would be scandalous."

"But it's all the rage on the continent." Anne assured them. "Lord Clarehaven says it's a most delightful dance and couldn't understand why no one danced it here." They neared the top of the stairs and she kept her voice low. "I told him that until danced at Almack's it would remain a continental dance only. Though I remember overhearing Lady Spencer tell my mother that Lady Charlotte Campbell and the Duke of Cambridge danced it during a garden party three years ago. She thought it a beautiful thing then, though it scandalized several of the guests. Unfortunately, I doubt tonight will provide an opportunity to attempt the exercise."

"So why did you ask such a question?"

"Because I wondered if it might make the evening a bit more eventful. Much as I enjoy meeting our friends, one ball has become much like all the others. Something so novel would be diverting."

Charlotte surveyed the room as the usual pattern of announced guests, dance requests, and mild flirtations settled throughout the room. What had at first fascinated her with its novelty now had the familiarity of comfort. Like Anne, she enjoyed the evenings where they danced, mingled and chatted about inconsequential amusing things. But she had to admit her breathless anticipation had waned with that familiarity and she recognized Anne's lively wish to create a spark of excitement. The musicians began a tune that warned dancers to take their places and she thought no more about it as Lord Bascomb claimed her first dance.

LUCIEN CHECKED THE room and saw that Anne danced with the Swathmore heir. *Safe enough there*– Swathmore was not yet ready to choose a wife, but neither would he tempt Anne to push the bounds of correct behavior. Anne knew the rules and generally followed them without much protest—though he couldn't claim she'd never found fault with the restrictions applied to females and not to males. Still, he'd noticed a restlessness in her lately that made him hope she received an offer acceptable to them both... and soon. Unfortunately, of the suitors he'd seen in his home, none had made any observable impression on her... nor had the three gentlemen who'd approached and been refused by him without him doing more than mentioning their requests to Anne.

Now that he had ascertained that Anne was properly occupied, he watched Bascomb lead Charlotte Longborough through the steps of the first dance with mixed feelings. Lucien generally avoided asking anyone other than relatives to dance the early dances. He knew better than to claim any young woman's first dance lest any mama take it as a sign of specific interest on his part. Marked interest at any ball inevitably led to expectation for notices in the Times and reservations at St. George's.

That Charlotte interested him he couldn't deny, but his interest had absolutely nothing to do with matrimony and everything to do with midnight kisses in the library. Clarehaven had described her as a delicious morsel when he'd first arrived in town and it had angered Lucien to hear another man say such a thing. But he couldn't deny that he wanted to taste her mouth again, or that he wanted more than mere kisses. He wasn't proud of his less than honorable desire for her, but he couldn't deny it either.

When Charlotte laughed at something Bascomb said, Lucien had the unaccustomed urge to stride onto the dance floor and remove Bascomb's gloved hand from hers and sweep her out of the ballroom where he could do exactly that.

He would not, of course. He was a proper man, and she was a proper young lady, and this was a proper venue. A stab of guilt pained his conscience that he'd gone from guarding his sister's attentions from unsuitable interest to lusting after his sister's friend. He wished the Swathmores offered something stronger than lemonade and ratafia.

He hadn't had occasion to speak to Charlotte privately since she'd stormed out of his study the night before. He owed her an apology, but apologies weren't easy, even when they were owed. He waited until the evening was nearly over before asking her to partner him.

"I wish to apologize, Your Grace," Charlotte said as he led her to the floor. "I shouldn't have said what I did the other night. I behaved no better than those who've judged my family for deeds over which we had no control." She took her place and curtsied as the music began and waited until they stepped together to add quietly, "But I'm still most disturbed that you would investigate my family as though my sisters and I might steal the family silver in the middle of the night."

They circled each other, and before stepping back, Lucien answered with the same formality. "I'm truly sorry to have caused you distress, Miss Longborough. I didn't fear for the silver, I assure you." He hoped his attempt at levity would be accepted as the peace offering, he knew he owed her. "But I can't apologize for acting as a responsible guardian to my sister. I couldn't chance putting her through the pain of ridicule and exclusion created by scandal."

Their steps brought them back together to circle in the other direction and allowed Charlotte to retort, "I believe I know the feeling. It is something like being investigated or assaulted for having an unconventional relative."

Her comment caught Lucien off guard, and he met her gaze. In it, he saw a depth of hurt he had not imagined his actions would cause. The dance required them to part and weave through the other dancers before meeting again at the head of the line and circling again. When they met, he said, "I never meant–"

"I know." Charlotte returned his gaze, then smiled at him for the first time that evening, "and I will allow I understand your motive so long as you now realize you are not the only one who prefers to avoid scorn because of what others do." She glanced away, then turned and gave him a teasing look. "From what I hear from the gossips, though, I should think *causing* scandal would be more fun than dealing with the results."

WHEN THE NEXT SET WAS about to begin, something in Anne's expression as she took the floor with the Marquess of Clarehaven made Charlotte uneasy. The musicians struck up a country waltz and she held her breath then closed her eyes. *Surely she wouldn't—?* A collective gasp confirmed her fear that Anne and the Marquess had taken the continental pose. She opened her eyes when her partner, Lord Swathmore, let out a startled, "Clarehaven must be mad," and halted any attempt to follow the music.

Across the room the duke stood at rigid attention, clearly furious, but restrained by his stepmother's hand on his arm. Three of the patronesses from Almack's had attended the Swathmore ball and now clustered together, clearly shocked and disapproving of such a display. The rest of the guests whispered furiously between themselves and watched in rapt attention as the Marquess and Anne whirled around the floor in a distant embrace that flowed with elegant ease to the time of the music.

The music came to an end and Clarehaven bowed to Anne before turning to their hostess. "Lady Swathmore," He gave her a rogue's smile as he bowed. "I pray you will forgive me my apparent error. Lady Anne informs me that the continental style of waltz is not yet considered appropriate on these shores, though it is popular on the continent where I've spent the past several years." He turned to her brother, his eyes twinkling. "I assure Your Grace I meant no disrespect and ask that you accept my apologies for any insult you might see in my inadvertent gaff."

The duke's jaw was clenched and his narrowed eyes pinned Clarehaven with unblinking fury. Charlotte noted the white line around his mouth as he obviously kept his anger in check. Still, the public apology left him no alternative other than a stiff nod of his head or the call for a challenge that would create a greater scandal. She could see he didn't believe for one moment that the dance had been a simple mistake of understanding. She doubted anyone else did either.

"I am sure you would not show my sister any calculated disrespect, or knowingly expose her to scandal." Lucien responded. His voice dripped with icy restraint. He sent Anne a look that clearly said she should have known better than to engage in such a pose. "But I must make clear I cannot allow my sister to participate in such a demonstration again."

Anne blanched. Then took a breath and said, "I, too, ask my brother and our hosts to forgive any perceived forwardness in following the Marquess's lead in the style." She curtsied to Lord and Lady Swathmore. "I believed it would be rude to refuse after accepting his request to dance."

Lady Swathmore looked to her husband who flicked a look at Lucien, then said, "I am sure no permanent harm has been done. Though, in future, we would prefer our guests to follow the traditional mode."

At his nod, the musicians struck up *Sir Roger de Coverley* to signal the end of the evening's entertainment. At least, Charlotte thought, the end of the dancing. The entertainment of gossip had only begun. By morning, every household in Mayfair– and she was sure, a good many other neighborhoods – would know Anne had danced the scandalous dance from the continent.

As they collected their shawls to leave the Hall, Lady Ridley approached Anne. "Oh, my dear, you've set the cat among the pigeons tonight."

"I am sorry if I embarrassed–"

"Don't be silly, child." She turned to her nephew whose jaw was still clenched and told him, "Don't take her to task for this little rebellion, Lucien. The Marquess told the truth, you know. They have been dancing that form of the waltz on the continent for years."

"That may be true, Aunt, but Anne's reputation will suffer for–"

"Balderdash!" The older woman thumped him on the arm with her fan. "You are in danger of becoming priggish. Come see me tomorrow at two. We need to talk."

# CHAPTER 16

The damp air and threatening weather matched Lucien's mood when his aunt's butler admitted him into her townhouse the next afternoon. He strode up the stairs to the drawing room, ready to defend his stance against Anne's flagrant behavior the night before. He'd been both shocked and a little hurt when she'd defended Anne the way she had. She should have supported him as head of the family.

Yet Lucien remembered how she'd stood up to the gossips when his father brought Tristan home, so he shouldn't be surprised that she'd shielded Anne from his displeasure. His stepmother, too, had subtly restrained him from pulling his sister from the dance floor before the dance was complete. Both understood his fears for Anne's reputation, yet had discouraged his protective reaction.

He crossed the room to where Aunt Ridley sat beside the fireplace. Above the mantle hung a painting of her and Lord Ridley that his late great uncle had commissioned shortly after they married. Her natural hair now was as silver-white as the wig she'd worn so many years ago, though her posture was as erect as ever. On the mantle were miniatures of various family members. Among them were his father, Lucien's stepmother, and each of his siblings. All of them.

"Good afternoon, Aunt," Lucien bent to kiss his aunt on the cheek. "I hope you are not going to call me a prig again." He smiled as he straightened.

"Indeed, I am," Lady Ridley retorted briskly. She pointed to the chair opposite her and ordered. "Sit down, my boy. It is time you learned that our family history is not so pristine as you think it is."

Lucien chose a seat opposite her and stated, "I believe Tristan is proof of that."

"I'm not talking about Tristan, though it is past time you forgave your father for being human. Ah, here is the tea."

A maid entered with a tea tray that she put on the table beside Lady Ridley. When they were alone, she poured out two cups and handed one to him. She added a teaspoon of sugar to her own cup, then sat back and took a sip.

"I do so love Oolong," she said. "It is so soothing in times of stress." She cocked her head to the side and smiled at him. "And I can see my criticism has upset you. Good. Now, perhaps you will pay attention to what I have to say."

"I accepted Tristan years ago." Her comment irritated him. "And I have never thought Father anything less than human."

She took another sip of the tea before correcting him. "You thought your father a saint until the day he brought Tristan home. Learning that he was not, hurt you." She set her cup down and leveled a look of compassion that made him uncomfortably aware of how well she knew him. "As a boy you were a mischievous imp who kept everyone on their toes and charmed us whenever you were caught playing tricks." A smile touched her lips before she frowned. "But since inheriting the title you've become an overly proper prig who takes life far too seriously."

He wanted to protest, but she held up her hand to halt his objection. "I've gathered, over the years, you think your father's indiscretion was the only irregularity ever committed in our family and that it is your responsibility to see that there is never another." She shook her head with a rueful smile. "None of them were saints, myself included, and it's time you were told a few family secrets."

"Secrets?" Lucien eyed her warily.

"Secrets." She nodded firmly. "For example, how do you think the first duke was granted the title?

"He uncovered a plot to poison Princess Elizabeth while she was in the tower. She thanked him by granting him the title when she came to power." Lucien stated without hesitation.

"True... so far as it goes, and so far as society believes," his aunt said. "However, he learned of the plot when hiding in an antechamber where he'd almost been caught in a tryst with the plotter's wife. Once Elizabeth became queen, she *knighted* him and made him a member of her inner circle as thanks." She raised an eyebrow and said, "The *duchy* was awarded after he kept her secrets for the next thirty years."

Lucien stared and his aunt nodded with a wicked smile. "Had he been a man of impeccable integrity he would not have taken up with a married woman, the Princess might never have become queen, and you would not now be a duke."

"How do you know this?"

"There is a collection of family diaries in a trunk with the old clothes we used for masquerades and theatrics when we were children." She took a nibbling bite of a scone. "I was a curious child. I read them." She looked him in the eye. "And I *kept* them. Lest you think that is the end of the irregularities, the first duke's diaries weren't the only ones packed away in those trunks."

Lucien eyed his aunt with a sense of dread. "I take it that was not the only story altered over time."

"Of course not. Gaining power and influence is not the result of happenstance. Nor is it always neat and tidy."

"Another way of saying my forefathers did not always act with honor?"

She smiled wryly. "They always acted with honor... but what may be honorable to some is treason to his enemy. One thing you may be sure of is that every one of them believed they were maintaining their honor when they acted."

"Whether they were or not? That doesn't sound particularly honorable. So, what other secrets should I know?" Lucien asked. "I take it several of my ancestors acted upon some inexplicable need to record their deepest secrets?"

"Some were quite frank." His aunt agreed. "Others used personal codes that could be worked out if one read between the lines. The men and women of our family have often been ambitious and extremely human. Fortunately, they were also discreet, *despite the diaries*... which is why you, and all but those involved, know nothing of their indiscretions."

"So far as the other secrets I know," Lady Ridley continued, "The diaries are now in a chest of their own which I am sending with you today. You can read them yourself if you choose or keep them to edify future generations once you fulfill your duty and establish your nursery." She wagged her finger. "Do not think to destroy them in an attempt to alter history, either. That *would* be dishonorable."

She leaned forward and removed the now cold teacup from his hands and placed it on the table. "You are too young to live like a monk. I encourage you to take advantage of your youth. You need not become a libertine to be human. Simply enjoy yourself and do something for the fun of it, like dancing in the continental style with that Longborough miss you are always watching." She grinned at his start of surprise. "If it shocks Sally Jersey or Emily Cowper, so be it. They wouldn't dare cut you or me." She chuckled. "I know a few of *their* secrets as well."

She stood, indicating their audience was done. "You are a duke, my boy, and dukes rise above petty rules set by gossip mongers."

LUCIEN CLOSED HIMSELF into his study upon returning from his aunt's house. If he opened the chest his aunt insisted he bring home, he feared he'd release a Pandora's Box of facts about which he'd prefer to remain ignorant. On the other hand, he acknowledged as he gave in and located the first duke's journal, he knew he could not ignore the challenge his aunt had thrown down. The deeds in these diaries were long past and of less personal impact than those revealed when he'd accidentally come across his father's diary and given in to curiosity when he was sixteen.

Nor was he the frustrated and angry youth who'd acted with immature defiance to the sentiments written by his father so many years ago. The result had made him determined never to keep a diary of his own, or to read one again. His father's diary had caused Lucien's still smoldering humiliation over Tristan's presence to flame into anger and revenge that had altered everything... and cost his father his life. Wary, but resigned, he settled into his chair and began reading.

It was late when Lucien returned his great-great grandfather's diary to the chest. The third duke had been a close friend to Charles the second and acted as procurer for tryst occasions and locations for the king's many mistresses. That revelation left Lucien shaking his head as he firmly locked the diary away. *Definitely not a saint.*

In his defense, it was clear Lucien's relative had believed himself honor-bound to comply with the king's need for life affirming celebrations now that he had power and no need for asylum. The duke had written of his friend and liege's need to live life to the fullest in the light of his father's execution.

Before settling in on the third duke's revelations, Lucien had thumbed through the first and second dukes' diaries, and acknowledged that the chest was, indeed, a Pandora's Box of scandal and intrigue. His ancestors were a collection of rakes and schemers who knew how to cover their indiscretions and bluff their way through the social and political maze with brazen unconcern for anything other than loyalty and a warped form of honor.

He had not perused those of his female relations, though he saw several of those in the chest as well. It relieved him that none of the diaries belonged to his Aunt Ridley. Still, he did not think he would ever be ready to pry into feminine secrets.

His male relatives had recorded commentary indicating his female relatives had not been particularly docile or compliant with the dictates of society, either. He conceded that they, too, were less than perfect though he preferred not to know *exactly* how imperfect.

Nor did he want anyone *else* exploring his family secrets. He stood and stepped to the bookcase flanking the right side of the fireplace where he removed a thick tome from the fourth shelf. Pressing firmly, he slid the upright side of the shelf forward, then reached up into the corner to release a catch. Silently, the bookcase to the left of the fireplace released, and Lucien carried the chest into the secret landing behind it. As he did, he smiled grimly. He should have known that the secret passage leading to the duke's chambers had not been the only secret his family harbored… just as the passage from his study was not the only passage in Wolverton House.

After closing the passage panel and securing the secret latch, Lucien climbed the front stairs to his room to change for the evening. Though he could have continued up the hidden stairs to his rooms, Jennings would be laying out his clothes and Lucien preferred to keep the passage secret, especially as it now held a trove of family secrets as well.

After Anne's flagrant behavior at the Swathmore's the night before, Lucien knew they could not miss the Sinclair's ball, or the incident would escalate the gossip. So, they would attend the ball and all other scheduled events that would undoubtedly test his great aunt's assurance that dukes had the power to ignore what they chose, and thus, cause others to do the same.

He was halfway up the stairs when Harry trotted quickly past him, something furry in his mouth. Lucien increased his pace, memories of young Sarah's rat query speeding him to reach the beast before he delivered his prize to an unsuspecting member of the household. He caught up with Harry in front of Charlotte's door, took hold of the leather collar and reached for the still moving creature in his mouth. As he did, Harry growled and dodged Lucien's hand. A moment later Lucien heard Charlotte's voice through the door. "Harry? What are you growling at?" The door opened and Charlotte gave a short gasp when she saw Lucien holding Harry's collar.

"He has something in his mouth," Lucien warned as he reached again for the dog's prize. Again, the dog turned his head away and growled.

Charlotte bent over and held her hand below the dog's shaggy head, "Drop it."

To Lucien's amazement, Harry turned and dropped a small, slobber-matted kitten into her hand, then slipped past her and into her room. Beyond the doorway Lucien was sure he heard the high-pitched mews of more kittens. Charlotte straightened and Lucien raised his eyebrow in question.

"I, uh... rescued a bag of orphaned kittens from a man who dropped them into the Serpentine last week," Charlotte confessed. Her gray eyes widened, and she pleaded with him "I couldn't let them drown."

Lucien recognized the futility of resisting her appeal. He didn't approve of drowning unwanted cats any more than he would condone abandoning a child. Still, he had to point out the obvious. "Dogs and cats are natural enemies, and you already have a dog the size of a small horse."

A glint of amusement lurked in her eyes. "Harry has adopted them."

"Are you sure?" Lucien asked. "He had it in his mouth."

"That particular kitten escaped the room earlier." Charlotte said. "Harry was bringing him back."

Lucien looked beyond her to where Harry now lay on the floor while a gray kitten with white sock markings stalked his tail before leaping to bat at the shaggy fur. Harry turned to his attacker and washed its face with a single swipe of his tongue before turning back to observe another, gray-striped, furry hunter attack a small ball of paper.

"I begin to see why rumors of witchcraft plague your family," Lucien said as he took in the scene. "Only magical charms could explain how you could get a male dog to behave like a female mother cat."

"It is not magic." Charlotte explained. "It is the most basic instinct of all...protecting those unable to care for themselves."

He settled his gaze back on hers. "Only you, and perhaps young Sarah and her dreams of odd menageries, would find Harry's behavior normal." He reached out and stroked the line of her jaw with his forefinger. "I have long scoffed at the idea of witches, but I think you wove a charm to protect them." Her breath caught and Lucien knew he had to taste her mouth again.

"Charlotte, have you seen my–" Elizabeth stepped out of her room across the hall and stopped abruptly.

Lucien dropped his hand and Charlotte quickly bobbed a curtsey and said, "Thank you for removing the smudge, Your Grace." Then she turned to her sister and asked, "Did you lose something, Elizabeth?"

Lucien turned as well, bowed, and retreated to his room.

# CHAPTER 17

"How good of you to come," Lady Sinclair greeted Lucien and his party with a wide smile and twinkling eyes. "She looked directly at Lucien before adding, "I hope you don't mind, Your Grace, that I have arranged for a dancing master to demonstrate the steps of the continental waltz with our daughter, Cassandra, after the supper dance. Everyone is so excited to have finally witnessed the continental waltz about which we had only heard gossip. Following his instructions, we intend to invite those who wish, to attempt it before the end of the evening."

Lucien returned her gaze and realized that her announcement offered him a chance to lessen any criticism of Anne's behavior. It was also clear that she gave him the opportunity to leave early if he did not wish to allow Anne to dance in that style again.

"I am sure that we shall find it most diverting once a dancing master has provided guidance." He said with an ironic smile. "How thoughtful of you to think of it."

Lady Sinclair nodded her head. "Lady Ridley assured me you would agree."

He should have expected his aunt to set things in motion after her disclosures earlier in the day. Family privilege and a steady gaze would get them past the shocked whispers and speculations. He'd perfected that distant demeanor long ago.

They passed into the ballroom itself and Lucien noted that his great aunt stood with Lady Jersey and several other ladies whose approval was deemed a necessary part of the social Season. Lady Jersey had seen Anne's dance at the Swathmore's but neither she nor the other Almack's patronesses had yet pulled Anne's vouchers... for which he suspected he owed his aunt his thanks. He assumed they'd move on to another ball venue before the supper dance. What they didn't witness, they could ignore.

A short time later, Lucien led Anne out for the first dance... a traditional, and popular, Scottish reel. He did encounter a few disapproving looks which he met with challenge, but most of his fellow guests behaved as though they didn't know of the previous night's events or didn't consider it shocking enough to comment upon. His aunt had not erred about the privilege of his title.

The set ended and Lucien led Anne back to her mother who visited with his great aunt and Lady Jersey. "Be ready to be humble," he said in an undertone. "But do not grovel," he added when her arm stiffened against his. "We are Caldwells, after all."

She glanced up in obvious surprise at his encouragement and her arm relaxed. "Yes," she agreed with a pleased smile. "We are."

Having made his public statement of support, Lucien intended to remain on the sidelines until he needed to again present a united front and learn the new style. He went in search of the card room.

"THE GENTLEMAN PLACES his right hand–so." The dancing master set his hand alongside Cassandra Sinclair's waist. A lean faced man of average height and precise dress, the master shifted his partner around so that everyone could see both the placement and the distance of their positions.

Charlotte watched his demonstration, well aware that the guests had all been warned of this... and those who did not approve had left the ballroom before the supper dance. The room was still crowded, however, and she suspected the waltz would be performed at a few more private balls during the remainder of the Season.

"The lady places her left hand upon the gentleman's shoulder–so."

He lifted Cassandra's gloved hand to his shoulder, keeping several inches of space between them as he joined their opposite hands to finish the pose. "When the music begins, the gentleman steps forward with his right foot to lead his partner to the measured count. One, two, three... one, two, three." He demonstrated the three-quarter time steps slowly, working the steps so that they turned in a circular motion. Then he nodded to the quartet, who began a waltz tune. He and Lady Cassandra began circulating the dance floor with the dance master calling out the time and further instructions as they moved.

Around the room, the guests stood in clusters, some whispering together, others visibly attempting to memorize the dance master's movements. The demonstration complete, Lord and Lady Sinclair stepped onto the dance floor and invited any who wished to try the steps to join in. Lord Chalmers led Lady Jane out, then Lady Millicent took her place with Lord Bascomb. Lord Norcross asked Elizabeth, and she saw Lady Ridley accept Lord Wentworth.

"Miss Longborough, would you care to try the steps?"

Charlotte looked up to meet Lucien's blue gaze and heat rose from deep inside. "I believe I would, Your Grace."

Lucien placed his hand on her waist and Charlotte felt the warmth of it from head to toe. When she placed her hand on his muscled shoulder she wondered if she would burst into flame. Certainly, her cheeks burned, and she had to consciously control her breathless reaction. She worried everyone must see her heart pound when Lucien took her hand in his. In the moment while they waited for the music to begin, she peered up into Lucien's face and saw that he was well aware of her nervousness.

"Courage, Miss Longborough," he chided her, "Aunt Ridley assures me that dukes are impervious to the opinions of others, so should we make a misstep no one would dare comment."

He surprised her with a teasing grin with those enticing dimples that stole her breath when the musicians struck up the same waltz they'd played during the demonstration. Lucien stepped forward in time with the music and Charlotte discovered that the face-to-face proximity made following his lead a matter of instinct. It also made her incredibly aware of how wonderfully exciting a man's embrace could be and wished the proscribed twelve-inch separation emphasized by the dancing master earlier did not apply. And that they were somewhere other than a crowded ballroom.

That notion made her face flame a deeper crimson. Unsure where to focus her attention, Charlotte let her gaze stray from Lucien's cravat to his strong jaw, then higher to his lips. Her own felt dry and she licked them. When she did, Lucien's hand at her waist tightened and she looked up to find his eyes blazing into hers.

"I predict," he murmured, "That the ladies of Almack's will be forced to accept this style of dance soon." His lips quirked and Charlotte's nerves jumped again. "Its appeal is undeniably clear."

Charlotte could not look away from his heated gaze and didn't object when his hand at her waist tightened slightly, moving them another inch closer. "It will certainly guarantee to bring many more bachelors to the dance floor."

She blinked in surprise. *Oh, my goodness, he sounds like a rake.* His hand tightened a bit more and now she couldn't pretend not to notice how much more familiar his embrace had become. "And should they forget to maintain the proper distance while dancing," Charlotte responded with a teasing grin, "to the alter, as well."

Charlotte bit her lip and regretted her comment immediately when he eased his hold on her waist with a rueful smile and broke eye contact to survey the other dancers before returning his gaze to hers. "The dance tempts, to be sure, and I suspect you are correct that the dance may encourage some gentlemen to make offers a bit sooner than they might have otherwise. From Chalmers' captivated expression I believe we shall soon be wishing Miss Pomphrey happy."

Charlotte turned her head toward the couple who danced nearby. Jane's eyes sparkled, her cheeks glowed soft pink... and the distance between them had also narrowed–to mere inches. Lord Chalmers said something near Jane's ear and her cheeks flushed to a deeper hue and Jane laughed as she nodded in response.

Watching the intimate looks that passed between them made the change in Lucien's hold following her flippant comment all the more disappointing. It had broken the intense awareness the dance sparked and caused him to assume his usual proper public demeanor.

LUCIEN STROVE TO BRING himself back into control. When Charlotte had licked her lips, his whole body had tightened, and he'd pulled her closer without thought. Fortunately, his glance around the room showed all the others focused on their own steps and no one had noticed his momentary loss of public awareness.

He hadn't questioned his decision to ask Charlotte to be his partner in the new dance, but now wondered if he should have chosen Charlotte's sister instead. He liked the elder sister well enough, but her presence didn't tempt him to pull her tighter, to breathe in her scent, or suggest that she meet him in the library after everyone else retired for the night. Now *that* was an action that would deliver him to the alter as soon as the banns could be read. He glanced down at Charlotte and another shaft of desire hit him. *Or as soon as a special license could be purchased.*

When this dance was done, he had best avoid future waltzes. At least with Miss Charlotte Longborough. Just because his forefathers had succeeded in suppressing the less savory aspects of their lives did not mean he intended to test his ability to do so. Much as he sympathized with the distress her family's reputation caused Charlotte, he didn't need to make it part of his own. However, he wouldn't permit dishonorable men to take advantage of her either.

The music ended and the chatter around them rose in volume as everyone shared their thoughts on the experiment. The ladies of Almack's had left before supper, but there could be no doubt that the popularly of the new style would demand they eventually allow the dance to enter their assembly room.

He bowed over Charlotte's hand and thanked her for the dance, then led her to his stepmother's side. Once there, he explained that he would be going on to his club with Ravencliffe once the ladies were on their way home in the family carriage. He had no real desire to go to his club but needed time to regain his equilibrium– and riding in the coach with one Charlotte Longborough would not allow that.

CHARLOTTE WATCHED LUCIEN take his leave with both regret and relief. Her pulse still raced with the thrill of his embrace and the intoxicating excitement that he had held her closer than defined by the dancing master. Before her foolish words about matrimony, his eyes had held that hot intensity she'd seen in the dim candlelight in the library. He'd wanted to kiss her again, she was sure of it, and she'd wanted him to. Desire had filled the air around them as they moved across the dance floor twirling to the measured cadence of the waltz.

When he announced he would be going on to his club after sending them home, cold reality chilled Charlotte's heart. Other than when they were alone together, the duke treated her with distant civility and sometimes amused tolerance. His interest was nothing more than the *needs* people spoke of. She mustn't look upon this attraction they had for one another as anything more than proof that men's needs had little to do with caring and everything to do with the acts described in naughty books. She reminded herself that Anne had once declared her obligation to make a suitable match was compounded by her brother's determination not to marry until both she and Rowena were settled.

Charlotte couldn't wait that long no matter how much her heart pounded when he was near. Was the reason she hadn't reacted to anyone else the same way was because he'd been the first to kiss her? Focused on him, had she ignored the chance that another gentleman might make her feel equally wonderful? Perhaps she needed to experiment to see if her reaction to the duke's kiss was no more than *female* need.

# CHAPTER 18

Lucien had just ordered a second brandy at White's when Clarehaven took a seat beside him. "I hope your participation in Lady Sinclair's experiment this evening means I am forgiven for upsetting tradition last night." He signaled his order for a brandy as well, then grinned. "I suspect the continental waltz will be performed throughout London this Season—except at Almack's."

"I should have called you out for exposing my sister to possible scandal, Clarehaven." Lucien glared at his companion. "Though you made that impossible by apologizing so publicly."

"Of course I did." Clarehaven agreed. "I'm not out to debauch your sister, charming as she may be. She is not my quarry, nor am I hers." The footman arrived with their brandies and he took a sip before telling Lucien, "I know it isn't gentlemanly to tell you, but you should know it was her idea to challenge convention."

Lucien sat up. "The devil you say."

"I only tell you this because you'll need to be alert to any other plans she might hatch to– and I quote her here—'*keep the Season interesting*'."

"You say she has someone in mind?" Lucien searched his memory for any male to whom he'd missed when they swarmed around his sister. He'd swear he'd seen no hint of special interest on her side, though it was clear several young men vied for her attention with hopeful intent.

"I believe she may be matchmaking for someone other than for herself," he clarified, "She only approached me to assist her because she believed I was audacious enough to do it and would be able to get away with it." He chuckled, and Lucien ground his teeth to discover how devious his little sister had become.

"If her target was Chalmers, he didn't need last night's encouragement," Lucien mused. "He's had time for no one but the Pomphrey chit since he laid eyes on her." He frowned. "You're sure she gave no hint about whose match she's attempting to secure?"

"None. But, so long as it's not me, I care not. I enjoy my freedom far too much. I'll leave it to my brother and his offspring to carry on the line. His heiress bride will keep them well coffered until my demise." He tossed back the last of his drink and stood. "As it is, I have a late-night visit to pay to a lonely *widow* at the moment."

As Lucien watched Clarehaven accept his hat and cloak from the footman and quit the club he wondered if he should find a willing widow as well. His deficiency of control around Charlotte Longborough made him acutely aware of how much he regretted his lack of a mistress.

WHEN JANE'S NOTE ARRIVED the next day, no one was surprised at the news that Lord Chalmers had called on her father that morning and that Jane had accepted his offer. Nothing would do but that they pay her a morning call to congratulate her. When shown into the Pomphrey parlor an hour later, Charlotte was pleased to see Jane had lost all her reserve and positively glowed with happiness.

"The first banns will be called on Sunday and Papa has sent word to our home Parrish to do the same," Jane told them. "St. George's is elegant and popular, I know, but–" She lowered her eyes, and her cheeks flushed a delicate pink, "I prefer a more intimate setting. We'll be married in the country and remain there for our honeymoon. The Chalmers estate is but ten miles from ours."

"That doesn't mean, however," Lady Pomphrey said with all the determination of one of the king's own guard, "that it will be any less of an occasion. We shall be inviting our friends from the city and provide accommodation and entertainment in the days before and after the nuptials."

"We don't wish to wait until the end of the Season," Jane blushed brighter and gave them a laughing glance, "but Mama insists that I have a full trousseau and a proper betrothal ball... and even a country wedding takes time to arrange."

Charlotte recalled how Lord Chalmers had whispered into Jane's ear the night before and envy filled her. Jane, who had begun the Season with dutiful resolve, and the least hope of a love match, was not only the first of them to accept an offer but had done so for love rather than duty. Lord Chalmers matched Jane's character– straightforward, thoughtful, yet not somber or rigid. He was solid—and he loved her. Theirs would be a happy union.

The first day Charlotte met her, Jane had posed the challenge to look around the ballrooms and observe the married couples of the ton, and Charlotte had. Without quite realizing it, she had noted which ladies appeared content, which ones seemed bored or restless, and which ones gave subtle clues that they were trapped in unhappy circumstances. Like Lady Dalton. Her experiences with Lord Dalton as a child had certainly made Charlotte aware that character, not appearances, counted most in harmonious relationships.

She had compared the ladies with their husbands. Those who were content had partnered with men with whom they shared affection and interests, though some of those shared interests were simply the children they raised. Those whose wives appeared bored or restless were those who had most clearly married for mutual social or financial status but without affection or any other shared interest. The resulting marriages clearly involved nothing more than a contracted joining of man and woman. Their children often were cared for by others while the parents attended social functions and engaged in flirtations, she assumed went further than the ballroom. Each fulfilled their contractual obligations and nothing more.

Seeing Jane's joy made Charlotte's eyes sting with unshed tears. How silly of her to have come to town with lists of titled gentlemen as though that was all it took to make a good match. Marriage was not a game. Nor was it a guaranteed shelter from gossip or unhappiness. If a husband and wife did not respect and love one another life would be emptier than spinsterhood.

Unfortunately, of all the men she had met thus far, only the duke attracted her. She admired his sense of family pride and responsibility. The droll sense of humor he sometimes revealed charmed her. *She enjoyed his kisses.* But while he found her physically attractive and occasionally entertaining, he did not respect or admire her. He saw her as a country miss with no understanding of the world and less sense than Harry. She merited acceptance to his circle only after investigation. Charlotte blinked to relieve the sting and refocus on the happy scene around her. Self-pity had no place here, and she was happy for Jane.

By the time they took their leave, Charlotte and her sister had agreed to accompany Jane and her mother to the modiste the next afternoon when she ordered Jane's wedding trousseau.

MADAME FOCHET BEAMED at them all when Lady Pomphrey announced their desire to see trousseau patterns. In addition to Anne, the duchess, Elizabeth and Charlotte, Millicent and Cassandra and their mothers had joined in the fun.

"Soon each of you will be making choices, as well," the modiste stated with a chuckle. "Once the first match is announced a flurry of others follow. Always it is this way." She gave a signal to one of the serving girls as she led them into the private parlor where pattern books filled the shelves and comfortable chairs surrounded a rosewood table.

A maid gathered a collection of pattern books while another appeared with a tea tray. "I have recently received a shipment of particularly fine silks," Madame Fochet told them as she opened one of the books and placed it in front of Jane and her mother, "So fine it fairly floats on the air." She eyed Jane's red hair and fair complexion. "The coral was quite stunning on you, but for a wedding… something more subtle." She stood silent for a moment, then murmured, "Blue is over-used for special occasions and green is too commonly worn with red hair—Something in between?" She gave a brisk nod, then snapped her fingers at one of the maids. "Molly, fetch the shot-silk teal with the silver warp threading." Her eyes gleamed as she added, "And the blue-violet shantung."

Word spread through the shop that Lady Jane had come to order her wedding trousseau. Soon Jane received good wishes from many of their acquaintances among them, Lady Ridley. Several of them lingered, adding their suggestions and opinions until the private room was more crowded than the main salon.

"I am glad to see that Lord Chalmers has not tarried in his duty to secure a wife and, soon to be hoped, heir." Lady Ridley said with satisfaction. To the duchess she said, "Wolverton is still dragging his heels, I notice."

"You know he believes Rowena must be wed before he takes a wife." Anne spoke up. She nodded to her mother and added, "And Mama tells me we must not tease him about how much older he will be than his bride by then."

"Wolverton is far more amenable when he believes he is acting on his own initiative rather than at the interference of myself or his sisters." Duchess Wolverton explained. "His father was much the same."

"As are most men." Lady Ridley said bluntly. "Those who are not independently minded are generally feeble minded." She gave a sniff of disdain, "A man of strong mind will only do what he wants to do–which is why we ladies know how to make a man *think* our wishes were his idea."

She rose and accepted her shawl from her maid. "Now I am off to pay my respects to Lady Rutledge and meet the latest in her brood. This new one makes number seven, I believe. An heir at last." She smiled at Jane, "Perhaps this time next year you will present Lord Chalmers with an heir as well."

She took her leave and conversation turned to several other ladies who had recently presented their husbands with offspring. Jane, her face pink after Lady Ridley's comment, excused herself to inspect the model of a dress style Madame Fochet suggested for the wedding. Once she was out of earshot, Lady Littlemarsh lowered her voice and said, "I would not dampen Lady Jane's excitement with sad news, but my maid told me this morning that Lady Dalton has suffered another miscarriage and will be unable to attend any entertainments for at least two weeks."

The Duchess released a brief murmur of sympathy before commenting, "I believe she suffered a similar loss last Season. She must be quite devastated."

"Nor was that her first." Lady Littlemarsh clarified. "According to my maid's sister, this makes four misfortunes for her in as many years. I believe she may be one of those unfortunate women who is unable to carry a child to term. My maid's sister has been employed at the Daltons since they married, and she holds out little hope for an heir."

Jane returned to the table and everyone turned back to the samples under discussion. Charlotte, though, found herself alarmed at the news that Lady Dalton was once more too ill—or was she again injured—to take part in the various parties and balls that remained of the Season. Was Lady Dalton unable to carry a child to term because of nature... or Lord Dalton's ill treatment? Martha Franklin had also suffered multiple miscarriages.

Charlotte would never forgive herself if she made no effort to rescue Lady Dalton from abuse–or death—at the hands of her handsome, but remorseless, husband.

# CHAPTER 19

It was nearing midnight when Lucien returned from dinner with Ravencliffe at his club. Timmons took his cloak and hat before clearing his throat and telling him, "Miss Longborough asked that I inform you she wished to speak to you in the library if you arrived home before midnight."

*In the library*? His body responded immediately to the memory of their last encounters there. "Is the Duchess with her?"

"No, Your Grace, though her maid was with her when she made the request. The rest of the ladies retired an hour ago."

*Nothing too personal then*. Charlotte Longborough might be a bit naive, but she was not stupid. If she needed to wait up to speak to him, it must be a matter of concern. "Then I suppose I must see what it is she wants."

He started up the stairs, then stopped and looked back. "Please tell me she has not rescued any more beasts—?"

"Not that I am aware of, Your Grace."

He looked down at his butler and gave him a wry grin. "How soon did you know of the kittens?"

Timmons drew himself up proudly, "Within the hour, Your Grace. Miss Longborough requested a box of dirt and a bowl of warm milk for her room."

"I've always admired your powers of observation and interpretation regarding matters of household operations," he said as he turned back to the stairs. "It is a bit late for swilling tea and I suppose whatever Miss Longborough has to confess will not take long," he added over his shoulder. "Go to bed, Timmons. I shall require nothing more from you tonight."

When he reached the library, he found the door open and Charlotte staring into the fire, an embroidery hoop lying neglected in her lap. He saw no maid.

His entry attracted her attention and she jumped up, dropping the hoop on the floor. "You are home," she said with a quick glance at the mantle clock.

"Timmons said you wished to speak with me?" Lucien didn't venture deeper into the room. With no maid in attendance, he didn't trust himself not to take advantage of the situation once again. Still, she did not look like a woman in search of further intimacies.

"I heard something today that greatly concerned me, and I hoped you might assist me to discover the truth." Charlotte said in a rush before she stopped, obviously unsure and a little embarrassed. Her eyes searched his and her cheeks flushed. She clasped her hands tightly together, her agitation undeniable.

She took quick breath and crossed the room to stand before him. "It is indelicate of me to speak of such matters—But, this afternoon Lady Littlemarsh reported that Lady Dalton has recently lost a child before term and that she will be bedridden for several weeks." She faced him with determination in her stance and anger in her gaze. "I believe it is her husband and not nature that has caused her loss."

"I know he behaved badly toward you," Lucien said cautiously, "But I made inquiries about him after he accosted you in the orangery. No one has ever seen him treat his wife inappropriately and all say that he is devoted to her. He may well have intended to give you a fright, and nothing more."

He stopped her protest with a finger to her lips. "I know the behavior I saw puts that in question. However, those same friends also assure me Dalton has consulted many physicians about his wife's fainting spells. The doctors believe a childhood illness has made her susceptible to heart palpitations and headaches. These make her dizzy and further prone to falls and mishaps. It could also make childbearing difficult or even impossible."

"That is according to Lord Dalton," Charlotte protested. "He might well have created the scenario of her childhood illness– I understand she has no family to contradict his description of her early health problems."

"Which the lady herself could deny."

"Many women are afraid to contradict their husbands or fathers lest they bring down further recriminations." Her eyes narrowed and she wrapped her arms around her waist when he didn't respond. "I see you are unconvinced."

"I admit it's hard to believe a peer would be so lacking in honor that he'd cause his lady actual injury. But you don't know if her situation is because of poor health or maltreatment, only that Lady Dalton has lost a child. Either way it is a sad situation, to be sure."

"It is more than, sad," Charlotte declared, "It is wrong. Lady Littlemarsh says it's not the first time Lady Dalton has suffered such a loss. I am sure Lord Dalton is beating her regularly. And to such an extent that she has miscarried. If he continues, she will lose her life as well." She crossed the room to stand in front of him. "We must stop him."

"If true, I wish we could," Lucien said. "But truth be told, Lord Dalton is within his rights to strike his wife if he so chooses. I find such behavior repellent, but it is his legal right."

"Even if he kills her?"

"No. Of course not. That would be murder."

"But he can cause her continuous injury so long as she doesn't die?"

"It's not right, but yes, he has the right." Lucien reached out and took Charlotte's shoulders, wanting to ease the shocked pain reflected in her eyes. "A man must take full responsibility for his household.

To do that he must have full control of those in his charge. That's why the law gives him the right to enforce his decisions in any way he deems necessary."

He watched her eyes, willing her to accept the reason, if not the occasional flawed result of the law. "You don't know that he caused her loss, even if we accept that it is possible. Some men," he told her, "do not deal well under pressure or disappointment. Wrong as it might be, her inability to carry a child to term might be a reason for his frustrated mistreatment."

She jerked out of his hold and her eyes suddenly sparked with anger. "So, it is her fault that he beats her?"

"No, of course not. But many men blame their loss of control on others rather than take the blame upon themselves." Lucien's frustration made his voice harsh. "His behavior with you might have been despicable, Charlotte, but it doesn't mean he has caused all of his wife's accidents– or this miscarriage."

"*I* am sure." Charlotte's voice resonated with conviction. "Whether directly or indirectly, it matters not. And there is no excuse that would make it pardonable. "

She stared up at him, her gaze demanding he give her hope that he couldn't give. Dalton had frightened Charlotte as a child long before his near assault in the orangery. It was no wonder she interpreted his wife's unhappy event in the worst possible light. Much as he despised men who treated their wives badly, he had no authority to intervene in another man's marriage. And even if he did, he had no proof.

"How can I discover if she has been injured in any other way?" Charlotte asked. "Perhaps she didn't lose a child, but he doesn't want her seen in public until the bruises heal."

"I believe you've allowed your dislike for Lord Dalton to elevate a sad situation into an overwrought event." Lucien gently stroked her cheek. "You imagine the worst scenario when it may be nothing more than an unhappy fact of nature. And if it is not, there is still nothing you can do. You have a good heart, Charlotte, but you can't rescue everyone and everything."

"I know that," her voice held a note of desperation, "But I can't let him get away with another murder."

Lucien's lungs froze. His gaze sharpened. "What do you mean, *another* murder?"

Charlottes gray eyes filled with unshed tears and their expression reflected both guilt and despair. "I saw him kill his first wife."

CHARLOTTE KNEW LUCIEN had believed her fears for Lady Dalton to be wild imaginings, but her stark confession clearly shocked him. He gaped at her, not blinking, not breathing. After an eternity of silence, he took her hand and led her to a chair, then seated himself across from her. "Tell me."

Gooseflesh rose as she remembered how deceptively charming Mr. Franklin, now Lord Dalton, had been. Where to start?

"Albert Franklin worked as the land steward for the estate beside ours. He married one of the estate housemaids, Martha, a few months later." Charlotte plucked at her skirt, pleating and smoothing the cloth as though it would soothe her chaotic memories. "The first time Mrs. Franklin told a neighbor about her dizzy spells, she claimed she'd blackened her eye when she tripped and fell against the edge of the door." Unable to sit calmly while she described that day, she stood, turned away from Lucien, wrapped her hands around her middle, and paced the room.

"What she didn't know was that I had been playing nearby and saw her husband backhand her for over-sweetening his tea." She stopped and looked back at him. "Neither of them saw me in the shadow of the large oak bordering the back of their garden."

She continued pacing, no longer making eye contact. "I was frightened at the force of his blow and crept away. When I got home, I told Elizabeth what I'd seen, but she didn't believe me, so I didn't tell anyone else. But some horrible fascination demanded I go back to see if he did it again. I saw him strike her many times after that. Sometimes it was a single blow, other times I had to cover my eyes when he used both his fists, and once, his feet, as she lay helpless on the ground.

One day, he saw me watching and locked me in the tool shed. He left me there for the whole day and didn't let me out until almost dark. When he did, he told me that if he ever caught me near their garden again he'd throw me into the river and let me drown." She shuddered and pictured his face shoved close to hers, his eyes hard and his voice a threatening whisper.

"Then he smiled in that way he had and told me he'd be the first to lead the search party for me when I went missing. He told me he'd extend his heartfelt sympathy to my family for their loss. He said he'd even put a posy of flowers on my grave, and possibly use his handkerchief to wipe his eyes in sorrow for so young a life to be cut short *by fate*."

The memory chilled and her pulse raced as if he still clamped her wrist, his fingers cutting off the circulation to her hand. "I was only eight years old but I knew he could, and would, do it. He always knew the right thing to say and who to say it to. He flattered and charmed everyone with his smile and no one would believe he could be so cruel. But," she again turned to face him and make her point, "that charming smile never warmed his eyes."

She rubbed her arms to warm them, still moving through the room, unable to sit in lady-like composure as she continued her story. "I didn't go near their property for several weeks after he caught me. But, then, I overheard the curate say Mrs. Franklin's dizzy spells were getting worse and that Albert Franklin had told him that he worried all the more because their cottage glaring was so near the river."

Charlotte's stomach clenched as it had then, the image of Lord Dalton's face glaring into hers created as visceral a terror as if she were again the eight-year-old he dragged to the tool shed. Her throat dried and she swallowed her childhood fear.

"After Elizabeth didn't believe me, I hadn't told anyone else what I'd seen. But when I heard what the curate said, I sneaked back, terrified that Mr. Franklin would catch me again. But I had to see if Mrs. Franklin was alright."

She clasped her hands together. "I hid behind a hedge when he came home, furious that his employer had dismissed him for skimming money from the accounts. I know this because he shouted at Mrs. Franklin that any estate manager worth his salt arranged deals that were of benefit to everyone, themselves included. Then he said that it was her fault that he had to sweeten the deals he made. It wasn't long before he hit her for asking where they would now live."

"The more he hit her the more his rage grew. I was petrified and dared not move lest he see me. He kept hitting her, and hitting her, and hitting—"

She suddenly realized that tears coursed her cheeks and that Lucien had crossed the room to take her hands. "In the end," she choked out, "He finally dragged her unconscious body to the riverbank and threw her in.

The next day," Charlotte shuddered, "when the magistrate told him they'd found her battered body two miles downriver, Mrs. Franklin's loving husband fell to his knees and sobbed. The day after her burial, he packed his things and quit the village."

Charlotte swallowed and fought back her tears. It was far too late to shed tears for Martha Franklin, but her heart ached for Lady Dalton. Lucien pulled her against his chest and held her while he stroked her back, murmuring reassurances while she regained her composure. She let him comfort her. He made her feel safe. He made her feel protected. But no one protected Lady Dalton.

In the quiet library with a fire warming the hearth and surrounded by the cultured trappings of rose-filled vases and fine furnishings, Charlotte's story of cruelty and violent death sounded implausible. Yet she knew the roses that scented the air had thorns, and a room without a fire in the hearth could be as frigid as the streets outside.

She straightened and looked up into Lucien's face. "You're sure there is no legal recourse?"

"I'm sure." Lucien spoke softly, but a grave note of warning emerged when he added, "Lady Dalton is neither a puppy nor a litter of kittens, Charlotte. Don't think to attempt some type of rescue. Stay out of it." He stared at her, his expression leaving her in no doubt that he expected her to follow his orders. "You must understand that if a lady leaves her husband, he can demand her return. Such an action would make her more vulnerable to his anger– especially since you've confirmed that he's violent and dangerous."

Charlotte lowered her gaze to hide her frustration. If she tried to help Lady Dalton and failed, she might well be the factor that led to the fate she hoped to avoid. If she did nothing, and the Lady suffered a fatal accident, Charlotte would be plagued with far greater guilt than she'd suffered for not speaking up as a child.

"Promise me you won't interfere." His finger lifted her chin and she looked back into his eyes. His expression softened. "I wouldn't like to see you hurt."

He drew her back into his arms and kissed her. The emotions of the day flared into desire, burying the hours of indecision she'd spent before admitting her need to confide in him. His mouth warmed hers and his arms sheltered her. He made her feel safer than she had since seeing Lord Dalton in the hallway at Anne's ball.

She nestled against Lucien's chest and slipped her arms up around his neck. His tongue teased her lips, and she opened her mouth to his exploration. A faint hint of brandy still clung to his tongue and intoxicated her senses. Her pulse beat faster, and the chill of her memories melted in the warmth of his embrace.

"Why is it," he lifted his lips to murmur, "that I forget rules of propriety and honorable behavior when we are alone together?" He kissed her again, trailing kisses along her neck and nipping the lobe of her ear.

She lifted her chin and angled her head to allow him greater access. When he kissed his way down to her shoulder, she yielded to temptation pressed her lips against the edge of his jaw, then instinctively touched her tongue to the beard-roughened flesh. He gave a low growl of pleasure and his hands shifted from her back to slide around and up until his fingertips caressed the swell of her breasts above her stays. At the same time, he took her mouth again, deeply, and she pressed against his hands, wanting more.

Lucien raised his head to lean his forehead to hers and she realized he struggled to slow his breathing as much as she. He shifted his hands away from her bosom, sliding them down to her waist, though she had not protested his familiarity.

"You should have kept your maid with you." He finally whispered. He gave her another long, drugging kiss, then broke away, his breath again short and harsh, his eyes hungry. "Go now, before I forget myself completely."

Still under the spell of his kisses, Charlotte made an inarticulate protest when he released his hold and stepped back. He kissed her once more, briefly and with finality. Just before she quit the room Lucien reminded her, "Life isn't always kind, nor is it often fair, Charlotte—Don't act rashly. You could greatly endanger yourself over matters you can't change."

# CHAPTER 20

Charlotte entered her room, her emotions once again tangled into knots of frustration and disappointment. Harry raised his head from his pallet when she came in, then did a nose count of the kittens nestled along his side before going back to sleep. She quickly changed into the nightrail the maid had draped over the coverlet for her and slipped into bed.

When Lucien kissed her, her mind had blanked, and she responded to the delicious, overwhelming pleasure of his mouth and tongue as he teased her senses and sent waves of desire to her core. He'd gone beyond kisses and caressed her breasts... *and she had let him*.

She knew a lady did not permit such familiarity, but the sensation of his touch had sent glorious fissures through her. When he'd pressed her closer, she'd felt a firm ridge against her stomach and realized that the drawings in the naughty book might be accurate after all. She'd wanted to press against the ridge, instinct telling her that to do so would ease the heated need his touch fired. If he'd wanted to do more, to do the things detailed in the books, would she have allowed that too? The question worried her and made her press her thighs together to ease the restless ache that made her embarrassingly aware of herself.

Lucien had stopped without attempting more, though. She couldn't help but wonder if he had kissed her to distract from her dark memories. If so, he had succeeded—until his parting words.

Frustration added to her disappointment over Lucien's assessment of Lady Dalton's situation.

When she'd decided to tell the duke her fears, and to confess the secret she had carried inside for so long, she'd hoped all would be settled. Once he knew the truth about Dalton, she'd been sure Lucien's title and standing could be brought to bear and make things right. She'd spent the hours until he came home imagining various scenarios wherein Lord Dalton was exposed as an evil murderer who would pay for his cruelties to both Martha Franklin and Lady Dalton.

Yet Charlotte was not so naive, as Lucien obviously believed, that she didn't know how unfair life could be. One had only to look around to see examples of it every day. However, that didn't mean everything must be unfair or that some things could not be made better. She couldn't save every mistreated dog, but she'd saved Harry. She couldn't save the cat by the river, but she'd saved the kittens. She hadn't saved Mrs. Franklin, but she *would* save Lady Dalton.

Lying in the dark, her thoughts jumbled, Charlotte searched her mind for some way to help. She needed to know exactly what had happened to Lady Dalton– but who would know the truth of the matter, and not simply what Lord Dalton told his friends? It struck her suddenly that Lady Littlemarsh had learned of Lady Dalton's situation from her maid... who had heard it from her sister... who worked for the Daltons.

She would call upon Millicent first thing tomorrow and ask to speak to her mother's maid. She would discover when the maid's sister had her half-day and when Lord Dalton would be away from home. Once she could do so without fear of Lord Dalton being present, she would call upon his wife to see how she truly fared. What she would–or could– do after that would depend on what she found. Lady Dalton had denied needing help at the Winterstone's musical evening, but would she now?

Charlotte rolled to her side, determined to settle into sleep. If Lady Dalton refused her help this time, she'd do as Lucien asked, and pray that Lady Dalton didn't suffer the same fate as Martha Franklin.

LADY LITTLEMARSH'S maid had described her sister as a sweet mouse of a girl who could disappear in plain sight. The girl at the teashop who slipped into the chair opposite her at her invitation fit that description– mouse brown hair, large brown eyes and slightly prominent front teeth that became more prominent when she smiled in response to Charlotte's greeting.

"You must be Margery," Charlotte greeted her.

"Good day, Miss." She bobbed her head. "Jenny said you wished to speak with me? Anne's maid had accompanied Charlotte on her errand and Margery glanced at her. The maid gave Margery an encouraging smile before moving to a table a short distance away. "She didn't say why."

Charlotte poured them each a cup of tea. "I hope you can relieve my concerns about Lady Dalton's health." She handed the cup to Margery and lowered her voice. "I understand she had a recent... *disappointment*... that requires her to remain housebound for some time."

The girl's eyes widened in surprise, and she nearly dropped the cup. "Beg pardon, Miss. You startled me." She surveyed the shop as though checking to see who might hear her answer. She looked back and Charlotte and said, "I didn't know Jenny said anything to anyone else... It isn't my place to spread gossip about my employers."

"I do not ask from idle curiosity, nor do I blame you for speaking frankly to your kin," Charlotte noted the way Margery's face paled and that she twisted the cloth napkin in her lap. "But it is of grave concern to me to know if the babe was–" She hesitated slightly– "The only health issue Lady Dalton suffered at the time of her loss."

She hesitated but continued when she remembered that this young woman had worked for the Dalton's for nearly five years. She must know the truth. "You see, I knew Lord Dalton's first wife before she died."

She watched understanding dawn in Margery's brown eyes and waited to see if she would deny what they both obviously knew about Lord Dalton and his violent temper.

"Oh." Margery put her hands over her mouth and tears glistened before she blinked them away. "You know– I mean–"

"How badly is she hurt?" Charlotte asked. "Can you arrange for me to see her without Lord Dalton knowing?"

"Oh, no, Miss. I couldn't do that." She leaned forward and whispered, "If I did, and he found out, he would kill *me*." She sat back, wide eyed and pale faced. "I tried to hide her from his wrath once and he swore he would kill me if I ever tried to interfere again." She shook her head, her eyes bleak. "I wish I could, but I dare not."

Charlotte understood the girl's fear. She, too, had been threatened by and lived in dread of Lord Dalton's anger. "Why didn't you seek other employment?"

"I thought about it, but even if Lord Dalton consented to provide a reference, Lady Dalton needed me. I have learned ways to redirect his anger without seeming to interfere. I tend her minor wounds and bruises. I believe," she let her gaze drift around at the ladies chatting with each other. "It sounds impertinent from a lady's maid, but I believe I am her only friend."

"Then as her friend," Charlotte implored her. "will you tell me Lord Dalton's schedule? I shall come to the back of the house when he is away. I promise to speak with her for just a short time and be gone. He need never know I was there, but I must talk to her."

Margery sat silently, clearly wrestling with her conscience and her fear. A serving girl approached and offered a fresh pot of tea and Charlotte realized that both cups sat cold and untouched on the linen covered table. The serving girl left to exchange the cold pot and Margery's lips firmed before she nodded her head.

"All right." She bobbed her head and her lips firmed. "He told his valet he will attend a sporting event in Southwark in two days' time. Cook will be at market at noon, though I'll still have to slip you past the butler. With the master gone, though, he and the valet will most likely share a tipple in the butler's quarters."

The serving girl placed a fresh pot of tea on the table and Margery took a sip of the fresh brew before adding, "He is to leave around eleven in the morning, and we don't expect him to return until perhaps four in the afternoon. He has an engagement at a gaming hell in the evening."

Charlotte breathed a sigh of relief. "Thank you." She noted Margery's shaking hands when the girl took another sip of tea. "If you ever do decide to seek new employment and Lord Dalton refuses to give you reference, contact me and I shall provide one." She nodded her head toward the Caldwell maid who'd accompanied her to the shop. "I am not able to offer you a position myself, as I must borrow my host's servants, but I shall do all I can to help you find a respectable place."

Charlotte rose from her seat, "No, stay and enjoy the rest of the tea." she said when Margery started to stand as well. "If Lord Dalton's plans change, send word, otherwise I shall present myself at the servant's door at half noon in two days. And again, thank you."

Leaving the bakery, she and her borrowed maid visited a nearby shop to purchase embroidery floss. She didn't need it, but she'd used the floss as a reason for her trip to Bond Street.

TWO DAYS LATER, CHARLOTTE slipped down the stairs to the servant's entrance of the Dalton's townhouse and tapped at the door. Several minutes passed and Charlotte feared the maid might have lost her nerve, but then the door opened, and Margery put her finger to her lips, and they crossed the kitchen to the back stairway. They passed the ground and main floors of the house to reach the second floor where the maid cautiously opened the door. Stepping out from the back stairs landing, she checked that neither the valet nor the butler were in evidence, then let Charlotte down the hall to Lady Dalton's room.

"I told her you were coming," she whispered. She opened it and stepped back to allow Charlotte to enter.

"Lady Dalton?" Charlotte walked across the room then stopped, aghast at the sight of Lady Dalton's battered face.

The woman lay against stacked pillows. Brilliant red, violet, yellow and blue bruises discolored her face and neck. A bed jacket hid the rest of the bruises that Charlotte knew had to cover her body and a splint supported her left arm. Lady Dalton opened blood-shot eyes that must have been swollen shut in the first days after the beating. The swelling had subsided, but the intense color told Charlotte her fears had been justified.

"I believe you were right about my husband," Lady Dalton's hoarse voice held an ironic note and she tried to smile, though her lip had been split and must be painful.

"I am so sorry," Charlotte said as she finished crossing the room to take a seat at the edge of the bed. "Did he know about the child when he did this… or when you–?"

Lady Dalton gave a dry chuckle that turned to a choke of pain. "Of course he knew. It is why he beat me." Charlotte took her hand as she explained, "He doesn't like children, nor does he care if the title goes dormant once he is gone."

Charlotte didn't know what to say to such a shocking sentiment.

"You once suggested that you wished to help me," Lady Dalton said. "But I don't know what you could do. He is my husband."

"Does he allow you a physician?" Charlotte noted that the splint anchoring Lady Dalton's arm had the look of a field dressing rather than the neater bindings she associated with a medical professional.

"Only if I am not marked badly. He is usually careful not to mark my face." She closed her eyes a moment and a tear rolled down her cheek and onto the pillow. "He had Margery tend to me this time." Another tear hit the pillow. "The babe came quickly... He took it away."

The door opened suddenly and Margery, her features drawn in fear, cried. "He has returned early. You must leave immediately."

Charlotte jumped up from the bed and turned back to Lady Dalton. "I don't know what I can do– but I will try to do *something*."

"Miss Longborough, hurry!"

Charlotte escaped the room, reached the back stairs, and started down as silently as she could. As she made her way, she could hear Lord Dalton bellowing for his valet and the butler, his fury enough to make Charlotte worry for Lady Dalton at the same time as Charlotte trembled to think what would happen if he discovered her in the house. She reached the servants hall and opened the door to the kitchen a crack to be sure the cook had not returned early as well.

To her dismay, the butler stood at the far end of the kitchen and she couldn't reach the door to the street unseen. When he turned and started toward the back stairs Charlotte drew back and looked around the landing in alarm. A door to the left caught her panicked gaze. She peeked around it and relief surged through her when she saw it was a linen closet. She managed to slip in and shut the door before the butler reached the landing and started up the stairs to answer Lord Dalton's demand for brandy.

# CHAPTER 21

Lucien studied the dossier he'd requested on Lord Dalton after Charlotte's revelations. It confirmed that Albert Franklin, now Viscount Dalton, had indeed been married and widowed before receiving the title he held. It raised no question regarding her death, though, listing it as an accidental drowning.

Lucien frowned. Children often misinterpreted what they saw, yet if Charlotte's story was true, Dalton had covered his guilt well. A body washed downstream in a fast-running river would be battered and broken by rocks and tree root snags. The incident at the orangery proved the man capable of striking a woman in anger, though, and Lucien accepted that Charlotte truly had witnessed a violent crime.

The report gave Lady Dalton's history as well. Orphaned the year before she married Dalton, she had no other close relatives to whom she might turn in need. He leaned back in his chair as he read. She'd inherited cash and properties from her maternal grandmother in addition to the generous dowry provided in her father's will. He turned the page as he reflected that it had made her all the more susceptible to unscrupulous fortune hunters like Dalton.

The Dalton title had provided him nothing more than a rundown estate. It didn't surprise Lucien that Dalton had offered for the heiress. Upon their marriage he had taken up residence in his wife's inherited townhouse but had recently placed both her other properties up for sale. Neither had yet found buyers.

The clock on the mantle struck the hour and he put the report into the drawer. It had revealed nothing of practical value. He didn't know if he'd expected it to, but he believed he owed it to Charlotte to discover if suspicion surrounded the first wife's death. He crossed the hall and climbed the stairs to dress for dinner. At the top of the stairs, he found Elizabeth and Sarah huddled together, engaged in a whispered argument. Hearing Charlotte's name, he suspected their argument was of a family nature and he pretended to be unaware of their altercation as he passed them on the way to his rooms.

"Your Grace," Elizabeth said. "We are worried about Charlotte."

"She is missing," Sarah explained. "We haven't seen her all day."

"I beg your pardon?"

"We haven't seen Charlotte since shortly before noon," Elizabeth said. I was involved in a project," she flushed. "I tend to lose track of time when I am. Then Sarah had a–" she shot a glance to her sister "*question*– for Charlotte, but she wasn't in her room. Nor was she with Anne or the Duchess. We've checked the entire house and she isn't here."

" You say she said nothing of an errand? Might she have taken Harry to the Park?"

Even as he asked, Harry nudged his hand, and Lucien knew that Charlotte must have gone somewhere on her own. Charlotte was determined to help Lady Dalton. He had no doubt as to where she had gone. *Little fool.* Dalton had already threatened her twice. He wouldn't warn her a third time.

IN THE LINEN CLOSET, Charlotte closed her eyes tightly and counted to one hundred before cracking the door open again. Upstairs Lord Dalton shouted orders, and rushing feet told her Lord Dalton's valet and butler feared his temper as much as had Lady Dalton's maid. Carefully, she checked the door to the kitchen ready to duck back into the closet if she heard footsteps on the stairs. At that moment, the door to the kitchen opened and the cook strode to the worktable at its center and set down the basket full of her purchases.

A footman followed with two more baskets. "His Lordship is home," he commented with a grimace when he heard the shouting from above stairs. "Something must have gone wrong to bring him home early on racing day."

"Then you'd best get yourself upstairs before he finds out you left your post to help carry the groceries."

"Aye." He glanced up at the ceiling and shrugged his shoulder. "Though he sounds like he'd not need an excuse to sack me."

Charlotte ducked back into the closet when the footman left the kitchen to climb the stairs. No more than a narrow rim of light around the door edge pierced the darkness of the closet, a dim anchor in the confined space. The storeroom was small. She felt around, noting that the shelves formed a tight "U" shape. *You're stuck, but you're not locked in.* Charlotte fought rising panic that clawed her stomach and hitched her breath. *You're not locked in.* She clenched her fists and settled down on the floor, her gaze locked on the ribbon of light beyond the door. *You must simply wait until things are quiet.* She heard the footman return with orders to bring hot water so his lordship could bathe before his evening out, and feared it might be hours before she could escape the house. She closed her eyes and repeated the one thing that kept her fear under control. *You're not locked in.*

Sitting in the dark, time crawled by. It made her acutely aware of the sounds of people rushing around, the scent of soap and linen, and the steady beat of her heart. She was also aware of the sharp edge of the shelf that pressed against her back. Shifting, she felt around until she located a stack of cloths, their purpose unknown in the darkness, but their bulk made her suspect a table covering. She slid it behind her like a cushion. *Much better.*

She must have dozed because the next thing she noticed was the aroma of roasting chicken. Her stomach growled and she realized it had been a long time since she'd eaten her breakfast of toast and coddled egg. Muffled voices alerted her that several people occupied the servant's floor and Lord Dalton had stopped shouting. She pulled herself up, her body stiff from remaining in the same position for such a long time. Again, she eased the door open and listened carefully. The voices came from a greater distance than from the kitchen, so she quietly left the closet and tried the kitchen door. Signs of preparation cluttered the space, but the servants took their meal in a separate room. Seeing the way clear, she gratefully made her way across the kitchen to the door. On her way out, Charlotte saw a basket on a hook by the door and grabbed it as she quickly exited the house.

The sun hung low in the sky when Charlotte hurried up the stairs to the street level. She lowered her head and tucked the basket under her arm, hoping that anyone seeing her would assume she was someone's maid completing an errand. She only needed to walk three blocks to reach Wolverton House. After the hours trapped in the linen closet, her brisk walk gave her a sense of freedom she'd never fully appreciated before.

Halfway there, a carriage pulled up beside her and Lucien leapt down. His firm hand clamped onto her elbow, abruptly altered her direction, and marched her to the carriage. "I thought we'd agreed that you were to stay away from the Daltons." He didn't wait for her response, but bundled her into the carriage, then signaled the driver to move off before he'd fully settled onto the seat. His gaze pinned her, his eyes narrowed, and his words clipped. "Did Dalton see you? Did he hurt you—?" He broke off and took a deep breath. "What were you thinking?"

"I had to see Lady Dalton myself. I made sure Lord Dalton would be gone. But then he came home early, and I had to hide until he left again. I couldn't let the other servants know her maid had assisted me." She caught her breath on a sob and blurted, "It was as bad as I feared. If Lady Dalton doesn't escape him, he'll kill her as surely as he did Mrs. Franklin." Her eyes filled. "I suspect from her breathing that her ribs are damaged., and her arm is in a splint." The tears crested and ran down her cheeks. "And her *face*—" She shuddered. "I must do something—I know the law says I can't—but I must." She wiped her eyes, then demanded, "What will the courts do to me? Will I be sent to Newgate?"

LUCIEN'S JAW TIGHTENED to imagine Charlotte held prisoner in filthy cages filled with both human and animal vermin. The idea that she might suffer such a fate while Dalton remained free to find more prey for his violence formed an icy resolve. "Not if I can bloody well help it."

Charlotte's eyes widened at his language.

"I'll not beg your pardon," he crossed his arms across his chest. "Strong emotions demand strong words."

The carriage stopped in the mews behind Wolverton House as he'd instructed when he'd plucked her from the street. It wouldn't do for anyone to see them descend a closed carriage with no maid in attendance. Lucien alighted to help Charlotte down. Charlotte might be a family guest, but they were both unmarried. He hurried her into the house and into his study. On the way, he told Timmons to inform the ladies that Charlotte was safe and would attend them shortly.

Lucien shut the door with finality and whirled Charlotte into his arms. "Don't ever take such a chance again." Before she could protest, his mouth came down on hers with an angry kiss fueled by worry and relief. He lifted his head from hers and muttered, "If it weren't bad enough you went to Dalton House, you told no one where you'd gone. Anything could have happened, and no one would've known."

"But it didn't." Charlotte's voice quavered. "I was on the way home when you found me."

"It doesn't signify," he ground out. "You were supremely fortunate you suffered nothing more than a few hours in a closet." His throat tightened and his voice nearly cracked. "You can't imagine my relief I felt when I saw you on the street. You can't imagine my fury when I saw you, alone at dusk, strolling along as though you'd done nothing more than take a walk in the park." He straightened and released his hold on her before pointing to the chair in front of his desk. "Sit down, Miss Longborough. We have a great deal more to talk about."

Charlotte blinked at him. Her lashes formed spikes, damp from her earlier tears. When she turned them toward him, her gray eyes were luminous in the half-light of the early dusk. Her mouth soft and still pink from their kiss.

*Bloody hell.*

Lucien walked around and stood behind the desk. He needed to distance himself from her, the appeal of those eyes, and the flavor of her mouth.

How in the name of all things holy could he want to throttle her as violently as Dalton and at the same time want to lay her down on the desk and ravish her like some raider of old? It made no sense. No more than the fact that he also wanted to hold her in his arms and soothe away the anguished sadness he saw in those luminous gray depths.

"I'm sorry–"

He cut her off with a gesture. "Do not say a word until I've done with you." He strove for calm. He strove for reason. He studied the intricately carved moldings that marked the edge of the wall cornice and counted to twenty.

"Now," he said at last, "As it is clear that you value others more than yourself," he signaled her to remain quiet when she took a breath to argue. "and that you will undoubtedly ignore common sense in your desire to rescue any and all things in need, I ask that you promise to do nothing more until a plan can be put in motion that will assist Lady Dalton without putting either of you in further danger."

He braced his hands on his desk and leaned forward. "From what you've told me, time may well be of the essence, though her injuries will require some delay for her to heal. I will think on the matter tonight, as I am sure, will you. I must investigate the practical possibilities before we decide on a plan of action."

He gestured to the door to indicate he was finished with the subject for the moment. "Your sisters have been particularly worried about you, as have Anne and my stepmother. I do not believe, however, that hearing where you were or what you found would relieve their concerns."

She stood as well. "You're right. I'll only tell them that I was visiting a friend on a private matter. I'm sorry to have worried everyone. It was my intention to be home within the hour." She moved to the door, then turned. "I know that I shouldn't have gone, of course. But you should know I'm not sorry I went." She left the study and Lucien sat heavily into his chair.

He didn't doubt that Charlotte was as determined to remove Lady Dalton from her husband's abuses as ever. So how did they get Lady Dalton away from danger and keep the man from finding her? And how did they do it without bringing attention and scandal to the family and guests of Wolverton House?

# CHAPTER 22

When the Daltons arrived at Jane's betrothal ball three weeks later, Charlotte's nerves skittered along her spine and made it difficult for her to breathe normally. Notes passed between the Littlemarsh maid and Margery had established that Lady Dalton would be attending the Pomphrey celebration, so the plan Charlotte and Lucien had made could be set into motion.

The lady was still pale, and Charlotte noted a less obvious splint beneath her long gloves, but the livid bruises had faded. Only someone who'd seen them in full bloom would realize the faint marks that remained beneath her powder were not shadows cast by candlelight. The drape of Lady Dalton's emerald green gown still set the gossips in the chaperone corner whispering, though it was not as low or daring as the red dress she'd worn to the opera. At her neck, a wide choker of emeralds, circled with diamonds, matched the earbobs and bracelet she wore. She'd been instructed to wear her finest jewels since they could, when broken apart, be sold as needed and provide Lady Dalton with the funds she would need in her new life.

Jane and her fiancé took their places on the dancefloor to begin the ball, and Charlotte experienced a pang of conscience. She hoped their celebration would not be marred by her attempt to rescue Lady Dalton. She and Lucien had planned for as many contingencies as possible, including a note to be delivered to Lord Dalton once he realized his wife was missing. He might still cause a scene, but Lucien said Dalton wouldn't endanger his reputation by allowing the situation to become public before attempting to gain her return.

Anticipation and trepidation combined to blur the evening entertainments as she danced with several gentlemen of her acquaintance. She chatted, smiled, and generally behaved like one of the automation machines she had recently seen on display. Her actions were directed by habit while her mind swirled with *what if's*. At every turn, she found herself watching for the moment Lord Dalton would finally seek out the card room.

"If you keep staring at them," Lucien murmured before taking a sip of champagne, "You will undo all our preparations."

"Are you sure he'll leave her alone for the card room? Though he's danced with several other ladies, she's danced only the first with her husband."

"Ravencliffe asked her for the second set and was told that though she wouldn't miss Jane's celebration, she didn't yet feel up to further efforts. If Dalton follows his usual habit, he'll go to the card room after the supper dance."

"If Lady Dalton is easily tired, might he take her home early? It would be rather unfeeling of him to stay late at cards when his wife is not dancing."

Lucien gave her a sardonic look.

"Of course he won't," Charlotte answered herself with a rueful expression. "We are speaking of Lord Dalton."

Charlotte thought it odd that time could move so slowly, and yet when Lucien came to claim her for the supper dance, the moment had come too swiftly. She wasn't ready, yet it must be in the next half hour that they put their plan into action. They must spirit Lady Dalton away to the carriage that waited in the mews without attracting attention. From there, Lady Dalton would take a ship bound for Canada.

Once supper was done, Charlotte slipped through the crowd as they made their way back into the ballroom. She quickly reached the retiring room where she had secreted an inconspicuous bundle during her visit with Jane and her mother the day before. Now if Lord Dalton would go into the card room so Lady Dalton could come to the retiring room.

The door opened and Lady Dalton came in, her face stark white, her eyes wide with anxiety. "Miss Longborough?" she whispered.

"Over here." Charlotte stepped from behind the privacy screen. "Let me help you change."

Lady Dalton's hands were cold even through her gloves when Charlotte clasped them in reassurance. They didn't speak as Charlotte quickly undid Lady Dalton's gown and removed her matching slippers. Lady Dalton's hands trembled as she reached to undo the clasp of her choker. Within minutes she stuffed the fine gown into a plain linen bag along with her shoes and jewels.

The dark gray traveling dress Charlotte drew over Lady Dalton's torso and fitted into place was of moderate quality. Neither fine nor coarse and with a high neck and long, plain sleeves the dress was plain and serviceable. Cotton stockings replaced silk, and sturdy walking shoes matched the genteel, but middle-class status that would make Lady Dalton less conspicuous when she arrived at her destination. In truth, she would easily pass as the lady's companion her manufactured references claimed her to be.

Lady Dalton removed the pins from her hair and, with Charlotte's help, quickly braided it into a single long rope that she then wrapped into a plain figure eight at the back of her neck. Charlotte bundled the hairbrush into the bag along with the remaining pins.

Lady Dalton turned to her and whispered, "Do you think this will work?"

Charlotte stopped tying the strings of the bag and placed her hand on Lady Dalton's arm. "It will if we hurry. His Grace has arranged everything, but we must have you well away before your husband notices you are gone."

"Thank you, my dear." Lady Dalton's eyes glistened. "Even if this should fail, I will never forget your kindness."

Charlotte's own eyes stung, remembering the woman she hadn't been able to help. But they had no time for tears or sentimentality. "There is a bonnet and cloak in the carriage along with a portmanteau with funds, identification papers– You are now Laurel Bennett— and personal necessities." Charlotte said as she handed Lady Dalton the cloth bag. "A trunk with additional clothing has been sent on board the ship and is waiting in your cabin. Margery is there as well and will travel with you."

She went to the door and peeked out. People danced and flirted with one another, Lucien stood by the card room doorway chatting with Lord Pomphrey. She didn't see Lord Dalton.

Charlotte beckoned Lady Dalton to follow and led the way to the back stairs and down into the servant's entrance. Maids and footmen scurried back and forth clearing away the supper things and setting out sweet meats, fruits, and pastries for the guests to enjoy throughout the rest of the evening. Other than a few glances, they paid little attention to the lady and her companion who left by the back door.

The carriage waited behind the garden wall, and as the driver assisted Lady Dalton inside, Charlotte told her, "I pray you God speed and a good life." Then she turned and hurried back to the ballroom before anyone commented on her absence.

"THEN SHE IS SAFELY away?" Charlotte asked Lucien when he joined her in the library long after she and his family returned home.

Lucien described Dalton's white-faced fury when he received the note delivered by the footman as he quit the card room before the final dance of the night. It had been Charlotte's idea to have Lady Dalton write a note that she had returned home early and would send the carriage back for him. Clearly, he had been angry that she would act independently, but he would be home before he knew his wife had left him forever.

"The ship left port an hour ago, and she and the maid were both aboard."

Lucien went to the side table and poured her a sherry and himself a brandy. When she took her glass, he held his up and tapped it against hers. "To a job well done." He took a sip, then gave her a stern look. "and may an occasion such as this never arise again. Rash actions rarely turn out so well."

Charlotte sipped her sherry and savored the exhilaration of their success. "Thank you for making the arrangements. You made it possible for me to save her life." She studied the amber liquid in her glass, then said, "As much as I wanted to help Lady Dalton, I know I wouldn't have succeeded on my own. You cannot know how much that lifts the burden of guilt I've carried for half my life."

"Perhaps I do." Lucien responded. Surprisingly, when he'd received the message from the captain of the ship confirming that Mrs. Laurel Bennett was on board, he'd had a similar lifting of guilt. "Making things right for Lady Dalton doesn't rectify the flaw in a law meant to establish order in society, but it does satisfy my sense of right and wrong."

He swirled the brandy in his glass, releasing its rich aroma before taking a final, fortifying sip. His thoughts swirled along with the liquid. After a moment he said, "When I was sixteen, I did something for which I have long been ashamed. Saving Lady Dalton doesn't undo my youthful rash behavior or the consequences," He raised an eyebrow and smiled. "But I believe it would have made my father proud."

"Whatever you did, it couldn't have been too terrible," Charlotte told him. "I don't believe you're capable of doing anything that would cause disastrous consequences."

His spark of pleasure faltered. Her gaze held warmth and admiration that he didn't deserve. Lady Dalton's rescue not withstanding, he was no hero. "It caused my father's death." He said bleakly, "and nearly that of my whole family."

Charlotte's teasing expression faded. "Whatever did you do?"

# CHAPTER 23

Lucien walked to the side table and refilled his glass while he sorted his thoughts. He wasn't sure why he'd admitted that to her, but it was a relief to say aloud what he'd kept inside for more than a decade. Still, he didn't make eye contact when he turned back.

"I was twelve when my father brought my half-brother home. Tristan was two years my junior. A scrawny, filthy gutter-rat who'd been conceived the year after my mother died and before he met my stepmother." Lucien shook his head and his lip curled in derision. "He told me it made no difference that he'd not married Tristan's mother, we were both his sons. And he insisted I accept my half-brother just as fully as I did my legitimate half-sisters." His lips tightened with the memory. "I was mortified to discover he'd fathered a child on my nurse. Nor did I believe him when he claimed he hadn't known of her condition when she left his employment."

He swirled the brandy, but didn't drink. "In my resentment, I saw everything he did for his other son as a slight against me. I was mortified to be associated with Tristan, who was an ungrateful streetwise ruffian from Seven Dials. Yet I fought the bullies at school who ridiculed my father for expecting people to accept a bastard in their midst. I nurtured my resentment long after I should have accepted matters." He paused, ashamed of his arrogant immaturity, and the actions he was about to confess. "One day I found a set of my father's old journals in an obscure corner of the library. Angry for being chastised because of my latest rebellion, I scoured them for anything about my mother, the nurse, or Tristan. Eventually, I found something my father had written that put Tristan's paternity in question." Lucien remembered the exhilarated triumph he'd enjoyed at the discovery before he downed the contents of the class and set it aside, then looked at Charlotte, his lips set in grim acknowledgement. "It wasn't enough that he was a bastard, I needed him to be someone else's bastard." He shook his head in disgust. "I knew he wasn't. We looked too much alike."

Charlotte nodded. "It would have made your life easier, and your father might have remained on his pedestal."

Aunt Ridley had said much the same thing.

"I left the journal where Tristan would see it. I knew he'd read it, that he still distrusted his good fortune, and that his pride wouldn't allow him to stay if he didn't belong. As I hoped, he was gone the next morning, taking little more than the clothes that he wore."

Lucien took a deep breath and caught the faint whisper of wildflowers that he would always associate with Charlotte Longborough. The clean, fresh scent was at odds with the sordid truths he revealed.

"My father went after him as soon as he realized Tristan was gone. He searched all hours, and in all weather, during the week it took to find him. He investigated every vermin infested hovel where street urchins gathered, he searched every vice house and gaming hell. When he finally found Tristan and brought him home, Tristan was ill with a fever. My father and sisters caught the fever from him. Tristan and the girls recovered, but Papa died." He met Charlotte's gaze. "I killed him."

Charlotte rose and came to stand by him, her eyes never leaving his. "You didn't intend for him to die."

"No. But I hoped Tristan would."

He froze, shocked at his words. Never had he admitted the degree of bitterness he'd born for Tristan. Not even to himself. Had he really hoped that Tristan would die in the dangerous streets of Seven Dials? He'd wanted him gone from his life, yes, but dead? Had he truly been so full of resentment and pride? He shuddered.

Slender arms wrapped around his waist, and he realized that Charlotte held him in a comforting embrace. Her head lay against his chest and her hands swept up and down his back in a soothing rhythm.

She lifted her face and told him, "You wanted him gone from your life, Lucien. But I don't believe you truly wanted him dead, any more than you wanted your father to die."

His arms came around her and he savored the warmth she brought to his chilled thoughts. Those glorious eyes held sympathy, understanding, and acceptance. He kissed her. It was a kiss of thanks. It was gratitude for listening to the confessions that had plagued his soul. For not turning away.

Then it changed.

His arms pulled her closer and one hand moved up to cradle the back of her head as he bent to deepen the kiss. Heat flared and she made a pleasured sound before she softened her lips, and he tasted the hint of sherry that matched the sweetness of her unique flavor. He plundered that sweetness, reveling in the unrestrained fervor with which Charlotte followed his lead.

Without thought, he scooped her into his arms and carried her to the broad wingback chair beside the fireplace and sat down, securing her on his lap and fixing his mouth back on hers. Her arms came up, one hand at his back, the other encircling the back of his head. He trailed kisses down her jaw, along her neck, then to the softness above the neckline of her gown.

"I have no right," he murmured, "But I must…" He brushed his lips along the upper slope of her breasts.

Charlotte gasped then arched in invitation. "Oh, yes."

His hand came up to press and fondle the plump flesh and they both exhaled with pleasure. He circled the soft mound with his palms then pressed the sensitive tips before he lightly nipped them through the cloth of her bodice. She moaned and he reveled at her reaction.

"You make me forget myself," He whispered when he finally raised his head and looked into gray eyes that were luminous with pleasure and desire. "I shouldn't have—"

She raised up and kissed him before he could say more. "Yes, you should," she whispered fiercely. "Do it again… please?"

Her bodice clung, moistened by his open-mouthed kisses. She took his hands and placed them against the dampness, and he flexed his fingers, pressing the flesh and feeling the nipples, hard and swollen, against him palms. With a growl, he slid his hands inside the neckline, tugging the cloth low to uncover the sweet flesh it hid from view. *Dear God, she was glorious.* He explored every inch of skin exposed to his touch.

Charlotte's moans combined with a low growl– but the growl didn't come from him. Nor was it a growl of pleasure. Hot canine breath made Lucien look up to see Harry, his stance protective, and his teeth glistening in the candlelight. Lucien sat up abruptly and released his hold on Charlotte's body.

*Damnation, he'd lost control again.*

"I believe your chaperone has stepped in, Charlotte." Frustration and a certain amused pragmatic fatalism colored his words.

Charlotte opened her eyes, their gaze unfocused, her expression confused. "Wha…?" She focused, then turned her head toward Harry, and sat upright.

Harry relaxed his stance and gave a kind of snort before nosing her arm.

"I think he is telling you it is time for you to go to your room." Lucien said.

WHEN TIMMONS ANNOUNCED Lord Dalton the next afternoon, Lucien was glad that Charlotte, Elizabeth and Anne had already departed for tea and gossip at the Sinclair home. His stepmother and great aunt had decided the younger girls would benefit from a bit of culture and had taken them to a concert at the park. Harry napped in front of the hearth. Again.

"Show him in, Timmons."

Dalton strode into the study, his eyes bloodshot and his body tense. He wasted no time on the niceties. "Where is she?"

"Won't you have a seat?" Lucien sat back and gestured to the chair opposite the desk before asking, "Whom do you mean?"

"I don't need to sit," Dalton declared. "I wish to speak with the Longborough chit."

"Considering what happened the last time you spoke with her," Lucien said coldly, "I am unlikely to allow you near her. State your business and I shall decide if you need to be admitted into her presence or not."

Dalton drew himself up, clearly unwilling to discuss his purpose with Lucien. After a moment of silence, he said grudgingly, "I wish to discuss something she may have said to my wife."

"May have?" Lucien raised a brow. "You don't know? I should think your wife could clarify whether or not Miss Longborough spoke to her." He watched Dalton's face redden. "Why don't you ask her?"

Dalton shot him a glance that suddenly sharpened with suspicion. "Because she is missing," he said through gritted teeth. "And I believe Miss Charlotte Longborough knows where she is."

"Missing?" Lucien feigned surprise. "But she was at the Pomphrey betrothal ball last night. I am sure I saw her."

"She left sometime after the supper dance while I was in the card room," Dalton struck his walking stick on the floor in frustration and Harry rose from the hearth and trotted over to the desk. "When I arrived home, she had not returned." Dalton leaned on his hands on the desk and said, "I know the Longborough chit played a part in this. I will speak to her– and I will speak to her now." Frustration finally won over attempted civility and he pounded the desk with his fist.

When he did, Harry barked sharply and leapt up, his front paws on the desk, his head taller than Dalton, his teeth bared. The low rumbling growl sent Dalton backing up and away from the desk in alarm.

"Harry, down." Lucien commanded. He stood and tugged Harry's collar to settle the dog back to the floor but did not order him to be quiet. Harry continued to issue a low warning rumble. "It would seem Harry does not care for your attitude," he observed. "Nor do I. If your wife has left you, I can only wonder why. But having witnessed your behavior toward Miss Longborough, I can guess." He leaned forward to make his point as he warned. "I would be most displeased if you make demands upon me in the future... particularly if those demands concern Miss Longborough."

Dalton maintained his distance from Harry but didn't back down. "I warn you, Wolverton, that I will bring charges of kidnapping and trespass to bear if I find proof of that meddling female's involvement in my wife's disappearance. The law is on my side, and I will see that she pays for interfering in my life."

Harry continued his threatening rumble, and Lucien maintained a hold on his collar as he stepped around the desk to open the door. "Timmons, Lord Dalton is leaving now. He will not be returning."

Dalton avoided Harry as he exited the room to where Timmons stood beside the open front door.

# CHAPTER 24

"Congratulations, Lady Montfort," Charlotte said as she followed the Wolverton party through the receiving line of the most recent betrothal ball.

Since Jane's engagement, the matrimonial damn had broken and matches with new celebrations occurred nearly every day. Lady Francis Montfort had accepted Lord Farleigh's suit to the extreme satisfaction of her doting mother. Lord Farleigh was a composer of some skill, she assured them, and he played the viola, so next Season's musical entertainments would reach record heights.

Charlotte moved into the ballroom where she, Elizabeth and Anne joined several acquaintances. As always, conversation soon turned to on-dits of the latest gossip. Lady Mary Strand was likely to receive an offer from Lord Plimpton and Miss Barbara Ogilvie had refused Mr. Williams but accepted Sir John Turnbull.

However, the most scandalous rumor was that Lady Dalton was missing.

"She was quite ill some weeks ago," Elizabeth commented, "She most likely returned to the country to recover."

Anne's cousin lowered her voice and announced, "Lady Templeton told us Lord Dalton banished her to his country estate. Not because she was ill, but for leaving the Pomphrey ball early."

"Oh, no," said a young lady, whose name Charlotte had forgotten, "My maid said cook had it from Lord Dalton's cook that Lady Dalton never even came home from the Pomphrey ball. She said Lord Dalton was fit to be tied when he discovered his lady gone and he ranted and raved for hours. He slammed out of the house the next morning and engaged a runner to track her down."

One gentleman chuckled and suggested that perhaps Lord Dalton had killed her and buried her in the back garden. No, said another with a jeering laugh, that would mean manual labor... and everyone knew Lord Dalton would not dirty his hands now that he'd risen from his obscure beginnings.

A chilled shiver ran down Charlotte's back as she listened to the low-voiced speculation and derisive jests. Until Lady Dalton's disappearance, Lord Dalton had appeared to be well liked by the gentlemen and rather a darling of the ladies. They had known nothing of his wife's abuse, though perhaps her chronic illness had not been as unremarked as she'd believed.

Either way, the sudden and salacious delight in which his former acquaintances gossiped about his embarrassment and his wife's fate stunned her. She didn't pity him in his infamy, he deserved it and more, but it amazed her nonetheless.

She danced several dances and caught snatches of similar gossip as she moved about the dance floor. From it she learned, Lord Dalton had been absent from many ballrooms since his wife's disappearance. He had, however, been seen at several of the most notorious gaming halls instead.

Just before midnight, the Montfort's footmen passed around trays of champagne. When she turned to accept a glass, Charlotte noticed several of the ladies in the chaperone corner whispering together with the animation only a fresh scandal could cause. Whatever sent their tongues wagging must be particularly shocking to distract them from speculating about the Dalton's.

Lord Montfort stepped up onto the dais and called for his guest's attention and made the formal announcement of his daughter's engagement to Lord Farleigh. After they raised their glasses and toasted the couple, Lord Farleigh led Francis into a continental waltz. Charlotte sipped the rest of her champagne and watched them while they danced.

Supper followed the dance, and Charlotte realized that she had not eaten a mid-day meal when she became a bit light-headed after finishing the contents of her glass. Lord Clarehaven took her in to supper, but nothing tasted quite right, and what little she ate did not ease the slight dizziness that that affected her when she moved too quickly. Once they'd filled their plates and found a table, the footman had placed another glass of champagne at her place.

"Are you one of those ladies who eats her meal before the ball so all and sundry believe her to be of small appetite?" Lord Clarehaven teased when he saw how little she consumed over the next half hour.

"Not at all," she denied, "It all looks delicious, but nothing quite strikes me this evening." She took another sip of champagne but found her fingers sticking along the stem of the glass. "If you will excuse me," she said. "I believe I need to wash my hands before the dancing begins again." She rose, steadying herself against the back of the chair before making her way to the hall and on to the ladies' retiring room.

At the door to the room, another wave of dizziness caught her, and she put her hand out to steady herself. A hand came from behind her and steadied her arm before turning her away from the door. "Why Miss Longborough, you appear to have taken too much champagne. Let me help you."

Charlotte had only a moment to register Lord Dalton's voice and face before he pressed a cloth against her face, and she breathed in a pungent odor. Her dizziness swirled into black.

LUCIEN EXCUSED HIMSELF from the card table and entered the main ballroom. He had led his stepmother out for the first dance after they arrived that evening, and Lady Montfort for the second.

They had hardly begun the steps before Lady Montfort said, "I see Miss Charlotte Longborough has been in your company a great deal of late." She smiled and her eyes twinkled. "Shall we be attending a second ball at your residence in the near future?"

A second ball? As in a *betrothal* ball? He shot a glance across the room to where Charlotte accepted a glass of champagne from a footman. "Miss Charlotte Longborough is a guest of my stepmother's and therefore under my protection," he responded carefully. "It is of little surprise that I am in her company, just as I am often in her sister's company as well."

"Ah, but I notice that you spend more time observing her than you do Lady Anne or the elder Miss Longborough." She tapped him lightly with her fan. "Deny it if you will, Wolverton, but I believe she has caught your interest."

"You will pardon me if I say your joy in your daughter's happiness has led you to see more in the interactions of others than there may be in fact." He smiled to soften his denial. "Lord Farleigh is fortunate in his choice of wife and mother-in-law, but I am not inspired to follow him down the aisle this Season."

He changed the subject by asking if Lord Montfort still planned to attend Lord Kendrick's hunting party in the fall. She gave him one last teasing smile before telling him that, yes, Lord Montfort looked forward to hunting grouse. When the dance ended, he excused himself and immediately sought the safety of the card room.

He wouldn't ask for a dance with Charlotte this evening. If tabby tongues were wagging with matrimonial speculation, he had best lay that issue to rest. The best way to do that was to return to his habit of dancing only with his stepmother, his hostess, or his sister.

He returned to the card room after supper. During the meal he'd noted that Charlotte took her supper with Clarehaven. That made him frown. Clarehaven's reputation as a rake was well earned, though he had not crossed over into the territory of the libertine. A supper dance did not particularly mean the man intended to pursue her. Nonetheless, he'd told Lucien someone other than Anne had his interest.

Lady Montfort's words echoed in his mind. He might not have danced with her, but Lucien realized he'd spent the entire meal observing Charlotte. He made a point of turning his attention away from her before someone else accused him of paying her particular notice.

An hour later, he felt he could return to the ballroom without anyone making suppositions about his intentions. As he strolled into the room he checked to see if Clarehaven still remained in her circle. He didn't immediately spy Charlotte, but Clarehaven now danced with Lady Middlesham. He continued to survey the room. Elizabeth sat with his stepmother and Aunt Ridley, Norcross partnered Anne and Bascomb danced with the Littlemarsh's daughter. He still didn't see Charlotte. He worked his way around the room. She was, after all not particularly tall and the room was crowded.

He had circled the room and was about to go out to the balcony when he overheard Lady Templeton and Lady Winterstone gossiping about the Dalton scandal. The subject had filtered through the card room where serious gamblers rarely discussed anything other than hands played or bets made.

"I don't believe the rumor that his wife is missing." Lady Templeton assured her friend. "After her recent disappointment it is to be expected that she would wish to recover in the country. Besides, Lord Dalton would not have come this evening if she were actually missing."

The hairs at the back of Lucien's neck rose. Dalton here? The man had avoided all ton entertainments since the Pomphrey ball. Why would he return to the social scene now? Yet Dalton's fury when Lucien refused him access to Charlotte might well have made him return to social venues to seek her out. Lucien's pulse quickened, and suddenly the fact that he'd not yet located Charlotte took on an alarming significance. His jaw tightened and he searched the dance floor again.

She wasn't there.

CHARLOTTE NOTICED THE musty scent of moldy straw first. As consciousness returned, she registered that she lay face down on coarse canvas, presumably the covering of an old straw mattress. Her head throbbed. She swallowed, and her parched throat ached for water. *The champagne... Dalton... suffocating cloth–* At some point she'd had the sensation of rocking movement and the sounds of carriage wheels on cobblestone, vague voices in the distance... of being forced to drink something distasteful. *Laudanum.*

She shifted and realized her hands and feet were bound.

Cautiously, she opened her eyes.

Dalton sat in a wingback chair, a bottle on the table, his hand cradling a half-empty glass of dark red wine. He smiled when he saw that she was awake. "I suspect your head hurts like the devil," he commented with satisfaction. "Are you thirsty as well?" He took a sip of the wine and she could not help the reflexive working of her own throat as he made a point of taking a deep swallow of the liquid. Her mouth felt woolly and her tongue cleaved to the roof of her mouth. "I see you are." He gave her an unpleasant smile. "You may have all the water or wine you wish once you have told me where my wife is." Charlotte closed her eyes rather than see the malicious intent in his expression. When she answered, her voice sounded hoarse. "I don't know where she is."

"Oh, I think you do." Dalton said as he stood. He put the glass on the table. He walked slowly over to where she lay. "I know you had something to do with her disappearance. She was less understanding of my occasional losses of control after you spoke to her at the Montfort's."

His glare revealed his rage that his wife had ceased blaming herself for his behavior. Had that been behind his last attack on her? She wanted to ask but suspected that anything she said would give him an excuse to give his temper free reign. He stopped beside the cot and she struggled to remain passive.

"What? No comment?" he asked. He knelt and put his face at level with hers. "I thought you had a great deal to say that day." His piercing gaze reflected the fire behind his artificial calm. "You know, she never looked at me the same way after that evening. She tried to act the same, but she no longer believed me when I said I was sorry."

He stood, grabbed Charlotte by the hair, and pulled her into a sitting position, then, slapped her. "That was your doing."

He bent down, grabbed her by the waist, and slung her over his shoulder. He carried her to the middle of the room before depositing her onto a hard-back wooden chair. She bit back a cry of pain when he wrenched her arms behind the chair.

"Feel free to scream if you wish," Dalton told her as he fastened a rope around the leg of the chair, her bound feet, and then around the other chair leg. "We are quite alone in the house, and well above the streets. You will not be heard." Charlotte's stomach churned. She'd seen what he could do, and fear made the nauseous after-effects of the laudanum worse.

"Nor will you be found by your friends or protectors." He bent low again to watch her expression when he added, "We are well and truly tucked away where people know how to mind their own business." He reached out and took her chin in his hand. "Now where is my wife?"

# CHAPTER 25

No longer concerned whether the matchmakers saw his actions as particular interest, Lucien sought out Elizabeth, Anne, and his stepmother to determine Charlotte's movements after he last seen her at supper. Each of his inquiries confirmed that no one remembered seeing her dance in the last hour. His neck prickled. It did not escape his notice that the occasion and timing echoed Dalton's experience. Lady Dalton had been spirited away following the supper dance... and he feared Charlotte had as well. The irony would please a revengeful mind.

He spotted Ravencliffe, Clarehaven and Norcross exiting the card room with Lord Montfort and made his way as quickly as decorum and the crowd would permit. As it was, he suspected more than one acquaintance noted his preoccupation as he brushed past without stopping to acknowledge them. By the time he reached his friends they, too, had noticed his haste and moved to meet him.

"Is something amiss?" Ravencliffe greeted him.

"Perhaps." he admitted. "I need to speak with you privately–Lord Montfort, may we use your study?"

"Of course." The older man assessed Lucien's expression and added, "Should I send for authorities?"

"No," Lucien summoned a practiced, social smile. "There is no need. It is a private matter."

"Then I hope it is easily solved." Lord Montfort said as he signaled a footman. "John will show you the way to my study. Feel free to take as long as need be."

Once in the study Lucien quickly explained the situation as it related to Lady Dalton's escape and his concerns for Charlotte. He did not speak of her childhood experiences, only of what she'd found when she called on the lady. Relating the severity of Lady Dalton's condition created tormented images of what Dalton might do to his captive.

"I need to find Dalton and Charlotte as soon as possible. I have searched the public areas of the house, but he could have taken her to the more private rooms... or, I fear, elsewhere entirely."

He paced the room, too on edge to sit still. The three men listening to his story looked at one another their expressions revealing they understood his agitation. "I need you to assist me in searching the house. Should we fail to find her here, as I am afraid we will, I ask that you allow me to borrow a carriage to go to his house." He stopped pacing and faced them, his gaze sharp and his voice bleak. "Dalton is an angry and violent man– and the information he seeks will only make him angrier."

He stared at each of them in turn. "I need not tell you that no one is to know about this. If I don't return within the hour, inform my stepmother and Charlotte's sister, but no one else, and take them home." He ran a hand through his hair in frustration. "If I don't find her at Dalton's I'll return home and we'll try to discover where he has taken her."

They left the room, careful not to attract attention, and quietly made their way to the private rooms on the third floor. At the top of the stairs, they split up, Ravencliffe and Norcross taking the hallway to the left, Lucien and Clarehaven the one on the right. The first door revealed a room of combined femininity and regal standing, obviously Lady Montfort's sitting room. The next, as expected, was her bedchamber and next to that, Lord Montfort's bedchamber. Clarehaven's exploration yielded the equally unoccupied guest rooms in addition to those of their two daughters. With the four of them working, it did not take more than a few minutes for them to verify that neither Dalton nor Charlotte were there.

"I will make my excuses to Montfort, then be on my way." Lucien said quietly, "Try to keep my family and Elizabeth unaware of the situation unless and until absolutely necessary."

Once back in the ballroom Ravencliffe and Norcross located the Duchess and Elizabeth and asked them each to dance while Lucien took his leave from his hosts.

Lucien thanked Lord Montfort for the use of his study and explained that he had been called away. No, there was no cause for alarm, just a friend who requested his aid. He gave Lord Montfort a conspiratorial smile and raised his eyebrow. "When one over-indulges, one should not attempt to ride home alone on a horse. If I am not returned within the hour, Ravencliffe has offered to see the ladies home."

"Oh-ho," Lord Montfort chuckled. "I see. Glad it is nothing serious, Wolverton."

Lucien collected his cloak from the footman and strode down the front steps to the street. Climbing in, he gave the coachman the direction and they set off at a rapid pace. He arrived at Dalton House to find all the windows dark. Either the servants were all abed, or Dalton had closed the house and taken Charlotte somewhere more private for his interrogation. Dalton might be rash, but he was not stupid.

As he exited the carriage, Lucien did not want to think about how a man of Dalton's disposition would go about questioning a stubborn woman. He strode to the front door and knocked loudly. When there was no response, he descended the steps to the servants' entrance. Leaves had gathered into a shallow pile at the base of the stairs, and the scent of coal fires drifted on the breeze that stirred them at his feet. The un-swept space confirmed that the house servants had decamped– but with or without Dalton?

He returned to the carriage and had it driven around to the Mews at the rear of the property. After confirming the back gate was locked, he climbed the wall and crossed the narrow garden to peer into the ground floor windows. The half-full moon provided little light outside, and none inside. Of the upper floors he could make out nothing at all. It was too quiet.

There was an emptiness to the atmosphere that made Lucien suspect that Dalton had closed the house and fled with Charlotte. Still, he had to be sure. Dalton could as easily have sent the servants away to give the appearance that he was not in residence.

A quick search of the area yielded a rock at the edge of the wall that he used to break the kitchen window. Reaching inside, he opened the latch and pushed up the sash then climbed over the sill. And stood, listening.

Silence. A lingering, slightly stale aroma of some savory dish hung in the air, but the kitchen hearth was cold. That meal had not been cooked today, or even yesterday. Nonetheless, he inspected every room. Dust covers protected the furniture, the rugs rested in rolled columns against the walls, and curtains closed against the light. He swiftly inspected the rooms on each floor. He'd suspected before he began that the house remained empty, but that knowledge didn't ease his sharp disappointment.

The properties that were his wife's inheritance would likely satisfy Dalton's sense as appropriate locations for establishing his rights. The family estate was in Epping, outside the city and a good four or five hours distant. He remembered the other properties were in the city, though he had paid no attention to the addresses when he read the report weeks earlier.

He saw no point in wasting more time in the empty house, nor in exiting through the window. If Dalton returned and found the door unlocked, it would make no difference. When he undid the lock, a fine wire connected to the handle caused the bell in the servant's hall to ring. Had he been home, Dalton would have known of the intrusion.

Lucien arrived at Wolverton House to find Ravencliffe, Clarehaven and Norcross waiting in the drawing room with his stepmother, Anne and Elizabeth. All three ladies stood when he entered the room, their faces pale and their expressions hopeful. They subsided back into their chairs and hope altered to distress when they saw he was alone. They waited for him to speak.

He did not waste time with soothing assurances– he had none to give. "Dalton has closed his house. There was no one there. He might have taken Charlotte to his country estate, but I doubt he would have the patience to travel that far."

He turned to Elizabeth. "I gather from Charlotte that you were unaware of his threats against her when he was your neighbor?"

" I remember she told me she'd seen him hurt his wife, but everyone liked him, so I accused her of making up stories. I didn't know about the tool shed until Charlotte told me of the connection after Lady Ridley's garden party." Elizabeth shook her head. "She was only eight-years-old."

Lucien debated telling them the rest of what Charlotte had seen, unsure if he should add to their fears by revealing exactly how violent the man was. If Charlotte hadn't told her sister what she'd witnessed, he didn't feel he should be the one to do so.

"He caught Charlotte spying on him and warned her off," he finally explained to the others. "After he recognized her name some weeks ago, and saw her speaking to his wife, he again warned her to mind her own business." His hand clenched at his side. He shouldn't have gone along with her plan. He should have known that any man who would beat his wife would seek revenge when thwarted. It was his fault that he hadn't foreseen that Dalton would not be warned away from confronting her. "When Lady Dalton found the courage to leave, he blamed Charlotte for encouraging her to escape. He believes she knows where Lady Dalton is."

"Does she?" his stepmother asked.

Lucien turned to her and could not lie. "Yes... and no."

The Duchess gave him the unrelenting glare he'd not seen her use since he'd taken on his title. When he was a boy it had released all manner of confessions. She waited, her gaze unwavering. *It still did*.

"She knows Lady Dalton is on a ship to Canada." he confessed. "She does not know the exact destination."

"Will she admit that she knows?"

Elizabeth spoke up, her voice a sad whisper. "Not willingly."

"Which is why we must find her– and quickly." Lucien agreed.

He turned to his friends. "After Charlotte confided in me, I had my solicitor compile a dossier on the former Albert Franklin. Dalton controls two other properties within the city that were part of Lady Dalton's inheritance and are currently unoccupied."

He faced Elizabeth and Sarah. "I will find and return Charlotte as soon as possible... but if he has taken her to his estate, it may be some days before we can retrieve her. I promise, however, that we will succeed."

He looked to his stepmother and Anne. "Until we do, we must keep word of this from becoming public scandal."

He motioned for Ravencliffe, Clarehaven and Norcross to follow him when he went to the study to retrieve the reports that listed the locations of Dalton's properties. A quarter of an hour later Ravencliffe and Norcross left to check one address while Clarehaven and Lucien hurried to the other.

"I TOLD YOU, I DON'T know where your wife is." Charlotte said. Dalton's eyes held hers as he'd bent to ask his question. Her scalp burned where Dalton had grabbed her hair and pulled her upright before depositing her on the hard wooden chair. Her arms, pulled tightly behind her, ached.

"I'm sorry you remain so stubborn," Dalton said. He straightened back from where he'd peered at her face. "Women are much like children. They are stubborn, willful, and in need of training." His eyes narrowed and his mouth turned down. He gestured vaguely. "Women do have uses once they have been trained, of course. They should be worthy hostesses for their husbands, obediently see to his creature comforts and provide heirs to carry on family name—though I never wanted an heir." He darted his gaze back to her and added, "If they cannot manage such wifely duties, they are of no more use than whores to ease a man's needs."

He paced slowly back and forth while he explained. "It pains me that I must teach you the proper manners a lady should show before a gentleman." He stopped in front of her again and held up a finger.

"Lesson number one– When a gentleman asks a lady a question, she should answer. *Immediately*. *Truthfully*." Then he backhanded her with a blow that rocked the chair and left Charlotte's cheek burning.

"For all her faults," Dalton told her, "Sophronia learned that lesson early." He slowly circled the chair and Charlotte fought the instinctive urge to follow his progress. He stopped in front of her again. "It is only because I love her that I must chastise her when she disobeys or argues."

Charlotte did look up at him then, not hiding the scorn in her eyes, and he shook his head. "You don't understand, do you?" His voice reflected sadness, but his eyes held no emotion. "I love my wife, but because I love her, I must do all I can to help her be the kind of wife she should be."

He spread his hands in a magnanimous gesture. "Unlike most peers, I do not insist she provide an heir." He let his hands fall back to his sides. "I try to be patient. I take the time to instruct her. I have repeatedly made clear what is expected of her as my viscountess."

He shook his head again. "But she simply does not fulfill her duties properly. I dare not even trust her to do something so simple as plan a dinner party for my friends. She is still like a willful child... and it is well established to spare the rod is to spoil the child."

His eyes changed. Charlotte could not name it, but it frightened her. Empty of the anger he usually projected, the eerie fire of fanaticism lit his eyes, but for what she was not sure. "Spanking did not improve her behavior." he said. "So, though I am sorry for it, I have had to employ more severe means of making her do as she is told."

Charlotte stared up at him, unable to hide the disbelief in her voice when she asked, "Did you love your first wife, then?"

He said nothing for several seconds.

"Do you know," He finally said, "I believed shutting you into that shed when I caught you spying would teach you to mind your own business," Dalton said. "But I see it takes more than threats to teach you not to meddle.

He circled the chair once more. When he stopped in front of her, he said, "I ask you again. Where is my wife?"

Before she could do more than look at him, he hit her again, this time the chair did tip and Charlotte hit the floor, bruising her other cheek and making her ears ring. Dalton lifted the chair back up, then came around to study her burning features. "Do you see what you did?" His question had a false note of sorrow and injured patience. "Had you answered me, I would not have had to chastise you... and you would not have hurt yourself."

Charlotte licked her lip, tasting the blood where it had split. Her face throbbed, her head spun, and she vaguely noticed that she'd lost a shoe.

Dalton walked over, picked up his wine glass, and carefully swirled it. The liquid left thin rivulets of clinging wine along the inside of the glass. As he had obviously meant it to, it made Charlotte again aware of the cotton-dryness of her mouth and throat. He finished the glass with audible gusto, then poured another generous portion and put it back on the table. "I find that wine takes the edge off my sorrow." He said with a faint smile. "And I am truly sorry for what I see I must do."

This time he used his fist.

Pain exploded and air left her lungs when he drove his fist into her stomach. Brilliant lights danced in a blackly swirling whirlpool of agony. She struggled to breathe, to take in air, but her body froze, and her mind screamed in panic. Finally, as the dancing lights flickered and nearly faded to black, her shocked muscles uncramped and air, *blessed air*, seeped back into her lungs. She blinked, her eyes watered, then the contents of her stomach shifted, and she vomited onto the floor and her lost shoe.

Dalton eyed the floor with distaste before asking, "Where is my wife?"

"I told you," she managed to whisper. "I don't know."

"The Thames might not be as swift flowing as the river at home, but it is deep and will be as anonymous as needed if you do not l tell the truth."

He stepped to the table and took another long drink of wine. "And if Wolverton suspects me– and his refusal to grant me access to you makes me suspect he is part of this as well–" He told her, "he will have no proof. You will have wandered off as mysteriously as did my wife." His eyes lit with the fire of revenge. "Yet he cannot accuse me of retaliating without disclosing his role in taking my wife. Which I remind you is against the law."

He fiddled with the glass, holding it up to inspect the wine's color in the light, then saying with assurance, "He will have gone to my residence to confront me personally– but I will not be there." He bowed to her, his hands wide to include the room. "I am here."

He took another sip of the wine. "I suspect he will have come and gone from my home within the hour as he apparently keeps a close eye on you. I will know when he has gone by the simple expediency of a trip wire set at the lower floor doors. Only after he has verified that my household has been closed and is truly empty of servants and master, shall I take you to my home." He surveyed the bare, neglected space of the room they were in with amusement. "Which, you might be interested to know, is connected to this one by way of a secret tunnel." His amusement grew and he chuckled. "It seems my wife's grandfather kept his mistress here and did not wish to be seen visiting her."

His amusement altered to cunning. "Wolverton will undoubtedly learn of the location of this property and search here when he discovers nothing at my home." He looked down at the congealing mess at her feet. "He will suspect you were here, but ..." He smiled again. "Any vagrant might have taken up residence in an empty house... and drunk too much." He leaned near and added. "Oh, and if you did not know, careless people fall into the river more often than one would think." He grinned with satisfaction. "Even if Wolverton dared accuse me, I will not hang– for I am now a peer."

He studied her carefully, then swiftly backhanded her in the eye, his signet ring breaking the skin on her cheek.

# CHAPTER 26

Lucien inspected the rundown building that sat between its recently renovated neighbors. Ironically, this building was but a block behind the Dalton home and located between Mayfair and the gentlemen's clubs of St. James. No light showed here, either. Still, that meant nothing since it would soon be dawn. An occasional carriage made its way from the clubs, late as it was. He and Clarehaven turned their horses toward the back. He didn't want anyone to see them enter the house.

The second property was a few blocks away, so Lucien had instructed Ravencliffe and Norcross to meet him at White's if they found nothing. They would send word if they located Dalton or Charlotte. One would contact the others while the second stood guard.

Lucien forced the lock on the servant door, and they entered the kitchen. It was as cold and empty as Dalton House. No kitchen scents lingered, only dust, mold and the slightly sour smell of old mortar and brick. Lucien lit the small lanterns he'd brought, then lowered the shades so that the light shone down at his feet but didn't send betraying brightness ahead of them. Silently, he handed the second lantern to Clarehaven and signaled him to inspect the current floor while Lucien took the back stairs to the ground floor.

A much smaller house than Dalton's, the first floor had a moderate sized receiving room across from a cramped study. The threadbare carpet-runner on the front staircase had once been of good, if not the best, quality. Cobwebs filled the space between most of the banister's spindles.

Clarehaven soon joined him and they ascended to the next level together.

That floor's sitting room opposed the dining room, both with open doorways connected by a broad landing. A wide window along the connecting wall at the head of the stairs provided light during the day, and now lent enough moonlight to show the rooms to be shrouded and empty.

At the third floor they again split up, Clarehaven taking the servant staircase to the attic where the servants' chambers were. The third floor contained one spacious and two smaller bedchambers. It was in the second of the smaller rooms that Lucien discovered a narrow cot that looked as though someone had used it recently. *Vagrants?* Lucien raised the lamp and studied the rest of the room.

A wingback chair sat next to the empty fireplace. The table beside it showed marks where a bottle and, presumably, a glass had rested. Whoever had used this room had made himself comfortable.

What struck a disturbing note, however, was the hard-backed, wooden chair that sat between the cot and the wingback. It didn't belong. Plain, wooden, and centered in the room, it looked like the interrogation seat of an improvised courtroom.

He held the lantern higher and saw the drying splatter of vomit… and a lady's dancing shoe. That sight sent cold shockwaves through him before raging fury had him yelling for Clarehaven. *He would kill Dalton for that.*

Together they hunted for clues to tell them where Dalton had taken Charlotte. Frustration fueled the tension that had Lucien reinvestigating the other rooms, but to no avail. When they finally admitted defeat and went to Whites, it was well past dawn. Ravencliffe and Norcross had already arrived and ordered an early breakfast.

They had found nothing to indicate Dalton had been at the other house.

Lucien still believed that Dalton would not retreat to his home estate. However, they could not take the chance he had not. Ravencliffe and Norcross agreed to leave for Dalton's country estate immediately. Lucien would make the rounds of the gaming houses to glean what he could of Dalton's habits and regular haunts.

Clarehaven went home, promising to return to join Lucien when he questioned Dalton's friends. Unfortunately, they could not do that until afternoon when the ton began to stir. Lucien had to return home. He would not distress his or Charlotte's family with the details of what he'd seen, but he needed to let them know that Dalton had temporarily eluded them.

No sooner had he stepped across the threshold, than Sarah met him, her eyes red from crying, and babbling about her dreams of Harry chasing the weasel and how Charlotte kept spinning around.

Elizabeth followed her into the entry hall, her eyes also red, though her words were calmer. "Please, Your Grace, you must return to Dalton House. Sarah's dreams are never wrong."

Lucien gaped at the two of them. Sarah rarely spoke directly to him. She struck him as a rather shy child, so it surprised him that she now clung to him as she tried to make him understand.

"Pardon me, Your Grace," Elizabeth reached out and gently released Sarah's hands from Lucien's sleeves. "I'll explain, but we must hurry." She glanced to where the duchess and Anne had joined them. "You see," she looked to where a curious parlor maid lingered near the stairs and lowered her voice. "Sarah has the sight."

Lucien raised an eyebrow at that, and she rushed on. "Stupid rumors circulate about our grandmother being accused of being a witch. She was not. But she did dream and know things before they happened, and it frightened people. Sarah dreams and knows things, too." She put her arm protectively around her sister. "I ask that you do not mention this to others, but I beg you to believe in her gift."

"Please, Your Grace." Sarah took a deep breath and looked up at him, her gaze direct and compelling. "You must go back to Dalton House. She is there. I know she wasn't before, but she is now. *I know it*– and she is hurt."

Lucien saw the real panic in Sarah's eyes and the desperation in Elizabeth's. Suddenly he remembered the questions the child had raised so casually, and the situations that had followed. The horse with shoe blacking and her request for oranges. He might have questioned clairvoyance if he weren't so desperate to find Charlotte himself, but perhaps the bond of sisterhood, at least, existed.

"We found evidence that Charlotte had been held at one of the locations but had been removed before we arrived." He told them. "I don't see how he could have gone back to his townhouse without us seeing him, but I'll do as you ask if it will ease your mind. I certainly have no other viable clues to follow."

As soon as he spoke, Harry's bark sounded behind the doors to Lucien's study followed by a loud thump and desperate scrabbling against the wood. The frantic barking and thumping had Lucien yanking open the doors before the beast could tear them down. As soon as he was released Harry leapt up, his paws on Lucien's shoulders until he was face to face with the frantic, whining dog.

"Harry, down." he ordered. The dog obeyed but continued to whine and move between Lucien and the door.

"We had to put him in there– he's been pacing in front of the door for the last two hours– ever since Sarah woke from her dream." Anne told him. "I believe he also knows Charlotte needs help."

Lucien turned to Timmons. "Have my horse brought back around and tell John to drive the coach to the mews behind Dalton House and wait for me."

"I must change, or I'll be noticed in the daylight. If Dalton has taken Charlotte back to his home I need to attract as little attention as possible." He took the stairs two at a time to his room where he stripped out of his evening clothes and into riding clothes as quickly as possible.

Within five minutes he mounted his horse and sent it in a brisk canter through the early morning delivery cart traffic. Halfway there he realized Harry followed. When Lucien ordered him home, Harry ignored the command, and Lucien reconciled himself that Harry would be part of his new search.

THE THROBBING PAIN woke her, but Charlotte kept her eyes closed. Or, rather, her eye. The other was swollen shut and would not open had she tried. Nor did she want to try. She didn't want to move at all. Lord Dalton had hit her several more times before she'd lost consciousness. At some point he must have moved her since she was no longer tied to the chair. And the cotton under her cheek was of better quality. It irritated her abraded skin less than the rough mattress where she'd been before. It smelled cleaner, too.

She kept her breath slow and even while she concentrated on listening for some sign that he waited for her to open her eyes. She listened for faint movement, for the whisper of his breath. Nor did she breathe in the cloying tobacco scent that had surrounded her when he had leaned down to make eye contact with her. She opened her uninjured eye... and recognized the room where she had discovered Lady Dalton. Wherever she'd been before, she was now at Dalton house– and three blocks from Wolverton House.

Tentatively, she flexed her wrists. They were still bound, but she believed the cords had loosened a bit. She tried moving her feet. The coarse rope chaffed against her ankles making them burn. She would have to free her hands in order to undo the bindings. Her arms ached as she worked her hands, twisting and stretching the cord. The movement caused her face to brush against the sheet and her cheek burned, too. The pulsing throb of her swollen eye did not relent.

Every few minutes she stopped and listened for movement from either the hall or the connecting door she knew must lead to the master bedchamber. She had no idea how long she'd been unconscious, and she had no idea how long Dalton would leave her alone. She only knew that she needed to free herself and find a way to escape before Lord Dalton could strike her again.

When Charlotte succeeded in narrowing her hand enough to pull it free of the loosened cords, she wanted to cry in relief. Instead, she took another moment to listen for Dalton before struggling upright. The movement made her head swim with dizziness and the throbbing in her eye to radiate into a headache that pounded as though her head would explode. She fought through the disorienting pain to pull at the knots that rubbed against the raw skin at her ankles. It took her an eternity to work the cords loose, but she finally managed to break them free. She lowered her feet to the floor and carefully stood. Fire laced needles flashed as the circulation returned to her feet, but that discomfort made little impression over the pain from Dalton's fist.

The first step was the hardest, but she managed to hobble to the window. Turning the latch, she succeeded in raising the sash. The pale dawn light, the rattle of wheels on cobbles and the distant calls from street vendors told her the working class had begun the business of the day. The room was too high for her to climb down, even without the beating she had endured, but if she could get the attention of someone at the ground level—

"You're awake," Dalton said from behind her. He crossed to the window and grabbed Charlotte's hair as he had earlier. "I see I'll have to tie the cords tighter this time."

# CHAPTER 27

As he had the first time, Lucien inspected the grounds and the windows at the back of the house. Early morning scents of damp grass and the distant calls of the dairy venders rose with the dawn. At the far wall, a cat slunk along its top, then jumped down and sauntered to a hedge at the far corner and disappeared beneath its foliage. He checked the windows on the upper floors and saw that one was open, a detail he'd not been able to see in the darkness the night before. He saw no movement behind its frame.

He traveled swiftly and silently across the path to the servant entrance. He slipped through the door he had left unlocked earlier when he found the house empty. He shut the door quickly, ordering the dog to stay outside. The kitchen was still cold and silent, but the scent that floated on the air had changed. A plate with cheese crumbs and a thin crust of bread on the table showed him that someone had been here, but whether or not it was Dalton he could not know. He took a step, then a soft *woof* made him turn back.

"Quiet, Harry." he commanded in a low voice. "Down... Stay."

The dog had kept pace easily, and Lucien had hoped the fence surrounding the yard would keep him from following further. He should have known better.

Harry ignored him. His great shaggy head poked through the broken window, and he whined. But he did not bark again. Lucien hoped the dog did not raise a commotion that warned Dalton he was here.

Lucien turned to the back stairs and climbed quickly and silently, not stopping at the first or second floors. He pictured the opened window and knew Dalton would use a room on the upper floor. Halfway up to the third floor he heard the distinct smack of flesh hitting flesh and a woman's cry.

Horror and fury rippled down his spine. *Charlotte!* He took the remaining stairs two at a time, no longer concerned about stealth. Behind and below him a great, howling bark. The glass splintered, and nails scrabbled against the floor as Charlotte's beast ascended the staircase. At the top of the stair, Harry passed him and leapt against a door near the end of the hall, barking frantically.

Lucien flung open the door and lunged across the room to grab Dalton by the collar and jerk him around. Charlotte lay on the floor, the sight of her battered face escalated his fury to rage, and he slammed his fist into Dalton's nose with his entire strength.

Dalton staggered, nearly fell, and his nose spurted blood. Shaking his head, he recovered and lunged at Lucien with a snarl that turned to a shout of pain when Harry leapt forward to clamp his great jaws onto Dalton's leg. Dalton went down with the force of the beast's attack then kicked out, trying to get Harry to let go. Lucien caught Dalton's foot, twisting and forcing his leg down so he could not retaliate. Harry growled, but did not let go.

Lucien needed all his concentration to restrain the struggling man whose eyes held the feral light of the vicious, cornered animal that he was. Finally managing to get Dalton face down in a grappling hold, Lucien ordered Harry to release him. For once, the dog obeyed, but stood ready to leap again, all teeth and growls. Lucien shifted until his knee was in Dalton's back and Lucien anchored his hands together. Dalton finally subsided, though his gaze was no less feral. Even a cornered beast ceased fighting when forced into submission.

"Here."

Charlotte's hand shook as she handed Lucien a length of coarse cord. The raw abrasions on her wrist and the dried rust color that darkened the fibers of the cord told him she handed him the same cords that had bound her. Dalton's wrists were far larger than Charlotte's, but Lucien managed to bind them together.

That done, he rose and gently brushed his fingers over the swollen, bruised, and broken skin on her face.

"I did not find you in time," he whispered. "I am so sorry."

"But you did," Charlotte assured him. Her voice a rasping whisper. "I am not floating in the Thames."

He caught her reference and shuddered. "I should kill him for this."

He gathered Charlotte into an embrace. Her right eye had swollen shut, the lid brilliant purple and red. The left one had been spared– But for how much longer? Lucien did not want to think about it. Scrapes across her cheek and little patches of dried blood left a striped pattern across the once smooth skin. He dared not hold her tightly, fearing cracked or broken ribs when she winced.

Dalton stirred and Harry's growl escalated from warning to threat.

Lucien lifted Charlotte into his arms and carried her to the bed. He started to seat her on it, then stopped. He searched the expression in her one clear eye, "You aren't– hurt in any... other... way?"

She shook her head. "His violence did not take that form."

Lucien released a relieved sigh. "Rest." He said as he lowered her gently to the mattress, "while I take care of this. Then I will get you home."

He turned back to Dalton and hauled him upright. "As a gentleman of honor," Lucien told him, "Society would not permit me to strike a man incapable of defending himself." He steadied Dalton onto his feet. "But honor," he said with a grim smile, "must sometimes bow to justice–" and Lucien drove one fist into Dalton's face, the other into his torso. Lucien then bowed, hauled Dalton up again, and tied him to the bedpost. His aunt's assessment of his forefathers' action made absolute sense, he realized. Socially prescribed honor, and private honor, did not always match.

"You've invaded my home," Dalton snarled, "You dare not send for the authorities over this."

"I don't plan to." Lucien said as he turned back to Charlotte, "Once Miss Longborough has been safely reunited with her family, I'll return with peers who can be relied upon to be discreet." He helped Charlotte to stand and supported her as he guided her around the end of the bed. "They'll decide your fate without exposing the lady to scandal." Harry came with them but growled when he passed Dalton. Before Lucien closed and locked the door he told Dalton, "Be glad it won't be left to me alone."

Outside the door, Harry fawned over Charlotte, whimpering and snuffling as she praised him for his actions while Lucien further secured the door by placing a chair under the knob. That done he turned and pulled Charlotte into a gentle embrace. Now that he could focus on her and not the immediate need to restrain Dalton, he experienced an awkward uncertainty. He wanted to kiss her but dared not touch her swollen mouth. He wanted to crush her to him in a secure embrace, but would not, lest she have injuries he could not see. He wanted to go back into the room and beat Dalton with as much ferocity and viciousness as Dalton had shown Charlotte.

He settled for kissing the top of her head when Charlotte leaned against his chest, her arms around his middle. He could feel the tremors that shook her in the aftermath of her ordeal. Then, he blinked in surprise to realize he wanted to weep with relief that she was safe from further harm at Dalton's hands.

"That was Lady Dalton's room," she finally said. She released her hold and stepped back and gestured to the door to the left. "His room connects with hers."

Reluctantly, he released her, then entered the next room and secured the connection with another chair under the knob. Once he knew the room had been barred, he helped Charlotte slowly negotiate the stairs down to the ground floor. She had refused to let him carry her, surprising him with the teasing comment, "I do not wish to chance a fall down the stairs in addition to my current discomfort."

In the kitchen, she sat at the table while he checked to see that the carriage waited, as ordered, in the mews. Before he led her outside to the carriage, though, he raised her hands and kissed them. "I will never forgive myself for not recognizing the full depravity of that man," he whispered. "Rest assured, though, he told her, "I will see that he never hurts you, or any other woman, again."

Charlotte's eyes grew wide. "You must not–"

"Don't worry." Lucien assured her. "Much as I want to kill him for doing this to you, I won't sink to his level." He kissed her forehead again. "Sometimes there are worse things than death." He smiled grimly. "I will endeavor to find precisely such a solution."

He chose to enter Wolverton House by way of the mews, as he had the Dalton residence, hoping to avoid the attention of the neighborhood. He feared it might be a lost cause to believe no one noticed Harry following the coach through the streets before it turned into the mews.

Short as the ride had been, Lucien recognized that Charlotte suffered every bump and sway of the carriage and that her brave front was beginning to crumble. As soon as he helped Charlotte down from the carriage, Lucien scooped her into his arms and Harry followed them as he carried her into the house past his housekeeper, and up the stairs to her room. It showed he'd been right in his estimation of her exhaustion that, this time, she made no protest of his actions.

"Mrs. Abbot, Miss Longborough will need bath water and a strong pot of tea... with sugar and brandy. Timmons, send for Mr. Lynch."

Charlotte's sisters, his stepmother and Anne had rushed to the landing at the top of the stairs as soon as he spoke. After their shocked exclamations when they caught sight of Charlotte's battered condition, they trailed after him, their silence as grim as his expression.

Once Charlotte was in her room, surrounded by caring females who could address her personal needs, they banished Lucien to his own room to bathe and change. While his valet laid out fresh clothing and he waited for his own hot water, Lucien sent a missive to Clarehaven asking him to meet him back at Dalton's within the hour.

"I could have used another hour or two of sleep," Clarehaven told Lucien with a wry smile when he arrived. "Your note said Dalton was restrained and Miss Longborough is safe. Is it so imperative that we deal with him immediately?"

"Safe is not the same as unharmed." He told Clarehaven. "He beat her without mercy and, while I believe she will recover, it will be weeks before the evidence of his abuse fades." He released the catch on the gate, grateful he did not have to scale the wall a third time in the hours since leaving the Montfort ballroom. "I will not rest until he is properly dealt with."

Lucien had hit upon a way to punish Dalton and guarantee he would not be able to hurt another woman in future. English law might not be quick to punish a peer, but many foreign locales did not defer to the peerage so predictably.

"I shall sign Dalton over to a ship bound for the disease-ridden tropics of the East Indies." Lucien told Clarehaven, "He will be a deckhand after I have had a word with the captain to guarantee Dalton does not escape the ship, here or in any other port of call. Nor will he be accorded the deference of a peer. If arrangement cannot be made for the East Indies," he said as they crossed the garden, "I will arrange for him to be transported to the Barbary Coast and its infamous dungeons. Either way, the man will not return to England's shores."

He entered the broken door to the kitchens and lead Clarehaven up to where Dalton waited. "We must keep him secure while I make the proper arrangements and the ship is ready to sail. It is too late for the morning tide and I won't chance his escaping the ship... particularly before it leaves England."

He opened the door and immediately saw that Dalton had escaped his bonds. A scrabbling sound turned his attention to the window where Dalton clung to the sill, his head barely visible, his hands gripping the wood frame.

Lucien shouted, "No!" and rushed forward, determined to prevent the man from escaping justice.

Dalton gave a startled oath as his hands lost their grip, then cried out in alarm seconds before his body hit the ground some thirty feet below. Lucien reached the window and looked out. His stomach lurched and he slammed his fist on the windowsill in frustration.

Dalton lay below, his back arched awkwardly over a low bench, his legs and arms splayed in unnatural positions. For an instant, Lucien thought him dead, but then he saw Dalton's chest rise and heard him groan in pain.

When they descended the stairs and reached the garden Dalton still breathed, though blood seeped from his nose and ears. The heavy bone of his left thigh poked through the dark fabric of his pantaloons. Pink spittle drooled from his lips, and he grimaced at the very effort to breathe. He did not move– Lucien doubted he could with his back so obviously broken. Dalton opened his eyes, looked at the two men, and muttered. "I knew that spying little bitch would make trouble the first time I caught her watching me."

# CHAPTER 28

It took him two hours to die.

Lucien would have experienced pity for any other man whose injuries were so obviously fatal, but he remembered Charlotte's battered face, and couldn't. In the end, Lucien recognized an ironic justice to the agonizing pain Dalton suffered until his last breath. He supposed it might be called divine retribution.

Clarehaven volunteered to report to the authorities that he found the house empty and Lord Dalton dead when he'd come to discuss a business matter. Since Lady Dalton's desertion was such a prominent subject of gossip, it would be a simple matter to explain the death as a suicide– which in a manner of speaking, it was. He had caused his own death by trying to escape from a third-floor window.

"OH, CHARLOTTE," ELIZABETH gasped when she helped Charlotte remove her dress before helping her into the bath. Her torso was marked with vivid red, purple and blue where Dalton had driven his fist into her stomach. Other, equally colorful marks showed at her hip, arm and shoulder from when Dalton had hit her hard enough to knock the chair over.

Charlotte's swollen eye would not open and the thickening of her lip, along with the sting where the skin had split, made it painful to talk. Nevertheless, it wasn't until she registered the shocked horror on the faces of her family and friends that she understood how much damage Dalton had inflicted.

The doctor, when he examined her, had assured her the wounds would heal and that the damage would not leave scars. However, he'd been taken aback when he entered the room. She touched her fingers to the misshaped skin and winced. The doctor had warned her that the bruises would become more vivid in the next several days. She dreaded facing a mirror.

At Charlotte's request, only Elizabeth stayed with her while she bathed. Sarah, though worried, was too young to be exposed to the fullness of Dalton's attack. Kind as Lucien's family were, she needed the comfort of her older sister. She missed her mother more than ever.

In the aftermath of Lucien's rescue, Charlotte felt more vulnerable than she had when under Dalton's control. It seemed odd to be the one rescued instead of the rescuer. She was less sure of herself than she ever remembered being. And right now, her eye hurt, breathing sent waves of aching pain through her body, even to the tips of her fingers.

The warm water stung the raw skin, but still felt like heaven as it eased the aches from her arms and body. The Duchess had insisted the water be sprinkled with herbal salts to further ease her abrasions, and the comforting scent of chamomile, comfrey, and lavender soothed her discomfort. She sighed and leaned her head back against the raised back of the tin tub. After a few minutes, she steeled herself to ask for a mirror.

"Are you sure?" Elizabeth asked. "I can wash your face for you. I will be gentle."

"I will do it myself," Charlotte said. "It is time I saw for myself how bad it looks."

Elizabeth handed her the mirror and Charlotte took a deep breath before holding it in front of her face. *Dear heavens.* No wonder everyone paled at the sight of her. She dipped the face cloth into the water and carefully applied it to the dried blood on her cheek.

It stung, but as the dampness dissolved the dried blood, the stiffness eased. She gingerly raised the cloth to her eye and commented, "I suppose leeches will be necessary, but they feel strange... and are quite disgusting."

When she was done, her skin no longer burned. She handed the mirror to Elizabeth and again leaned her head against the back of the tub. Charlotte's scalp was tender where Dalton had pulled her hair and each tug stung as Elizabeth undid the remaining pins and brushed out the tangles.

Charlotte was tempted to remain in the water until it grew cold, but she found her eyes growing heavy and the lure of clean linen and the soft feather bed had her rising to use the towel Elizabeth offered. Within minutes of climbing between the sheets, she drifted into sleep.

WHEN LUCIEN RETURNED, he told his stepmother and sister how Dalton had died. He'd intended to spare them the gruesome details of Dalton's injuries, but they surprised him with their insistence that he tell them everything. More disconcerting, he discovered that females were every bit as vengeful as men.

They assured him the doctor had seen to Charlotte's injuries and verified that Charlotte was not permanently injured. Only after he stopped by Charlotte's room and saw for himself that she slept, and that Elizabeth watched over her, did he seek his own room and much needed rest. Before crawling into bed, he sent word to Ravencliffe, Norcross and Clarehaven inviting them to dinner in order to resolve any remaining issues to deal with Dalton's death.

Several hours later, rested and in a much better frame of mind, Lucien again checked Charlotte's room. Sarah sat with her now. She glanced up from where she read a book in a chair by the bed while Charlotte still slept. Harry lay on the floor between them both. Four kittens lay curled against his side. The fifth chased a ball of yarn under the bed. He nodded at Sarah, then quietly closed the door and made his way downstairs.

"I hope you are rested," His stepmother said when he joined her, Anne, and Elizabeth in the sitting room. "Because we have another problem."

Lucien accepted the cup of tea she handed him and took the nearest seat. He took a sip of the tea and discovered she had added a splash of brandy to the cup. He raised his eyebrow and he saw her nod before she continued. "Lady Templeton paid us a visit this morning to inquire if Charlotte was taken ill last night."

His sister gave an inelegant snort. "She came sniffing around for gossip. She noticed you were gone, too."

That stone weighed again, but now it sank to his belly.

"We told her Charlotte had developed a headache and that you had gone on to meet friends at your club," his stepmother said, "But I don't think she believed me."

"She didn't *want* to believe you." Anne declared. She turned to Lucien. "She all but ordered us to have Charlotte make an appearance while she was here, but Mama told her Charlotte was still recovering from her headache. Mark my words," she told him grimly, "She will have Lord Templeton checking the clubs to verify if you were there."

"And if that woman ever discovers that Charlotte was missing all night," Lucien finished for them, "Charlotte will be ruined."

They looked at each other in turn. "It will be weeks before Charlotte can be seen in public." His stepmother voiced what they all knew. "Word will soon leak that something is amiss, which will only fuel the fire."

"And Lady Templeton will be only too happy to supply the fuel," Anne said.

"Perhaps we can say that she and her sisters were called home or are needed to help care for their cousin," his stepmother suggested. "Though it would mean Elizabeth and Sarah would be unable to take part in any activities until Charlotte is recovered."

"Word would leak out that they are still here." Lucien countered. "No matter how loyal our staff, it would be impossible to conceal the presence of three additional females for so long."

"That is true," the Duchess admitted.

"Then we shall claim illness." Anne suggested. "Something contagious to prevent callers."

"A contagion would put the entire household in quarantine," Lucien reminded her.

"Then perhaps I should take a page from Lady Dalton's book and claim a fall down the stairs." Charlotte's voice came from the doorway.

Startled, Lucien stood and hurried to the door where Charlotte leaned against Sarah's arm. He recognized the dark blue dressing gown she wore as one his stepmother occasionally wore when she felt poorly but could not remain in her room. It did not bind but covered her properly should someone other than family see her. Charlotte's hair hung in a long, braided rope down her back.

"She woke shortly after you left and insisted on coming down," Sarah told Lucien when he reached them. He added his support and led her to the chair he'd vacated.

"You should not be out of bed."

"I am sore," Charlotte told him, "but I am not broken." Her uninjured eye sought his gaze. "I had to know what happened."

"He is dead." When she gave a start and her eyes riveted on his in question, he explained Dalton's bid for escape.

Charlotte's shoulders bowed for a moment, and she took a deep breath. "He will not be able to hurt anyone again." Then she slowly straightened. "Is there any way to inform Lady Dalton that she is truly free?"

"I suggested she write, using her assumed name, to let you know she had arrived safely. If she does, you will be able to send her word."

She tried to smile but winced when it pulled her lip. She turned to the Duchess. "Perhaps we should invite Lady Templeton to tea. I could drape myself dramatically at the base of the stair when she arrives so she can verify my story. I shall claim that Harry knocked me off my feet and I fell."

That made them all chuckle.

"I don't believe you need to go quite so far as that," the Duchess said. "It does occur to me, though, that as the doctor was called, we might encourage the servants to spread the word that Charlotte fell after coming home with that imaginary headache." She smiled wryly. "Everyone knows that the gossip one hears from their servants is more trustworthy– and scandalous– than the official story." She stood to leave the room. "I shall speak with Mrs. Abbot."

Lucien stood, too. He bent down and scooped Charlotte from the chair. "You will return to your room and rest." He straightened and carried her to the door.

"I've been asleep for hours," Charlotte told him as he carried her up the stairs. "I don't need to rest."

"You will tire more easily than you think."

"At which time I could rest. But for now, I prefer to remain in the sitting room."

"And I prefer that you remain in your bedchamber."

WHEN CLAREHAVEN, RAVENCLIFFE, and Norcross arrived that evening, Lucien discovered Charlotte in the drawing room again. She thanked them all for their roles in trying to find her. The swelling at her lip and eye looked only slightly less garish since being washed, but the ravages of her treatment filled Lucien with remorse that he had not protected her. He should have anticipated her danger and kept her in sight no matter how many eyebrows raised and or teasing remarks were made. He'd been a fool and Charlotte paid the price.

After she thanked them, Charlotte excused herself with the rueful comment, "I shall not be joining you at the table as I find chewing a bit of a challenge at the moment. Cook has prepared a fortifying bowl of soup for me, however, which is awaiting me in my room."

Elizabeth escorted Charlotte up the stairs, then rejoined them when Timmons announced that dinner was served.

After dinner, they settled into Lucien's office to report on the aftermath of the day's events. Ravencliffe and Norcross had been informed of Charlotte's condition and Dalton's fate before they arrived at Wolverton House, but now expressed their shock at the severity of Charlotte's injuries.

"An hour after my contacting the authorities about Dalton I went to Whites and word had already begun to circulate about his death. The air of ridicule that surrounded the gossip last night has altered to sympathy that he could not face life without his wife."

As incorrect as that assumption was, Lucien was grateful that Charlotte's name was not linked to either of the Daltons.

His gratitude was proven premature, however, when Ravencliffe warned him, "Templeton has been asking about you and your whereabouts last night. Our meeting at Whites was noted, but that was several hours after you left the ball. I gather that he is raising questions about where you were before we arrived... particularly after it was noted Charlotte also disappeared around the same time. I do not doubt his wife sent him to sniff out scandal."

Ravencliffe leaned back in his chair and crossed his legs at the same time as he said, "I reminded Templeton that as the lady in question was a guest in your home, it was unlikely you would need to spirit her away from a public ballroom."

"I appreciate your pointing out that bit of logic." Lucien stood and paced the room. "But gossip mongers always like to plant the seeds of doubt." His lips curled and he gave a depreciating sigh. "I told Montfort I was called away to assist a friend in the hope that the story would be accepted in simple terms. It seems a falsehood made to avoid scandal is of little use to those who believe only what they want to believe." He turned and directed his gaze to each of his friends and told them. "As to Miss Longborough, the duchess told Lady Templeton that Charlotte developed a severe headache, and it was she who sent the lady home."

"That story may be disregarded by some." Norcross said with a frown. "Marshburn claims he saw Harry following a closed carriage early this morning. He holds the Longborough's in low esteem, so he took great delight in raising suppositions as to what that signified. In fact, he has placed a wager that Miss Longborough has surrendered her virtue and offers a reward to anyone who can discover to whom."

# CHAPTER 29

Lucien's ire rose again. He was all too aware that Dalton might have inflicted that particular insult to the injuries Charlotte had suffered. To hear it spoken aloud and with such salacious curiosity made the wager all the more obscene. Nor would the insults end there. The snide looks, smirking laughter, and taunting remarks that had followed his father's actions would pale to what Charlotte faced from the notoriety of the betting books. His family had survived the gossip over time, but a woman's reputation would not recover.

He thought back over the hours since Charlotte had gone missing as, according to the Templetons, had he. No one, other than the men sitting with him now, had seen him during that time. If he made an appearance in public while Charlotte remained out of sight in order to heal, his name would not be linked with scandal, but it would seal the smear on hers. *Unless...*

His lips shifted into an ironic smile.

It would cause a scandal.

He'd spent more than half his life rigidly adhering to the mandates of society, but scandal mongers never rested and did not care about truth. Nor did they care about what was truly right or wrong. Providing a means for Lady Dalton to escape her husband had been right... just as his father's sense of responsibility to both his sons had been right. Certainly, saving Charlotte's reputation rose above the socially correct course he'd plotted for his life and was the right thing to do.

Inspiration doused the angry fire that had eaten at his insides since Charlotte's abduction.

*He would do it.*

"How much of a reward is he offering?" Lucien asked.

All three men looked disconcertedly at him and then each other. "A hundred quid." Norcross finally answered. "Did Dalton–?"

"No." Lucien said firmly.

His friends visibly relaxed. "Then why did you ask?"

"I wondered how much he was willing to chance on so questionable an answer. Does one trust the word of a man who would tryst and tell for reward? He would certainly not be a gentleman to do so." He raised an eyebrow and added, "Though if the lady were wed, the answer would be obvious, would it not?"

If he had not shocked them with his first question, he did so with his second.

"It occurs to me that the time it would take to travel to Scotland and back would be ample time for Charlotte's bruises to fade." Lucien stood and leaned his hands on the desk. "It is the only logical solution." He grinned. "You may wish me well, my friends. I am about to become leg-shackled."

"YOU HAVE DECIDED *what*?" Charlotte clutched the arm of the drawing room chair where Lucien had seated her.

"We shall take the journey in short stages so as not to tax your strength, of course." His expression was one of smug pride that he had hit upon such a witty—make that *witless*–plan to save her from ruin.

A ball of something tight and hot formed in her throat. She forced herself to take a breath. "You expect me to agree to an elopement in order to save my reputation from Lady Templeton and the betting books of Whites?"

For weeks Charlotte had fought the secret yearning that Lucien's kisses had been more than fleeting temptation. After he'd rescued her from Dalton and had treated her so gently, she'd foolishly allowed herself to hope he might care for her on a deeper level. But to *elope*?

She'd never imagined he would make such a suggestion– for it was not an offer. An offer meant banns and betrothal balls, St. Georges, and wedding breakfasts. Elopements meant scandal and disapproval and sly questions for months following the return of the couple—if they dared return to polite society at all. He could not seriously believe she would agree.

Besides, Lucien hated scandal.

She blinked away the sting of tears as her gaze flittered around at the crowd in the room. He had not so much as granted her the courtesy of a private audience.

The duchess and Anne smiled encouragingly though their eyes darted between her and Lucien with concern. Elizabeth and Sarah eyed her with wary sympathy. The three gentlemen she had so recently thanked for helping to free her looked between themselves, not quite able to meet her gaze at all.

The ball of heat at her throat expanded, until fury drove it outward and her fingers curled into fists.

Humiliation burned deep and she narrowed her eyes.

"Absolutely not," she declared.

Lucien's eyes widened in shock, then his eyebrows drew together, and his broad smile flattened. "You can't mean that. You would have my protection and respectability. It is the most logical solution to the situation."

"I shall not be a *situation*." Charlotte said. The stinging in her eyes turned into angry tears. She dashed them away and pushed up from the chair. "As I said before, I'll claim a fall down the stairs and dare the Lady Templetons to malign me to my face." She turned toward the door. "I shall return to my room, now. I feel the need to apply a cold compress on my eye so that I may look at the dragons directly when I relate my *accidental* fall."

Elizabeth and Sarah started to join her, but she waived them off. With as much dignity as she could muster, she made her painful way out of the room and up the stairs. Once in her room she sank down on the bed and let the tears fall freely.

LUCIEN WATCHED CHARLOTTE leave the drawing room with a sense of disbelief.

Not just no or, No, thank you, but *absolutely* not.

What's more, she had looked insulted to be offered marriage and respectability. Wasn't marriage the reason why she'd come to London in the first place? He, on the other hand, had planned to wait until Rowena married before choosing a wife. If he was willing to change his timetable to protect her name, how was that an insult?

He became aware of the absolute silence behind him. Not only had she refused him, she had done so in front of his family and friends. Heat climbed his neck, rose to his ears and fired his cheeks.

"I believe Miss Longborough was caught off guard," Clarehaven's voice held a note of amusement.

"Perhaps it was the pressure of so many witnesses," Ravencliffe suggested. "I shall take my leave."

"I shall be appropriately surprised or sympathetic, whichever scenario prevails," Norcross said as he moved toward the doorway with Ravencliffe. "A note, perhaps, would allow me to react accordingly."

"Perhaps we should retire," his stepmother said. "It has been a trying day for all of us."

Lucien turned around. No one made eye contact with him but his sister, and it was not a friendly eye.

"Charlotte doesn't want to be a noble duty." A note of disgust colored her words. "She deserves more than that." Then she stepped up and gave him a hug. "You both deserve more than that." She turned and followed the others out the door.

Lucien sank into the nearest chair. *Noble duty?* Marriage would save Charlotte's reputation. If that was noble duty, how was that wrong? It was the right thing to do, and he would have sworn Charlotte would agree. *It made sense.* She responded to his kisses, so he did not repulse her– and she had shared her family secrets, which meant she trusted him. He frowned as the clock struck ten o'clock.

*He had come to her rescue, damn it.*

CHARLOTTE WIPED AWAY her tears and took stock of her options. She admitted she had very few, but she was determined to defy the gossips. Particularly Lady Templeton. She would write notes to Lady Jane and Lady Millicent describing the terrible tumble she'd had down the stairs and assure them that she would rejoin the social scene once her injuries were less hideous to look at. At least that way it would not be such a shock when she did appear in public again.

When she finished, and had the footman take them downstairs for the morning post, she sat by the fire and wondered if that would be enough. She'd just begun to doze when Martha, Anne's maid, knocked on her door. "His Grace asks that you join him in the library, miss... if you will." She curtsied. "I am to assist you down the stairs."

She knew he would try to change her mind. Not because he wanted to marry her. He didn't want to marry anyone for years to come. Not until both his sisters were married and settled. Everyone knew that.

She stood with Martha's help, and accepted her arm for support as she reluctantly left the room. She moved slowly, as much as to delay the meeting as to spare her battered body. She didn't want to speak to him again tonight, but there seemed no point in delaying matters.

When she reached the library, she found him standing by the fireplace, a glass of wine in his hand and bottle with a second glass on the table.

"I am sorry to have called you down when you made it clear you would prefer to be alone." He nodded to the maid and she left the room. "But I did not feel it right to come to your room."

He stepped over to the table and raised an eyebrow in question while at the same time inviting her to have a seat on the settee in front of the fire. "Would you care for a glass of wine?"

Charlotte preferred to keep her wits about her but saw the advantage of having something to do with her hands, so she took the offered glass and studied the deep red color so she would not have to look at Lucien.

He took the seat at the other end of the settee, and for several seconds, said nothing. When he finally spoke, the quiet, bewildered note in the question made her raise her gaze to meet his. "Why not, Charlotte?"

What she saw was a vulnerability she'd never seen in him before.

"When you first came to London you had a list of gentlemen– strangers– you were willing to consider for marriage. You told me you wished to see if they would suit, but I got the impression you would have taken any respectable offer so long as the man was not offensive, would not treat you or your family background with disrespect, and would bring you an established title. I flatter myself that I fit those criteria. So, why *absolutely* not?"

Did he honestly not see how abhorrent his plan was to someone who had done nothing of which to be ashamed? Silence stretched and she finally said, "I wonder if I can make you understand how humiliating it is to be a situation to be solved, and not a woman to be desired as a wife?"

She looked away, unable to let him see how much it hurt to admit that fact. "Yes, I came to find a match– a *love* match. And, yes, I had a list. I believed it would be as easy to fall in love with a titled gentleman as an untitled one. Whomever I married, however, would care for me and I for him."

"And what if no one ever met your criteria for what caring—*love*—is," he asked. "Would you deny yourself a woman's place in life? Would you deny yourself children? Would you deny yourself the security of marriage for a dream of some perfect scenario?"

Charlotte looked back up at him and he held her gaze, not blinking, as though the steadiness of his gaze could force her to tell him the truth.

"I don't know," she finally admitted. "This is my first Season. I knew I might not make a match this year." She sighed. "Elizabeth didn't. In fact, it is why I made the list. I did not expect to meet every eligible gentleman in a single Season."

His gaze did not waver. Hers did.

She took a nervous sip of her wine then admitted, "I suppose, in time, I might have settled for affection if not love… if there were no other option."

"Charlotte, there is no other option."

Lucien sat forward and caught her freed hand in his. "If we do not marry, you will be ruined. There will be no introductions to eligible men for respectable connections. There will be no genteel, comfortable life for a woman whose reputation has been savaged by the Marsburns and Templetons of society." His thumb stroked the back of her hand. "It is not your fault, but it will be your fate if we do not marry."

He spoke softly and shifted until their knees touched. "As for affection, I believe we have formed a friendship of sorts. I believe you are comfortable with me. How is this option different from what you might have accepted in two or three years had you not found a love match?"

Charlotte struggled to find the words to explain. "Duty is not comfort, it is an obligation. It mixes gratitude and resentment into an already unequal bargain." She twisted the stem of the wine glass in her hands. "I cannot be an obligation. Nor will I bring more whispers and ridicule to your door."

"Then it is the idea of additional scandal and the belief that I see you as a duty, and not my person, that you refuse?" Lucien took the wine glass from her and put in on the table beside him. " Let me tell you something I have recently learned. Duty and honor are not obligations, they are the very foundation of what makes a person's life meaningful."

He took her hands and coaxed her closer, then lifted them to his lips. "You are proof of that. It is not duty or honor that drive you to rescue living things." He kissed her fingertips a second time. "You care and are honorable through that caring. You don't expect gratitude or obligation. You don't resent your role in it. You don't do it *because* it is honorable but because you need to make things right."

He lifted his hand to slide gentle fingertips along her jaw and his eyes never left hers. "If you will have me," His finger traced her swollen lip. "I'll not expect gratitude or obligation. I'll not resent my role in it. Yes, I want to make things right... But most of all I want to marry you because I want to." He whispered. "And not only for propriety."

He leaned forward and pressed his lips to the corner of hers as lightly as a butterfly wing. "I would have banns read and do things in full celebration if it were possible, Charlotte. I would get a special license and marry you from the drawing room if I did not suspect the cleric would reveal the physical trauma you have suffered. No one would believe your injuries to be the result of a fall. They are too numerous and severe."

He kissed her lips again, still taking care not to cause her pain. "An elopement is not the way I would see it done, but it is the only way I can see to do it." He took a deep breath. "Run away with me, Charlotte. If we are to face scandal, let us make it worthwhile and make Marshburn pay for the privilege." He grinned when that made her sit up and look at him in surprise. "We can make it work."

His grin nearly convinced her. Charlotte could not deny the sincerity in the clear blue eyes that had captured her attention from the first moment he'd looked at her.

Despite her assertion that she would face down Lady Templeton, she knew he spoke the truth. There would be no respectable offers once the gossips had savaged her reputation. Her only choices were a scandalous marriage that would fuel tittering whispers or a return home and the ruin of both her sisters' dreams as well as her own. She really did have no choice.

Lucien believed the promises he'd just made. He liked her and was kind enough to care what happened to her. Dared she hope his affection would turn to love? She swallowed her pride and prayed he meant what he said, and he would not come to resent their marriage... or her.

"Very well."

# CHAPTER 30

Charlotte looked around the back hall and decided hers must be the oddest elopement ever undertaken. The only clandestine factor in their run-away marriage was the lateness of the hour and the closed carriage waiting behind the house to avoid the notice of neighbors.

As soon as she had agreed to his proposal, Lucien summoned Timmons and gave instructions that the carriage be readied within the hour. He insisted she remain in the library while he informed the duchess that Charlotte had seen reason. The duchess supervised her maid as she packed Charlotte's things and roused the rest of the family. While his valet packed his things, Lucien had written notes to Ravencliffe, Clarehaven, Norcross, as well as his solicitors.

"We shall host a ball in your honor when you return." The duchess assured her while Lucien checked that all was ready. "Once you are Lucien's duchess all will be as it should be, for I believe the two of you will suit each other well."

Everything was happening too fast and Charlotte feared they would overlook something important, though she could not say what that was. She turned to her sisters. "You must write to Papa and Uncle Aubrey so they won't be alarmed if they hear of this," she told Elizabeth. "You'll have to walk Harry and be sure to have the dirt in–"

"We have cared for your rescued animals before," Elizabeth told her. "We know what to do."

She took Charlotte's arm and turned her away from the others. Her face flushed before she lowered her voice so Sarah would not hear. "I am more concerned to know if *you* understand what to do—what to... *expect*?" She shot a quick look at Lucien who was directing the footman as he tied a trunk to the back of the carriage. "Perhaps you should speak with the duchess for a few minutes before leaving?"

Charlotte felt her face heat as she whispered. "Do you remember what Anne told us about the naughty books in the library?" Elizabeth gave her a startled look. "The one I read was quite detailed." Charlotte's face flamed hotter. "I am willing to discover if it was accurate."

"I thought she was teasing us." Elizabeth's eyes lost their worried expression and her mouth relaxed into a genuine smile. "Perhaps I should explore the library myself."

She kissed Charlotte's cheek when Lucien came to take her arm and lead her to the waiting carriage. "Be happy, Love."

Inside the carriage, Charlotte found that Lucien had provided several pillows and a thick quilt to ease the discomfort of the long trip. There was also a black cloak and widow's veil. She would use them to hide her bruises until they faded. He took the opposite bench seat then tapped the roof of the carriage and the coach lurched forward.

He cleared his throat. "I'm sorry our beginning must be hasty and that it isn't the celebratory occasion ladies dream of, but I hope we'll find things to celebrate nonetheless."

"It is my wish as well." Charlotte looked away, flustered and embarrassed. "Though I know not what to say for the moment. I believe I'm still somewhat in a daze."

"Don't worry about that now," Lucien said as he unfolded the quilt and settled it over her shoulders. "You have had little sleep in the last two days and the trip is tiring even when one is in the best of health. I suggest you rest."

Charlotte burrowed under the quilt and adjusted the pillow against the wall of the carriage then closed her eyes. Tired as she was, she didn't want to sleep, but for the first time since meeting Lucien, Charlotte found she had no idea what to say to him. How could she hold a conversation when he was to be her husband? All she could think of was that he would soon expect her to share his bed and engage in the activities pictured in the naughty book. What could she say to him, knowing what they would be doing? Her mind chased her questions round and around in circles. In time, she did fall asleep.

THEY'D BEEN ON THE road for more than an hour before Charlotte relaxed against the pillow and Lucien knew she finally slept. He sagged against the squabs of the carriage and for the first time admitted to himself how terrified he'd been that she would not agree to this. The one thing he had not said—what he had not been able to say—was that he loved her. Why would she believe in something he had only discovered for himself during the past twenty-four hours?

He crossed his arms and shifted on the seat. Each time they'd kissed he had assured himself that it was merely attraction and circumstance. Yet, she had intrigued him from the start with her mix of thought-provoking questions and naïve enjoyment of the most mundane of London's entertainments. She was innocent, but not insipid. Funny, but not silly. Curious but not nosey. She made him shake his head in rueful amusement with her need to rescue dogs and kittens... She made him face his conscience when she begged him to help rescue a woman who had no way to save herself.

It seemed wrong that she was soon to be his wife, but he had never paid her court. In fact, he had scrupulously avoided it. He'd convinced himself she was simply a distracting guest of his sister's.

And she *had* distracted. Of that, there had been no doubt.

Until he met Charlotte, home and family had been kept fully separate from amorous pursuits and seductions, and those seductions had never included an innocent, or anyone sheltered under his roof.

He studied Charlotte as she slept and bit back a curse. He'd blindly refused to entertain the notion that she might be more than a pleasant acquaintance. He'd been so determined to follow the path he'd set for himself, he had ignored the subtle change in his feelings.

Until Dalton took her.

The carriage dipped, then jerked when they hit a rut and Charlotte winced in her sleep. He leaned forward and adjusted the quilt that had slipped when she shifted.

*He loved her.*

Oh, yes, he had wanted to bed her from the first time he'd looked up from his doorway and recognized the danger of those clear gray eyes. Marriage had nothing to do with that, though honor had demanded he restrain his urges where she was concerned. The times he'd lost control in the library had only fueled the unrelenting ache of desire that bedeviled him whenever he caught a whiff of that elusive wildflower scent. It floated in around his senses now, teasing him. Taunting him.

Guilt caught him by the throat when anticipation rose, and his body followed suit. Her battered face made no difference to his desire other than to swear he would not add to her pain. He wanted to hold her in his arms and soothe her hurts with kisses and caresses. Yet, the lightest and most platonic of touches still caused her to flinch. He vowed not to touch her until she had healed. He shifted in his seat. His personal code of honor demanded he wait, but his body knew nothing of honor.

THEY ARRIVED AT THE border near dusk of the sixth day. Charlotte had heard the trip could be made in as little as three days, but Lucien had instructed the coachman to keep a steady, but less hurried speed to spare her the rough jostling of a faster pace. During that time, he had told her about his various properties and related amusing stories about his family, including a scandalous one about the first duke. It was as if he courted her, though she admitted there was no need. She had agreed to his mad plan. But it pleased her to think he wanted to make their marriage work.

Each morning she had checked her face in the mirror tucked in her valise. The swelling had subsided by the third day and the deep red and purple bruises continued to fade as yellowed edges formed. Her body no longer ached other than from the constant motion of their travel. The cut on her lip was little more than a red mark that was only slightly tender.

As her condition improved, an undercurrent of rising expectation pulsed along with the swaying carriage. She knew Lucien watched her when she napped, and she sometimes feigned sleep so she could study him in return.

She arranged her hat and veil before Lucien helped her from the carriage. She was acutely aware of his touch and the flash of heat in his eyes. She fought the shocking urge to take advantage of the moment to lean a bit closer, to pretend to stumble so that he would slip his arm around her to protect her from an imagined fall.

The inn was full so late in the day, but the proprietor quickly offered to shift patrons to other rooms in order to provide his finest accommodations for his honored guest, the duke. He assured them their things would be taken upstairs while they had their dinner in the private parlor downstairs.

Charlotte noticed several of the male patrons studied her as Lucien guided her to the private dining room. Their grins and sly chuckles told her they knew that she and Lucien were eloping. She blushed behind the black lace that hid her identity as well as her fading bruises.

Once in the parlor, Charlotte took off her hat and held out a black ribbon she removed from it. Lucien took it, his eyebrow lifted in question.

"In our haste to be on the road we forgot something." She stepped to his side and tied the ribbon around his coat sleeve, turning the bowed knot to the inside to make it look less contrived. "Though perhaps it is a bit late to remedy."

"Ah, yes." He shook his head and smiled with a rueful sigh. "A widow's escort must also be in mourning or he is not a proper escort...and she is not a proper widow." He sobered. "No one noticed before. Why would they now?"

"We are in Gretna Green. I suspect I am not the first to hide her identity behind false widow's weeds until a marriage takes place." She blushed. "I suppose I shall need to become accustomed to such stares when we return to London."

"I am sorry you will be subjected to curiosity and gossip, but we shall weather the storm. Once it is clear you are not breeding—" he stopped when Charlotte gasped and turned pale. "I am sorry, Charlotte. I should not have been so blunt."

"Don't be. It's nothing more than the truth." She stepped away and looked out the window to the busy street. "I must face the fact that Lady Templeton and her cronies will keep close watch on my waistline until well after Christmastide."

When they finished their meal, they went upstairs. To Lucien's dismay, they discovered their valises had been placed in the same room. Lucien called for the innkeeper who apologized for the misunderstanding. He eyed Charlotte's heavy veil and Lucien's recently acquired black armband, then returned his apologetic gaze to Lucien's.

"I did not think Your Grace would object to this arrangement," he stammered.

Lucien stared at the innkeeper with all the icy arrogance of his title. "In future," he said coldly, "I suggest you do not presume to know what I do or do not object to. The lady requires the privacy of her own room."

"I have no other room," his face paled as he protested. "As it is, I arranged for two of my other customers to share a room to make room for Your Grace." He looked between them, his agitated consternation clear in his strained voice. "I can arrange for a cot to be assembled and brought upstairs," He looked at Charlotte, "and another privacy screen?"

Lucien turned his gaze in her direction and Charlotte gave him a minute nod. It made little sense to object over a shared room when they would be married in the morning.

"Very well," Lucien finally agreed.

The innkeeper visibly relaxed. "I shall see to it immediately, Your Grace." He gave Charlotte a quick bow and scurried down the stairs calling instructions to a pair of manservants.

The room afforded a chair on which Charlotte seated herself while the inn's servants arranged the cot and screen. When they completed their task and left the room, Lucien took her hands and raised her up to stand before him.

"I'll keep my word, Charlotte. We'll find a different inn tomorrow so that today's misunderstanding does not feature into our wedding day." He hesitated. "But the situation reminds me that I must ask you something that's occurred to me since our journey began since I did not think to ask my stepmother to speak with you before we left." He cleared his voice.

"She did not need to," Charlotte stopped him with a finger to his lips, touched that he worried about what she might or might not know. "You see, Anne told me about the naughty books in the library... and I found them... and read one." She blushed. "It was quite... informative."

Lucien's expression changed to one of incredulity. "Naughty books in the library? And how would Anne–?" He stopped suddenly. A wicked look lit his eyes.

"How naughty?"

"Very." Charlotte admitted. Her face flamed even more. "I am not sure how much is true and how much is the result of an overactive... and odd... imagination."

Lucien gave a choked cough. "Imagination is good."

"Is it?" Charlotte asked. "Some of those drawings were quite scandalous."

Lucien grinned in a way that Charlotte had never seen, but that sent deliciously tingling fissures of excitement from her head to her toes. "I am sure they were."

"They... made me feel most peculiar." Charlotte whispered.

Lucien's eyes darkened. "I recall you once said that it might be more fun to make scandal than to avoid it." He coaxed her closer. "We have taken the first step by eloping, and another by sharing this room." His eyes took on that heated look she'd glimpsed before. "Were it not for my promise, we would share the bed as well. As it is, I hope you will forgive me if I give in to the need to do this." Then he lowered his head and kissed her.

Charlotte closed her eyes and savored the warm pressure of his mouth against hers. She lifted her arms to encircle his shoulders and raised onto her toes, then she tentatively softened her mouth, hoping he would press the kiss deeper as he had in the library. Gloriously, and with a growl of pleasure, he did.

He coaxed her with his tongue, and she sighed then met his exploration with equal ardor. His hands stroked her, sliding up and down her back, along her hips, then up her ribcage until he filled his hands with her breasts. Charlotte gave a gasp and pressed herself closer to his hand, lost in the incredible pleasure of his touch. When he brushed his fingers over their tips, raising them to rigid peaks, she moaned.

"You have a scandalous effect on my good intentions," he whispered.

Charlotte snuggled closer. "I release you from that promise." She raised her face to his again. "There is no need to wait."

He eased back, though his gaze still blazed with desire. "What that book may not have explained," he cautioned, "is that a woman's first time usually causes some degree of pain." He ran his fingers lightly down her cheek and assured her, "I have been told the pain quickly gives way to pleasure, but I would not have you be unprepared."

"If that is the case," Charlotte whispered against his lips. "It does not matter whether I experience discomfort tonight or tomorrow. I suspect the pain I recently endured was of greater magnitude than that of giving up my virtue." She pressed her lips to his. "Show me the pleasure that will follow the pain."

He slid his arms around her again. "I make you a new promise, then." He kissed the faint discolorations that still shadowed her skin. "I shall protect and cherish you from this day forward."

"I shall make you a promise as well," Charlotte said. "I shall do my best to make you proud and to overcome the questions of our scandalous marriage."

Lucien studied her, then smiled broadly before he kissed her. "I love you Charlotte. I am proud of who you are, and I only hope the day will come when you feel the same about me."

"But I do," Charlotte declared, "You are everything I hoped for when I came to London, and more."

"Then we shall share the bed and make it legal in the morning." He said before kissing her again. "Then we shall share it again in the afternoon... and the evening."

His grin grew wicked. "Tell me, which illustration did you find the most intriguing?"

# Don't miss out!

Visit the website below and you can sign up to receive emails whenever Leslie V. Knowles publishes a new book. There's no charge and no obligation.

https://books2read.com/r/B-A-BEDN-ANGLB

BOOKS 2 READ

Connecting independent readers to independent writers.

# Also by Leslie V. Knowles

**The Wolverton World**
Scandalizing the Duke

Watch for more at https://www.leslievknowles.com/.

# About the Author

I live in Southern California with my husband, who is also my best friend. Together, we raised two children, one of whom is married and the parent of three wonderful boys. The other is an aerospace engineer who made watching The Big Bang Theory seem oddly familiar.

I first started writing when a co-worker challenged me to write my own book after I complained about a disappointing story I'd read. When I attended a chapter of Romance Writers of America, I learned a lot from the speaker, and left the meeting with a new story idea. I was working as an interpretor-aide for the County School's Deaf Program at the time, and the new story, about the reconciliation of the parents of a deaf child, evolved from that experience.

At the urging of friends and critique partners, I entered the Golden Heart Contest for Unpublished Writers. *Silent Song* was one of six finalist in the short contemporary category, and it eventually sold to Kensington Publishing.

I earned my BA degree with teaching credentials in art and English, and taught both disciplines at the high school level. Between the regular changes of teaching assignments, and family obligations, writing was put on hold for several years. Once I retired, however, characters and story ideas began dancing in my head again, but now they danced to Regency music. Soon, *Scandalizing the Duke* was born, along with *Chasing Scandal* (book 2) and *Scandal's Choice (book 3)*

Be sure to go to my website, **leslievknowles.com**, sign up for my quarterly newsletter, and follow me on Facebook.

Read more at https://www.leslievknowles.com/.

www.ingramcontent.com/pod-product-compliance
Lightning Source LLC
LaVergne TN
LVHW021657060526
838200LV00050B/2392